A Tide for Renata

2647-LEOD

BY GUS LEODAS

(THE MITCHELL PAPPAS MYSTERY SERIES)

THE FORGOTTEN MISSION
(KENSINGTON/XLIBRIS)

A TIDE FOR RENATA (XLIBRIS)

A Tide for Renata

Gus Leodas

2647-LEOD

To order additional copies of this book, contact:
Xlibris Corporation
1-888-7-XLIBRIS
www.Xlibris.com
Orders@Xlibris.com

... TO MY FIRST LITERARY AGENT, JAY GARON—DECEASED— WHO LAUNCHED ME AND OTHER WRITERS (INCLUDING JOHN GRISHAM) WITH PERSISTENCE AND DEVOTION.

HE WOULD BE PLEASED TO KNOW THAT I'M CONTINUING TO WRITE.

MY THANKS ALSO TO JEAN FREE, JAY'S ASSOCIATE FOR HER CONSTANT NURTURING.

I WISH FOR ALL NEW WRITERS TO FIND SUCH RESPECTFUL AND CONCERNED PEOPLE.

'Dwellers by the sea cannot fail to be impressed by the sight of its ceaseless ebb and flow, and are apt to trace a subtle relation, a secret harmony, between its tides and the life of man. The belief that most deaths happen at ebb tide is said to be held along the east coast of England from Northumberland to Kent.'

The Golden Bough
Sir James George Frazer

PROLOGUE

Monday, May 6.
Pinelawn Memorial Park.
Long Island, New York.

HE STOOD OVER her grave as a wilted flower.

His world was immobile, except for the twitch in his right thumb, and silent to the audible grief of a mother and young daughter kneeling by a new marker five graves to the left, and to the private plane overhead departing nearby Republic Airport.

The sun no longer warmed him and the mild southwest breeze, scented with gravesite floral, went unnoticed. He was immersed in his grief, drowning. Nothing overcame his sense of loss.

He imagined her pulsating through the ground into his feet and body as his soul migrated into the mourning field, through the grass and earth and casket to lie down beside her, to savor closeness, to enfold his beloved, to be with her again, sharing laughter and happy moments.

Consuming the fantasy, his body shuttered to stifle the need to weep. His eyes had blurred before he entered the cemetery, but now the tears came, though restrained. The anguish collapsed his breathing as he tried to stifle sound. He turned his back to his mourning neighbors in an effort to be un-heard . . . and unrecognized.

The saline eyes started to dry before movement and the returning soul began straightening a body easing from the receding weight of sorrow. Deep inhales energized his system to surge and return to normal, to turn and head with quickened steps to the car, his hand covering his face.

Suddenly, he had to get away from there; to go on with his life with purpose, to dream his dreams and fantasies without her. Impatience had come demanding a pound of flesh for his loss.

* * *

Saturday, May 25.

AT SIX IN the morning, Luke Samuel, a broad shouldered student from Stony Brook University, guided his twelve-foot outboard boat up Hunting-ton Harbor's narrow S-shaped channel that was bor-dered by hundreds of boats on moorings; primarily sailboats. A group of swans inhabited the shallow cove north of the renowned Eastern Shore Yacht Club, gliding on the water to make arrow-shaped ripples.

The horizon clouds in the sunrise sky were pas-tel shades of cream and silver; a contrast to the se-vere thunderstorms two days ago that gust winds to fifty knots and churned the Sound. Luke loved be-ing on the water at dawn when the world was less chaotic and less polluted.

Luke steered to the northern edge of Lloyd Neck by the red buoy where the bottom dropped sharply to form a ledge; his favorite spot for fishing—with a three-pound magnet, ordered from a direct mail nautical catalogue. The advertisement claimed the magnet could lift one hundred eighty pounds.

To add variety to his time on the water, he began using the magnet and had raised a knife, pliers, screw-driver, car parts and a shattered wristwatch—worth-less.

He found magnetic fishing more exciting and intriguing than regular fishing. Who knows what metallic treasure the water would yield from sunken ships? The underwater turbulence caused by the recent thunderstorms may have dumped new booty near the ledge.

Luke lowered the magnet, securely tied with 3/8 inch docking line, into the water. The boat moved slowly over the bottom, the magnet glancing off rocks.

The boat crept forward towards Morris Rock, a submerged hazard noted on nautical charts. Luke dragged and pulled, dragged and pulled; a proce-dure he termed the best method of utilizing the magnet. The pull indicated a change in weight.

This procedure continued without metallic re-wards until within a hundred yards off Morris Rock. When pulled, the magnet didn't move. Caught be-tween rocks, Luke thought.

He tightened his hold and pulled harder. The tension remained. He steered the boat in a circle hoping to free the magnet from the rocks. The re-sistance remained taut. Another method was needed.

He increased the throttle while gripping the line. The magnet began to move, stuck to something. He pulled and dragged for ten yards. A heavy metallic object, he reasoned. What was it?—Another part from a car?—From a ship? *Could it be a treasure chest?* The possibility evolved from tales that Captain Kidd, the famous pirate, had sailed in The Long Island Sound and buried his treasure in various spots. Did some fall overboard?

Bracing and using both hands, he tried to raise the magnet. He hoisted four feet of line when the magnet became free of the underwater captive. Luke raised the magnet and examined for damage. Finding none, he lowered the magnet again, maneuvering until the magnet attached to metal. How could he raise his heavy catch?

He decided to maneuver the object to the shallow end. If he could raise the catch over the ledge, he'd drag it to shore. The magnet had lifted the object four feet, perhaps higher, if he didn't pull hard.

Reaching the base of the ledge, he hoisted carefully, hand over hand until sensing that the object cleared the ledge, then pulled forward and stopped. The magnet and prisoner cleared the ledge. He strained to see the bottom, but visibility was limited to five to six feet. The depth was ten feet.

Cautiously, he headed for shore and shallow water, dragging the line. The magnet and object moved without encountering rock. Having no desire to share his treasure, Luke searched the shore, the cliffs and tree line to assure no one was watching. This would be his secret for now. He saw no one. Then he smiled at his new sense of greed and scolded himself.

At six feet depth, he could vaguely see that the magnet was attached to a long, dark object. What was it? Doesn't look like a treasure chest. Images were distorted underwater. An old British cannon from the Revolutionary War? The cannon had to be worth something to a collector. That made it treasure.

Wild with curiosity, he gazed at his catch seeking

identification as it moved towards shallow water until the depth was three feet.

Then his eyes widened and his breath stuck.

The magnet was attached to a chain that was wrapped around the body of a man whose hands were tied behind his back.

ONE

Saturday.
Memorial Day Weekend—
Aboard the yacht, *Coyote*

"A COLLEGE STUDENT using a powerful magnet fished a man's body, wrapped in chains, out of
the Sound last week. The victim was Arthur Dryden,
an officer of my yacht club and a prominent attorney. He had been in the water only a few days," related Professor Josh Trimble, the owner of the 47-
foot Chris Craft. *Coyote* was tethered to its private
mooring in Lloyd Harbor.

"Did they find the murderer, or murderers?" inquired his guest and investigative author, Mitchell
Pappas, as he sipped his breakfast coffee on the aft
deck.

"Authorities express confidence to the membership that they soon will."

Mitchell sat up, amazed. "What are the odds of
that kid finding the body? How many people go fishing with a magnet? Was he shot? Knifed?"

"Drowned, according to the autopsy. His wife
reported him missing for two days. The police questioned all club members and employees and have

no suspects. Dryden's car was at the club. They assume the killer met and then kidnapped, or lured him from there. The impact is compounded because that's the second murder in the club this month."

"You're full of good news this morning," said Mitchell, shaking his head.

"My dock neighbor, Renata Tredanari, was found knifed and possibly raped on her yacht. Her death remains unsolved. The Commodore held emergency meetings to calm the scared membership. The police patrol the club around the clock. There's a squad car in the parking area and a police boat in the channel.

"The police questioned me and all of Renata's neighbors on the north dock who slept on their boats that night. We are the primary suspects. I have suspects, but can't prove a thing. In my need for self-preservation, I'm not saying anything to the police."

Silence.

Mitchell leaned forward. "What are you saying? Speak up if you suspect someone." His voice was adamant. "They were fellow members, not strangers. You have an obligation to their families."

Unfazed, Josh rejected the retort. "I am not sticking my neck out. For me, it's a no win situation. I can justify my isolationist attitude."

Mitchell raised his palm for Josh to wait until he poured another coffee. Josh's position bothered Mitchell. Josh usually thrusts into matters surrounding him.

"Fire away, Professor. It better be good, or I'll drag you to the police."

"You'll find my comments better than good and will agree I'm right."

"Your tale better be exceptional then. Proceed."

"Renata was a dear friend and neighbor, a widow, about forty-two, no children, plenty of dough, attractive, a happy, fun loving and wonderful person, and I adored her. And before you ask, we didn't have a romance; purely neighborly and platonic. I accepted that and valued her friendship."

Mitchell noticed increasing anger in Josh's face while reflecting on Renata. "That's sufficient reason to tell the police. As her friend, you owe it to her."

Josh shook his head in disagreement and continued. "When I can't sleep, I usually take *Coyote* out late at night for long rides on the Sound. Other times, I'd sit on this deck and gaze mindlessly over the marina area. Periodically, I'd see her bringing one or two of her drinking buddies to her yacht after the club bar closed. They couldn't see me from where I sat. They would leave an hour, or so later. One was the guy whose body was discovered with the chains, Arthur Dryden."

Mitchell's expression and interest changed. He formed a T shape with his hands and sat up. "Time out. This is fiction and you're testing a new book premise on me. Right?"

"You know how strange reality could be."

"Was Dryden married?"

"A terrific wife and two teenage daughters, and she couldn't have done it. She can't handle their yacht to take the body to the Sound. That excludes her unless she had an accomplice. The police are not charging her. She probably never knew of his involvement with Renata. Maybe she did," he shrugged, "and didn't want to upset her status quo. Some women can absorb their husband's infidelity to keep a marriage going. Her name is Valerie. She's a high school teacher of English and American literature."

"How about Renata's other drinking buddies? Could they have been involved? What's your opinion on them?" Mitchell reached over and grabbed another cinnamon roll and held it with a paper napkin.

"I have a good idea who killed Renata," continued Josh. "No, I *definitely* know who killed her and Dryden. Their deaths are connected."

The statement was heart stopping, leaving Mitchell open-mouthed. The cinnamon roll stopped in mid-air. "And you won't tell the police? That's not smart."

"It is smart and intelligent." Josh was secure in his decision.

Mitchell remained mystified. "Keep unrolling your rug and let's see if I agree."

"Another visitor was the club's rear commodore, Alvin Dean Horatio, who's also married. Another was an honorary member, Douglas Deever, Commandant of the Coast Guard station at Eaton's Neck, married. And the fourth, who's not married, hold on to your coffee and roll, is Edward Marlowe, Director of the Central Intelligence Agency. Area resident and club member."

Mitchell swayed his head, amazed. "How strange can this get?"

"The night Renata was murdered, I saw Marlowe leave her yacht at about two in the morning. Students who cleaned her yacht discovered her body the next day, Saturday. Arthur Dryden, Commandant Douglas Deever and Alvin Dean Horatio signed affidavits that they and Marlowe were on Marlowe's yacht playing fourhanded pinochle beginning at ten o'clock Friday night to five in the morning. Those bastards lied to protect Marlowe and one of the most powerful offices in the land." Josh whacked the table, saying; "They lied!" He adjusted his jarred eyeglasses.

"Calm down, Professor. What time did Marlowe visit Renata?

"I only saw him leave. I was on deck a few minutes."

"You don't know whether he was there five minutes, ten minutes, a half-hour, or more?"

"Right."

Mitchell became pensive, mulling the conversation.

Josh inhaled several times, taming anger before continuing. "Renata's investigation is waning. Marlowe is connected and regarded here in Suffolk County—no one's about to implicate him, or make the remotest connection without evidence. Also, Marlowe, Dryden and Horatio were partners in a law firm here in Huntington. When Marlowe went to Washington, he took a leave of absence from the firm—possible conflict of interest stuff. His ex-partners were also protecting themselves and the firm."

Mitchell digested every word with the cinnamon roll with more than story-telling interest. He leaned on the table, involved and curious, and consumed.

"How does Deever fit in with the legal trio," Mitchell asked. "What's the connection? CIA and Coast Guard?"

"I don't know. Maybe Renata's friendship and the yacht club were what they had in common."

"You're convinced the police won't continue to investigate Renata's death?"

"They'll implement a sham to satisfy public opinion . . . and then, nothing. To inflict negative publicity to a native son and the pride of Huntington because he's the neighbor of a murder victim is not going to happen. He's coincidence with an alibi fully corroborated by reputable witnesses."

"Tell the media and to hell with Marlowe. How could you not go public? Do it for Renata and let the powers that be take care of things!"

Josh wasn't moved by Mitchell's pleas. "Renata will forgive me if I don't oppose the CIA. I'm a professor, not a guerrilla. If Marlowe abuses his power and authority, I'll be a clandestine operation, chained and lost at sea. And probably thrown in alive like Dryden to experience the anguish of drowning with my hands tied behind my back struggling to breathe, unable to prevent the inevitable. No thanks. Maybe you'll solve the following riddle that may offer a clue."

"Sounds like you're taking this to another level."

"The Board of Trustees received an anonymous note at the last regularly scheduled board meeting. All mail is read at the meeting and noted in the minutes. I'll get a copy of the minutes so I quote correctly." Josh left.

Mitchell remained captured and impatiently waited for his return. Maybe Josh was right. Abusive government power is terrifying. The director of the CIA being a murderer was incomprehensible to Mitchell. Nevertheless, he was at the crime scene at the approximate hour Renata was killed.

The mist began to fade, as the sun grew stronger. He could now see the eastern shore and the four LILCO towers two miles away, the entrance to Centerport Harbor, Huntington Bay and the concrete lighthouse in the foreground. The blue sky was taking over.

The mist was heavier when Mitchell came aboard

early this morning from Manhattan, arriving at the Eastern Shore Yacht Club at 6:30.

Mitchell had lost ten pounds in the past two months, enough to eliminate him from a stocky build. He had a firm six-foot body and gray hairs were beginning to dominate near the ears. He was a handsome man with full, dominantly brown hair. He wore a colorful Hawaiian shirt and white shorts.

Josh returned with a manila envelope. Josh wore rimless glasses, was slight in build, balding and mild mannered; not the athletic type, but rather scholarly befitting his profession. He wore a white designer T-shirt and blue shorts.

"Ah," Josh sighed, diverting his focus. "There is nothing so beautiful as morning on the water. Look out there," he added, sweeping his arms. "Look at this beautiful nautical tapestry."

"You've been living alone too long. If Melanie didn't live on the west coast, she'd straighten you out."

Josh's daughter, Melanie, lived in Santa Monica, remaining in the Los Angeles area after graduating from UCLA.

"She's into the show biz and California life, but she'll visit for two weeks in August with her fiancée," said Josh. His wife died four years ago from an aneurysm.

Josh Trimble and Mitchell had worked together for several years at the leading advertising agency at the time, J. Walter Thompson. After Mitchell left to undertake a writing career, Josh continued in the creative department area for another two years writing advertising copy before teaching English and creative writing at New York University. Periodically, Mitchell would be a guest lecturer to Josh's students.

The students were thrilled to be lectured by a famous and best selling author.

Josh removed the minutes from the envelope. He shuffled a few pages. "Here we go. 'To the Board of Trustees. It's now his turn and I say unto you— Secret guilt by silence is betrayed.' No one could interpret what that confusing warning meant, or why sent. Three days later, Arthur Dryden's body was found. The killer, for some reason, was alerting and warning the board with this cryptic message. Rather sadistic, don't you think? And defiant?"

Mitchell massaged the message. "Secret guilt by silence . . . is betrayed. Obviously, his killer knew that Arthur Dryden kept quiet about Marlowe. I would logically suspect the remaining three—Edward Marlowe, Alvin Horatio and Commandant Deever."

As an author of actual murders that he fictionalized when necessary to stimulate added interest and suspense, what Mitchell heard had the makings of a potential story idea that was easily written if the murderer was found. Or he would add fiction to create the story he wanted and cleverly implicate a fictitious CIA director.

"Josh, does Marlowe have bodyguards? He must."

"He has two, sometimes more who go with him everywhere. I don't know if they're CIA, or Secret Service. They check around the marina and clubhouse until he leaves then go with him. When on his boat, which is to the right from me across the dock, they monitor the north dock ramp. Occasionally, one walks to the end to monitor the water approach."

"Did detectives question them? They must have seen Marlowe enter and leave Renata's boat."

"Two were on duty in the parking lot monitoring the ramp. They verified what the others said—that

Marlowe was on his boat all night. They saw no one enter the ramp after midnight, or see anyone on the docks though lacking a clear view from where they sat."

"Two more eyewitnesses to verify for Marlowe."

"They further stated that he hadn't left the boat until noon. The way everybody is protecting Marlowe, my coming forward will be discredited and will put me at risk. I know how you operate, Mitchell. If anybody can find another way to expose Marlowe, you can. A well-known writer may be granted some attention and people may speak openly to you, as they've done in the past—to be part of the book's creative process without needing a lawyer present. On the other hand, you may jeopardize yourself." He shrugged. "If that's no concern, you can write and call attention to the case for Renata's sake."

"Professor Josh Trimble, I'm interested in everything you said. I'm uncertain about investigating. But I'll talk to Lieutenant Ken Mullins when timely. And why would Marlowe talk to me?"

TWO

AT TEN O'CLOCK, they dropped the mooring line and cruised to Port Jefferson to a slip at Danforth's Marina. On route, Josh pointed out the Coast Guard station and lighthouse on the bluff at Eaton's Neck, home of Commandant Douglas Deever.

They returned to the Eastern Shore Yacht Club at close to six o'clock. Secured to the dock and the water, telephone, cable and electrical lines connected, Josh hosed down the topsides and hull. Their schedule was cocktails and snacks on the aft deck, then dinner in the club's dining room after a change of clothes.

Renata's 46-foot Silverton, with *Champagne Lady* painted across the stern, was opposite Josh's *Coyote*. She rocked gently, firmly held in place by six docking lines. The yellow Do Not Cross police tape kept the curious away. Her personal flag, with a blue outline of a champagne glass, fluttered in the wind.

"Renata's yacht sleeps there peacefully," said Josh, "betraying the violence that occurred within. From here, I don't miss much, even when the plastic siding is down. I can view most of the dock in both directions. The majority of the yachts and boats are backed in and aft deck activity is visible."

"Do you have a photograph of Renata?"

"I may have from club functions—probably in a group shot. Why?"

"To see what she looked like. To make talking about her personal."

Josh left and returned holding a few group shots. He pointed her out when they sat together with other couples at one of the monthly social functions in the dining room.

"This is Renata." Renata Tredanari was smiling at the photographer, raising a glass of champagne. She had long black hair, attractive features and a green dress with a V neckline.

"Quite a looker, Josh. The champagne lady has a face."

"This was taken this past March at the Saint Patrick's Day gala. The guy on her other side is Matthew DiBiasi, who owns a sports boat on this dock, towards the ramp. Matt doesn't spend much time participating in club activities because of business travel. He's an independent investor, entrepreneur type. He spends his time here only for social and boating activity. No committee assignments."

Next to Matthew DiBiasi, another woman's shoulder was in the frame. "That shoulder," added Josh, "belongs to Matthew's fiancée, Gina Ferrara. I add that to underscore that he and Renata aren't on a date."

"Did you tell anyone what you told me? Or do I have an exclusive insight that may lead to nowhere."

"Convinced the police were hedging, I mentioned seeing Marlowe to Renata's cousin, Mario Colarossi, who's a club member. He was family. On the other end of the Marlowe spectrum, he also has friends and influence. He's a prominent businessman—restaurants, construction, oil depots, barges plus other assortments. He's a philanthropist, and a friendly and likeable guy. A wing at Huntington Hospital is named after him for donating five million dollars."

"When did you tell Colarossi?"

"A week before Dryden was found."

"How can Colarossi convince the authorities to expand the investigation? What influence does he wield?"

"He has a long and convincing reach. He's also the godfather of Long Island."

Mitchell's eyes widened. "As in Mafia?"

"Yep."

"This is too much." He slapped his knees.

"That description isn't used in this part of the world where his donations reap respect. They take his gifts and never say Mafia. He owns the seventy-two foot Broward at the end of the dock, by the channel. On Long Island, *he* is the powers that be. That's why I told him. I needed someone who can counter Marlowe. In instances like this, it's good to be on his side.

"Yes," Josh continued, "we have two powerful suspects in a locale that's logical for them to share. The Eastern Shore Yacht Club is the best in the region for yachts. The other major yacht clubs are basically sailing clubs without slip accommodations. We have about seven-dozen slips. If you own a large motor yacht, the Eastern Shore Yacht Club is the place to be. Marlowe and Colarossi own motor yachts. There's also a state senator, a judge, a top ten singer, an award winning actor, corporate leaders including a Pulitzer Prize winner in medicine. The contrast of Marlowe and Colarossi is part of the people mix."

"You've recruited me and Colarossi to get Marlowe. You plan to recruit others?"

"No others. Mario knows Renata and I were close friends. He loved Renata, but she was afraid of him. He told her he's loved her since she was a teenager, that she was his intended soul mate, his fated love. His profession aside, he's a romantic. He'd visit her occasionally, but never spent more than a few minutes below. They spent time on the aft deck, primarily. He'd stay for an hour, or so then leave, or they would have dinner at the club. She enjoyed his company, but kept him at arms distance romantically.

"*If* she was sexually active, he was exempted as I was. She told me that he asked her to marry him. She didn't want his world. He can be a suspect as the one avenging Renata. The star-crossed lover assumes the role of her avenging angel. He had motive and the wherewithal. Drowning people with heavy weights is a common procedure in his world."

"And you spoke to him a week before Dryden was murdered," added Mitchell. "The plot thickens! This is a story you must write. I couldn't invent this cast of characters."

"We'll do it together and you can give me an acknowledgement if you want. It'll be your book because you may have to add fiction to complete it."

"Let's keep going," Mitchell said. "You must include Marlowe as a suspect for killing Dryden, who knew too much. Now we have another suspect for Dryden's murder. The questions remaining are—If Marlowe killed Dryden, would Marlowe also kill Deever and Horatio? And shouldn't we warn them?"

"Then Marlowe will know I saw him. If he kills them, they deserve it for lying and defending him. The police wouldn't believe them, either. You can't say anything bad about Marlowe in this part of the world. Deever and Horatio also have to worry about Colarossi. I couldn't care less if they lived or died. My concern is Renata. I'm for the best course that brings Marlowe to justice other than my coming forward. I will, as a last resort if all else fails."

"Was DiBiasi on his boat the night Renata died?"

"Yes. He said he was asleep."

"How about Colarossi?"

"He was on his yacht that night."

"What's his alibi?"

"He was asleep, also."

"How about the others?"

"They were all asleep."

"What happens to Renata's yacht now?"

"Her sister, Sophia, and husband will come from Florida to claim it once the police issue a release. Renata hasn't moved *Champagne Lady* from that slip since I changed the oil nearly two years ago. She couldn't handle her well. She would start it every now and then without leaving the slip. When she did go boating, she would go on another boat, usually with a group. The club was her social haven, her pied-de-terre. After her husband died of a sudden heart attack, she remained as a member using *Champagne Lady* as a second home during spring and summer. She owned a co-op in the city overlooking Central Park. That 50-foot Chris Craft in the next slip," he continued, pointing to the *Legal Tender,* "belongs to Marlowe the untouchable. Marlowe the butcher!"

Mitchell studied the two yachts, visualizing Renata's guests coming and going and Marlowe sneaking out of *Champagne Lady* in the late hours heading for the safety of his yacht. His investigative mentality began to hum.

"Professor, after you saw Marlowe leave, how much longer before you went to bed?"

"Maybe three, four minutes. Tops."

"Let's assume Marlowe didn't kill Renata, that they had sex and he left. Leaving his card game for a quickie."

"Is this an extreme theory?"

"Everything has to be considered. You know that's what I do. Call them loopholes."

"Proceed. I forgot for a moment."

"You didn't see him enter so we don't know how long he was there. Maybe nothing happened. Maybe he went for a cup of sugar, or something. Assume that someone else visited Renata *after* you went below. Suppose the second visitor was Colarossi."

"That's an interesting supposition." He raised his brows.

"Deprived of the love of the woman meant for him and desperate for her affection, maybe he waited for Marlowe to leave. From his yacht, he could also see the *Champagne Lady's* aft deck. Right?"

"Right," Josh confirmed.

"Renata resisted and a struggle ensued making Colarossi the rapist murderer. We now have two high-powered candidates who may have killed Renata. Maybe Colarossi then killed Dryden assuming he was having an affair with Renata. Love does strange things. Without a confession, we may never learn the truth. What's your prognosis now?"

"That love does strange things." Josh slapped his hands. "I knew I was right getting you involved. You have the investigative mentality for this. It's like you told my students—Writing is an ongoing mosaic; all the pieces eventually make the whole. It could be Mario, except he loved Renata too much to kill her. If anything, his love would kill *for* her. Do anything *for* her. I'm betting on Marlowe all around. I saw him. Since his agents lied to protect him, they could be capable of killing Dryden for him."

"I doubt they'd kill anyone for private reasons. They're government agents. But you never know. Colarossi also has his own protective and obedient soldiers."

"Marlowe's more than the heavy favorite."

"Also, I and Colarossi know you were a witness. What if Colarossi is the murderer? Can he gamble that you didn't see him? You can trust me, but can you trust Colarossi?"

Josh became pensive, nodding with the acceptance of this additional logic. As he continued to nod, his concern grew. The concerned look was obvious to Mitchell and he issued a warning.

"Professor, beware of Marlowe *and* Colarossi. Include DiBiasi and everyone who slept on their boats that night. Be careful and guarded my friend and assume nothing. You could be on somebody's hit list."

THREE

AT 7:15, THEY LEFT the aft deck to shower and dress for dinner. Below deck, in the guest stateroom area, Josh opened a closet next to the twin-engine room and withdrew a Ruger M-16 semi-automatic rifle with a folding metallic stock.

"I keep this aboard for sea pirates. Thieves don't only steal on land. There's valuable electronics on boats that fetch more than car radios or television sets. Most boaters have a weapon of some kind on board. I'll keep this handy in case you're right about me being a possible target."

The sun was waning as they left *Coyote*. Mitchell believed Josh's frustration with the authorities and Marlowe's ability to evade responsibility were the underlying reasons Josh invited him on the yacht. Josh was now alerted and defensive against other possibilities for protection from possible danger and attack emanating from Marlowe, or Colarossi orders. Josh was reaching out for help to bring a friend's murderer to justice, something that Josh wouldn't do.

He liked and respected Josh, a close friend and best man at his wedding to Helene. Mitchell called him Professor and referred to him as Josh. Helene preferred Josh. Helene, Mitchell's wife, held him in high regard. Josh was more than an occasional dinner companion in the city. Helene was also Josh's agent having placed two texts on creative writing with McGraw-Hill as well as several short stories in the New Yorker magazine. She was urging him to try fiction since he was deft at grammar and in short stories, to use his imagination and concoct a novel length story. Josh wasn't mentally prepared for fiction, to commit to such an intense and time-consuming project. Not yet, but promised he'd try to accept the challenge to motivate him.

Having started a novel, he had difficulty continuing with consistent intensity. If nothing else to do, he'd write as much as his attention span permitted. He knew that as the improper approach to finishing the story. If he had graded himself, he'd get an F . . .for failure to retain interest. If he couldn't get interested in his story, how could a reader? For now, fiction had no reservation in his future.

* * *

THE UNPAINTED replacement floating dock of weatherproof lumber was installed last month and supervised by Josh as soon as the cold days faded and the April wind brought the scent and memories of last year's boating season.

Josh and Mitchell headed for the clubhouse, passing the officer's reserved parking spaces; one of the benefits of devoting spare time to club management.

"Marlowe's here tonight and earlier than usual. He must have had a slow day in Washington," said Josh. "Those two guys in that black Taurus are his agents. Good, you'll see thy enemy."

As they turned right by the closed swimming pool to head for the entrance, a whistle blew.

"What's that?" asked Mitchell.

"Retreat. They're about to lower the colors. We've a touch of military tradition."

Two dock assistants dressed in white shirts and slacks prepared for the ceremony at the flagpole. The agents exited their car and stood facing the American flag, their right hand over their hearts. One dock assistant fired a loud cannon burst and the other lowered the flag. Together, they folded the flag. The remaining flags were club officers' flags to indicate that the officer was on the premises. All but one of the flag officers was here tonight—the missing officer being Arthur Dryden, the victim.

They entered the modern, two-story structure and took the right side stairway to the crowded bar. Josh chose to sit at their reserved table. He waved hello to several members. They were escorted by a hostess and seated at a table for two on the north side of the dining room overlooking the marina, the sunset and the weaving channel lined with boats. Mitchell could see *Coyote*.

The view of Huntington Harbor was exposed on three sides. About a mile to the south, the lights of the commercial waterfront were coming on. To the west and north, the sun was creating a colorful sunset of pinks and purples to herald departure. The dining room decor was nautical; trophy cases with names etched on trophies, anchors, sea and sailing ships paintings and rivets to emulate the interior of a luxury liner. A blue rug with anchor designs bordered the gleaming dance floor. The west side was designed in an arc, like the stern of a liner with a balcony wrapping around the three sides with white

plastic chairs to sit, drink and enjoy the surroundings. Mitchell deemed it a perfect nautical dining
environment with great views. The piano player was
an added touch to the reserved murmurs of diners.

The members whom Josh wanted Mitchell to see
were already seated.

"The three large tables in the front are for the
three top officers. The middle one is the
commodore's table. He's facing you with the blue
club jacket and emblem. Immediately to his right is
his wife and next to her is Mario Colarossi." The table
of ten was full. "Next to Mario is Gina Ferrara, who's
a criminal defense attorney and . . ."

" . . . And next to her is Matthew DiBiasi. I recognize them from the Renata Saint Patrick's Day photograph."

"Right you are. The table to the Commodore's
left is for the vice-commodore. There's no one there
you need to see. The other table, behind Colarossi,
is assigned to the rear commodore and contains our
cast of characters. Alvin Dean Horatio is facing you,
with the horn-rimmed glasses. His wife is to his left.
The woman to his right is Marlowe's companion, Clair
Roseman and Marlowe is next to her, in the blue
club jacket. I've seen her with him several times.
She's a local attorney. The uniform next to Mrs.
Horatio is Commandant Douglas Deever and wife.
The others are associates and wives from the law firm.
They usually go to the bar after dinner. Until then,
what else would you like to know about yacht club
life?"

"Nothing. I hate boats and everything nautical
except yours, of course."

The Commodore's guests finished dinner and
headed for the bar to continue their social evening.

The Rear Commodore and his guests had preceded them by a few minutes.

Colarossi was conversing with Gina Ferrara and Matthew DiBiasi when he spotted Josh and his guest.

"Josh, how are you doing, buddy?" he said approaching the table. Gina and Matthew followed. Josh waved.

"Evening, Mario. Gina. Matt. This is Mitchell Pappas. Mario, he's the writer I told you about."

"Hello, Mitchell, a pleasure to meet you. And this is Gina Ferrara and Matt DiBiasi." They greeted.

Colarossi, forty-nine years old, had pre-mature shocking white wavy hair, a prominent round nose, strong features, wide mouth and a perfect set of teeth. His appearance was dignified.

Gina Ferrara had a wide smile that made her green eyes glow. In her thirties, she had shoulder length dark hair and pronounced dimples. She was five feet six inches tall, two inches shorter than Matthew was. Matthew DiBiasi was handsome, well built in his mid-thirties with dark combed-back hair Mitchell thought was a fair resemblance to the actor, Al Pacino.

"I've heard of you, Mitchell," said Colarossi, "but never read your work. Now, I will. That upsetting subject with Josh is for another venue. Josh, call me and we'll set a dinner date. Until then, Mitchell, I look forward to talking with you. Goodnight." He left. Gina and Matthew smiled, waved, and followed.

Josh turned to Mitchell. "Shall we join them for a drink in the bar?"

"Let's not. I want to stay at arm's length until we meet with him."

* * *

THE NEXT DAY, Mitchell returned to his East Side apartment that overlooked the East River and Manhattan south to the Twin Towers in the financial district. The night view was dramatic, profuse with lights and four bridges.

He had witnessed the characters in Josh's drama; the powers in Washington, the Coast Guard and on Long Island. What did they have in common besides Renata and boating? Did Commandant Deever or Colarossi have something to do with Marlowe—something out of the past culminating in desperate action?

Possibilities. Speculations. The best approach to seeking answers, while keeping speculation and fantasy in focus, was to deal with current events and reality and let the drama unfold. His mind was dominated by concern for Josh. He believed Josh should protect himself by keeping quiet. But, if Marlowe killed Renata and Dryden, exposing him now may save a third life.

In the spacious and windowed apartment, his wife, Helene, was at the dining room table with the Sunday New York Times puzzle, a weekly ritual for her. She challenged the puzzle after digesting the Book Review section, one of the Bibles of her industry. The other sections covered most of the walnut table. She gave a cursory review to the main section front page without any story demanding attention.

When Mitchell entered the apartment, she rose to greet him, wrapped her arms around his neck and kissed his lips; a greeting and departing custom their partnership required; kiss when one comes home from work, or a trip, kiss when one goes out.

Mitchell believed tradition was part of stability in a marriage.

She wore a long, man's white T-shirt and white panties, and was barefoot.

"Home is my sailor, home from the sea. How'd it go?"

"My time with Josh was intriguing, to say the least. I need your help. Let me grab a cup of coffee and I'll tell you why." He patted her rear and left.

Helene had dark brown eyes surrounded by a vibrant complexion; a straight nose with pronounced cheeks and a full mouth that he loved kissing.

Mitchell returned to the dining room, moved the newspaper sections and glut of advertising flyers to make room and sat opposite her. He then proceeded to explain what Josh told him and the various theories regarding Colarossi, Marlowe, Arthur Dryden, Commandant Deever, and Alvin Dean Horatio.

"Keep in mind that this note was sent *before* Dreyden was killed. I quote—Secret guilt by silence is betrayed—end of quote. Is that in any way familiar? Does it sound like English literature?"

Helene had sat spellbound by the events, characters and then the message.

"I haven't a clue. That's a more intriguing puzzle than The Times," Helene said, setting the Times puzzle aside. "The description fits Arthur Dryden for covering up for Marlowe. If the killer wanted the trustees to know his victim in advance, they couldn't tell from that. Odds were against anyone at the club knowing unless they were immersed in the field of literature."

"The quote also applies to five others—Marlowe, Deever, Horatio and the two agents," added Mitchell. "They all covered up."

"Who knew they covered up?"

"Marlowe, Colarossi and whoever he may have told, and Josh."

"The message is too broad for others," she said, thoughtfully. "If we find the literature from where the passage was excerpted then we'd know who the intended victim was to be, who we now know was Arthur Dryden."

"Correct. It has to be that direction. If we can solve this puzzle, then we might have direction on solving the next one, if there is another message and another murder planned. We may save someone's life. Probably one of our cast of characters, including Josh."

"That's almost like seeking the needle in a barn full of hay. I'll have Alicia try the local colleges' literature professors. That'll be an intelligent beginning. If not, I'll keep probing. The New York Public Library's Reference Library may be able to track it. They're an excellent source. I used them on numerous occasions when searching for data for you. How's Josh? How's he coping?" Her expression showed concern.

"Scared."

"He sure as hell should be. He's terribly wrong in withholding evidence or information, whatever the technical term maybe."

"He's convinced Marlowe killed Renata and Dryden. He's afraid of the CIA's clandestine operations. Has no doubt he'd be killed if Marlowe knew he was an eye-witness that night."

"I can't imagine the director of the CIA committing murder. How did Josh react when you said he might be a victim?"

"Surprised. Stunned, I'd say. He hadn't figured

the problem further than just talking to Colarossi. Can you believe that cast of characters?"

Helene nodded and sat up as if seated behind her desk in a business demeanor. "There's a book in all of this. Do you think the material will work for you?"

"My agent, my wife. Right there with the opportunities. Josh should write this. The subject could be his elusive novel. Nothing better than writing from personal experience. I'm intrigued by the possibilities and would love to tackle the subject someday, but my intention is to pursuade Josh to get over being overwhelmed by long fiction. This drama is his life. He's entitled to the story."

"I agree. As your agent, what's your commitment here, and will it sidetrack your current project?"

"I promised Josh I'd help with private investigation. You know, snooping and probing around and see what unearths. I'll take the covers off some garbage cans and see what's inside. Somewhere down the line an opportune opening will occur and I'll jump in and begin the process. Primarily, I want to focus on that cryptic message. If we can find the clue, a lot of doors may begin to open up to me, especially with the police. The solution may also stimulate club members to come forward with relevant information. I promise to avoid getting sidetracked from my current projects."

"Why don't you call Lieutenant Ken Mullins? He's a friend."

"He's out of town. I don't know his other people. I will when he gets back in a few weeks."

Her business demeanor vanished. "Did you get a chance to meet any of these characters?"

"Saw them all. Marlowe was impressive. Josh is a

sitting duck on that yacht of his. He has a weapon, however. Maybe that will help."

"Not from a sniper."

"And not from a crazy loon who sends cryptic messages. A crazy who knows cunning phrases."

"I'm becoming frightened for him. Can't the police protect him?" said Helene, more concerned.

"Not at this time. He's a reluctant witness. By telling the police he saw Marlowe leave Renata's yacht, he exposes himself to retaliation from Marlowe. And, if Colarossi killed Renata, then he's another threat who knows Josh was an observer. I'd say Josh is stuck in deep shit, in neutral . . . and the batteries are about to go."

"Then tell him to leave that damn yacht club and come back to the city. He doesn't have to be alone in his apartment. He can move in with us until the crisis passes."

"He won't listen to me, or to you. He's scared, defensive and optimistic of surviving at the same time."

"Mitchell, you must force him to leave. You have to protect him from himself."

"He's stubborn."

"So, what's next?" Helene asked.

"Josh is going to arrange dinner with Colarossi. I've also asked him if we could meet with Dryden's widow to get her view. We took a trip to Port Jefferson. Ever been there?"

"No."

"Let's find time to go. You'll love it. It's a renovated waterfront and village with restaurants and perfect for walking around. We can even take the ferry to Bridgeport and back."

"Sounds great. Let's find a Saturday or Sunday

and log it in this summer." She wrote Port Jefferson on the puzzle page.

"Better yet, let's go with Josh on his yacht. Speaking of that, his club is having a cruise to Newport at the end of July for a week and he asked if we'd join him."

"Well, you tell that stubborn idiot that if he's still alive by then, we'll go."

* * *

MITCHELL DECIDED to keep notes, a diary of the characters and events. He went to his computer and entered what he recalled of Josh's story and characters.

He would keep notes on any discussions and events related to the murders and maintain a newspaper file. He was certain Josh wasn't keeping notes. Should Josh decide to write a book, he would give the files to him.

FOUR

Wednesday.
June 4.

A NORTHWESTERLY breeze rippled the harbor as Marina Chairman Josh Trimble inspected the work in progress on the third dock. His inspection was fraudulent motion because his mind reverted to Colarossi and Mitchell.

Colarossi visiting Renata after Marlowe, and after Josh had gone below to sleep, should be considered, but was rejected by Josh. He saw Marlowe. Marlowe had some explaining to do. If he didn't kill Renata why did Dryden, Deever, Horatio and the two agents say that he was playing pinochle?

Marlowe may hold a high position, but he wasn't above the law. Josh was firmly secure in the belief that Marlowe killed Renata. He'd like to know why Marlowe would risk everything to kill her. And why he had to kill her. *There's always a reason for killing somebody.*

The ugly looking dredge and pile driver were at work blowing out the bottom of the sinking pilings with water pressure to firmly establish the pilings. Half the floating dock was in place and connected to the imbedded pilings, including the fingers. In three weeks or so, the balance would be finished. When completed, he'd run water, electrical and cable lines to berth another forty boats.

The Town of Huntington, the Army Corps of Engineers and the State Environmental Conservation Department in order to dredge and build out to the channel granted riparian rights. Commandant Deever readily agreed. The influential membership assured the Eastern Shore Yacht Club of prompt approvals. The club, being over one hundred years old, was one of the town's historical and prestigious assets.

The festering and questions continued, returning doubt. After Marlowe left *Champagne Lady*, is it possible that Colarossi visited Renata? Did Colarossi see Marlowe, or wait for him to leave? Colarossi wouldn't kill the woman he loved, Josh speculated.

He had confided in Colarossi in hoping his help would expose Marlowe. How would he do that? Josh didn't know, but felt that others—Colarossi and Mitchell—might know. His priority in life was to convict Marlowe, to knock him off his high and powerful perch that was making him an untouchable.

What if Marlowe didn't kill Renata? Maybe they had a customary sexual encounter and his friends protected him to prevent exposing his innocent, but possibly career destructive visit to Renata's boat prior to her death and to protect him from rabid media. If this theory was sound, then Mitchell's theory on Colarossi visiting later may have substance.

The conversation with Mitchell began to escalate into concern for Josh. Did he make a mistake by confiding in Colarossi? Mitchell offered good advice when he said beware. Would Colarossi tell

Marlowe?—Two, who represent the opposite poles of power. Again, he could find no logic in that.

But power makes strange bedfellows and leads to secret meetings, secret agendas. Any sub-rosa affiliation between those two was dangerous to remotely threaten.

A sudden terror began to clothe him with the possibility he might be a target from two independent sources, or by a collusion of Marlowe and Colarossi.

He hoped Mitchell's theory was only theory.

He became aware and sensitive to his surroundings. An internal alarm went off. His focus returned, looking for possible bushwhackers. He scanned the parking area and the houses on the hill across East Shore Road. A sniper there would have a perfect view of the club's marina. He left the unfinished dock, went back to *Coyote,* opened the galley pantry door, took out the M-16 rifle and placed it by the aft door as a measure of security from the unseen, and unknown. He re-checked to make sure the safety was on. It was.

Doubts might be erased if he called Colarossi and accepted his invitation to meet for dinner. Mitchell also wanted to talk to Valerie Dryden. Mitchell would ask the hard and direct questions. He was more experienced and could be viewed as an insensitive stranger.

Being Wednesday morning and his day off from the university, only the construction crew, and a police squad car by the gate, restaurant, and office staff and dock assistants were on the premises. If members were on the grounds, or on their boats, he didn't see them. Marlowe and his agents were in Washington and would return again for the weekend.

Josh hadn't been on *Champagne Lady* since the murder. As marina chairman, he was empowered to enter all boats in the marina in safety and emergency situations. Copies of keys to all boats were kept in a locked closet in the dock master's office. Josh had a key to that closet.

He sat on his aft deck looking across at *Champagne Lady* thinking of the good times with Renata and visualized her happy and smiling face. A sadness came . . . and a yearning for her company. He decided to board her yacht and look around for the last time before *Champagne Lady* was moved to Florida; a gesture to bring Renata's memory close; to make sure everything was secure below decks; to let Renata know he was taking care of things for her.

He took the long walk to the dock house by the south dock, enjoying the breeze ruffling his remaining hairs. He greeted the dock master, Titus Banks, told him he needed the key to *Champagne Lady* and helped himself, adding "Just checking to make sure there are no leaks, or build up in the bilge."

Titus Banks had been the dock master for eight years, a position he accepted after retirement from the navy as Chief Petty Officer. Now in his sixties and energetic, he moved as agile as his young dock assistants who helped secure and untie boats, pump fuel, run the launch to the sailboats on the moorings, help members cart supplies and maintain the club in neat appearance. He worked closely with Josh in keeping the marina operating at maximum efficiency and establishing new procedures in the processing of transient boats from other yacht clubs. Josh Trimble was his boss this year. And anything Josh wanted was fine with him.

"Josh, any further news from the police regarding Renata? Have you heard?"

"Nothing new, Titus. I can only hope they catch the killer."

"Me, too. Every time I look across the marina at her yacht, can't help thinking what a great person she was. It's a shame. I liked her a lot. We had some good times up at the bar with her. One of these days, you and I should visit her grave and bring her flowers."

"We should do that. She was the friendly type, Titus. Warm and outgoing. I think we all miss her."

"She was one of my favorite people. You want me to go with you?"

"No, thanks. I'll do a fast check. The boat should be okay. There's no listing and she's not below the water line—a preventive maintenance visit. Keep prodding that dredge, Titus. I want that dock finished by the July Fourth weekend. I'll see you later."

He accepted what Titus Banks said about Renata. She and Titus were socially friendly. Many an evening was spent when he, Renata, Titus and others closed the bar, broke into song and had a merry time all in good fun and camaraderie. With Renata's passing, those mirthful vignettes were gone. Lovely memories. Renata's zest for life was irreplaceable within the membership. When Titus said he missed her, his feelings were genuine.

Josh passed under the police tape and boarded. In the marina, he had the authority to by-pass the tape claiming an emergency. This wasn't an emergency, but what the hell. He made a cursory review of the salon, the galley, heads, the engine room, the bilge—which was dry, the guest staterooms, and then entered Renata's master stateroom. Feelings of nostalgia returned. He could see her smiling face as she raised a glass of champagne. The vision faded.

The room was neat and orderly and the bed made, as if nothing violent happened here—not a residue of the violence of that night. The police straightened up after taking evidence and photographs, but he and Titus helped. Her clothes and personal effects remained in the closets and drawers.

Whenever he looked at the bed, he could envision the naked Renata beckoning her lovers and imagine them in multiple positions. Then he saw her struggling, being raped and stabbed and he hurried out of the room into the fresh air with a hollow pull in his stomach.

You had no business going to her stateroom at this time, he thought. *Don't come back here again!*

* * *

Thursday.
June 5.

VALERIE DRYDEN watched her teenage daughters, Tina and Elizabeth, board the school bus and leave for the local high school for the first time since their father's funeral, ready to go on with their school work and future.

The worst was over; the funeral, the police questioning, the incessant local media in front of her house had gone and last night's meeting with one of the young lawyers from the firm to review the estate was beginning to put Arthur's murder behind her. She had taken last week and this week as personal time off from work. She wasn't ready to return to teaching—to face a room full of teenagers. She knew the substitute teacher and was confident she'd maintain her level of teaching and assignments.

The calls from the press had stopped, *finally*. All she wanted now was to be left alone to get on with her life, in her own way—to re-trench and plan for her economic future and her daughters' education. She had decided not to sell the house until both daughters graduated with their current friends.

When Josh Trimble called yesterday saying he wanted to meet with her with Mitchell Pappas, the famous author—a close friend who was visiting—she agreed to see them at ten o'clock today. They preferred to meet tomorrow, but she had to be in New York City all day. They agreed to today. She didn't ask why they wanted to see her. Josh was a friend. No reason why he couldn't visit to pay his respects with a companion. The thought of him writing a book never entered her mind.

With the kitchen straightened after her daughters' hurried breakfasts, she went upstairs in her spacious two level home—situated on four acres in the West Hills section of South Huntington—to shower, dress, have breakfast, read the delivered Newsday and await her guests. Eventually, when her daughters accepted their father's death, she'd gather his clothing and make a donation to a local charity, or church, or to the Salvation Army. That was practical.

In her early forties, Valerie Dryden was strikingly attractive with long, dark hair, a perfect five foot seven figure, naturally tanned skin and dark eyes set in a wide cheek face with full lips; a Roman classic, indicative of her Italian ancestry.

* * *

MITCHELL AGREED to meet Josh at the yacht club at nine that morning, drive to Valerie's, and then lunch at the club. Josh also made a dinner appointment at the club tomorrow night with Mario Colarossi. Mitchell would return tomorrow for dinner and stay overnight.

On the way to West Hills, they discussed the questions Mitchell would ask Valerie, concluding that the visit may be a waste of time. But some insight might be gained as to who may have murdered her husband—Maybe a disgruntled client and not a connection to Marlowe or Colarossi? A valid thought to consider. Also, Josh wanted to be sure they didn't offend Valerie with the questioning at this sensitive time.

They turned into West Hills Road, a forested two-lane road with countrified homes on multiple acres with stables and horses, making a right at the fork by the stop sign. They saw the Dryden house, passed a white post and rail fence and pulled into the long driveway leading to the white structure with red shutters. The Drydens didn't have horses.

The area was serene with occasional bird chatters and without evidence that death had paid a visit. Valerie had seen them turn into the driveway and was opening the front door when the car stopped.

Josh introduced Mitchell and she welcomed him to her home. Valerie and Josh touched cheeks as she smiled warmly. They sat in the living room whose decor was modern with glass and steel and bright colors accenting the white furniture. They offered their condolences and she offered coffee and breakfast, which they refused. The huge picture windows framed the forested surroundings.

"Valerie," said Josh. "We won't keep you long. I brought Mitchell because he may be able to help find Arthur's killer. In that regard, he has some questions. I hope you don't mind. If you do, we'll save the discussion on Arthur for another time. I know these two weeks have been extremely difficult for you."

Valerie smiled. "Not a problem, Josh," she said, discreetly crossing her legs. "Your taking the time to visit is appreciated. I'm rebounding pretty well. And I do know Mitchell's work and how he writes. Actually, he's in my library like an old family member— one of Arthur's favorite authors. Mitchell, it's a privilege to meet you and anything you do will be appreciated. Are you planning a book about the murders at the club?"

"No, I'm encouraging Josh to do that. He asked me to help regarding Renata and Arthur because the police have no answers. Sometimes, I find something the police don't. Or ask questions the police don't, or forget. From what I hear from New York City Homicide, Suffolk Homicide is one of the best squads. Honestly, I probably won't find anything new. Do you care to talk about the murder?"

Valerie quivered. "The word murder has such a horrible sound. But that's what it was. Sure. Help from all quarters is welcomed. What would you like to know?"

"Let's start with the basics. Who would want to murder your husband?"

She shook her head. "I've gone over every conceivable thing having the slightest, the most remote possibility . . . and nothing makes sense. I reiterated that to the media and the police. I absolutely have no clue why anyone would want Arthur dead, or what he did to justify his dying that horrible way—so sadistic. I also talked to his associates. They had no ideas and no unhappy clients, or adversaries who'd have motives. Arthur lived an honest and normal life. No enemies, a good father and husband. He made a good living; business was continually increasing and looked brighter thanks to Edward Marlowe's ascension as director of the CIA and connections in Washington. Did you know that Edward and Arthur were partners?"

"Josh told me. I saw Edward Marlowe at the club."

"Edward was devastated by Arthur's loss. They were close friends. Everywhere you looked in our life, there was a bright and happy light. Life was blissful, you could say."

"Valerie, Mitchell has some theories—and I want to emphasize—that's all they are," said Josh. "He'd like to state them. If they're sensitive in any way, tell him to stop and he'll change the subject. We don't wish to offend you. In his investigation to find the truth, he has to probe the sensitive to exclude possibilities—a process of elimination in formulating theory, which may prove to be realistic. That's his style."

"I agree. Theories may find the road to the truth. Fire away," she smiled, and prepared for the first salvo. "I'm ready for anything the future dares."

Mitchell hesitated a bit before beginning, wanting to start with less sensitive questioning. "Prior to the theories, Valerie, there was a cryptic message sent to the board of trustees warning, or alerting of a possible murder. Then Arthur's body was found. It's probable and logical that the pre-meditated message foretold Arthur's death. Are you familiar with the total message?"

"Yes."

"Does it mean anything to you?"

"No."

"I ask because—Secret guilt by silence is betrayed—sounds like some passage from English literature and knowing you teach the subject, there might be recognition from where its excerpted."

"English literature is voluminous. From many centuries, filled with great writers. It's difficult to know who wrote that disconnected sentence. It could be Shakespeare, Sir Francis Bacon, John Milton, Sir Walter Scott, Keats, Browning, Tennyson, ad infinitum. Maybe it's American literature, also extensive. Sounds familiar, but can't recollect from where."

"When you can, try to find out. It may help us."

"I'll delve into my library, here and in school— But where to begin to look? Josh, I see why you brought Mitchell. Even the police didn't ask me about that message. Proceed on any ground, Mitchell, sensitive, or not. A lot of questions have to be answered. I want the dog who murdered Arthur."

Josh got excited. "Good for you!"

"From the beginning," Mitchell continued, "when did you realize Arthur was missing."

"The first night. I assumed he had much to drink at the club and fell asleep on the boat. I wasn't with him. I called the yacht, but no answer. In the morning I called his office. I called all day. He never showed up. His car was at the yacht club. When I couldn't locate him there and when he didn't come home that night, I called the police. A day later, maybe two, I'm uncertain of dates now, his body was found by extraordinary luck. I'd still be wondering where he was. Also, his insurance is over two million dollars. Better to have it now than waiting for the official period for him to be declared dead."

"Did your husband play pinochle?" Mitchell asked.

"He loved the game. He'd drop everything for pinochle: single or double deck, one on one, or partners. He, Edward Marlowe, Alvin Horatio and Doug Deever where playing pinochle on Edward's yacht during the time Renata was attacked and killed. Is that why you ask?"

"Yes."

Valerie looked quizzical "Are you exploring a connection to Renata's death? The police questioned Arthur and the others. They didn't hear, or see anything."

"Maybe." He put his palms out to indicate patience. "We'll get to that. First, where were you the night Renata was killed?"

"At the club. My daughters and I slept on our yacht. The girls loved the change on weekends."

"Did you see anyone on the north dock after midnight?"

"No. We went to bed around eleven thirty. The next day, we were having lunch at the club when Renata's body was discovered."

"Valerie, now I would like to ask some personal questions."

"No holds barred in this discussion. Go ahead, no matter how personal."

"I appreciate your attitude. Did you love your husband?"

"Very much. I always considered him the perfect mate."

"Did he love you?"

"I would say so. He was outward about showing his feelings." She smiled. "To be blunt, he wanted plenty of attention and affection and he got it. He had no reason to go elsewhere. His daughters were his joy, as they are mine, and he and I were totally compatible. He was the only man I needed and wanted in life and I believe he felt the same about me."

"You don't think he had outside affairs? Not plausible at all? I have to ask in case there's a secret lover who found reason to kill him."

She hesitated and uncrossed her leg as she mulled his comment. "Hadn't thought of that. Good question. Arthur's time, for the most part, was accounted for. He had no time for promiscuity. I can't account for the hours he spent without me at the club. I didn't spend much time there. I can't help thinking that since he disappeared the night he went to the club, he might still be alive if I went with him." She displayed signs of a guilt demeanor. She straightened. "Too late now." Her eyes were damp.

"Valerie," said Josh. "Don't blame yourself. The killer was determined."

"Maybe with time I'll overcome the guilt."

"Let's assume," continued Mitchell, "that he was having an affair at the club. Let's say the dead woman, Renata. Renata was murdered. Arthur was murdered. What do you think of that?"

"A relationship between Arthur and Renata was unrealistic. Improbable."

"I accept that. Let's add a third party."

"The proverbial triangle?"

"Only this time, it's not romance, but intrigue. Suppose Edward Marlowe was involved with Renata and he killed her, and Arthur and the others cov-

ered up with the pinochle story to protect him. And
that Marlowe may have killed Arthur if Arthur stated
that he was going to tell the truth to the police. Or
had someone kill him. Marlowe would then have a
lot to lose. That's a motive."

Valerie shifted. "Whoa. That's grasping, but I accept the premise and extreme theory. What comes
next?"

"Marlowe goes free. The others will remain loyal.
If something happens to the others, then Marlowe
has to be scrutinized and questioned. But will he be?
Would the police protect him? Now, I'll add another
player into this scenario. I've learned that Mario
Colarossi loved Renata that he wanted to marry her,
but was rejected. Let's say Mario learned that Renata
was having affairs at the club with a member, or members. Mario may believe that one of her lovers killed
Renata. Maybe he thought Arthur. Mario may have
had him abducted, wrapped in chains and dumped
overboard in a manner consistent with people involved with a mob. I heard rumors he's involved. Now
we have two theoretical suspects. Can you conceive
of Marlowe killing Arthur?"

"You just put a lot of balls in the air, Mitchell. No
chance at all. They grew up together, went to the
same schools, started the firm together. They were
more than brothers."

"How about Mario?"

"We've known Mario for years. The man is gracious, a prince and a good friend who has helped
Arthur obtain some prosperous clients. He was also
Arthur's client, on occasion. Arthur's firm did a lot
of business out of the club. Others do, also, like ac-
countants, stockbrokers and others who are members for business contacts as well as pleasure boating.

Intriguing as your theories may sound, they do have a place in fiction, but not in reality. I cannot fathom Marlowe or Mario being involved. Maybe Marlowe and Renata did have an affair. Why not? They were both unattached. As for Mario, whoever said he loved Renata was speculating. Mario dates on and off and Arthur and I dined with him and his dates many times. Mario, ever since I've known him, never expressed a serious comment about sharing his life full time with any woman . . . including Renata. They were cousins only. Family. And he's close to his family members and very protective. His family concern may have been mistaken for romantic love."

Mitchell was satisfied with the conversation. "Valerie, I thank you for your frankness and appreciate your tolerating my curiosity, fictitious or not."

"I respect your writing, and now I've gained respect for your intriguing thought process. I believe that in the future, teachers will be discussing your literature as one of the great American novelists."

Mitchell smiled. "I hope so, too, but unlikely. I thank you for the compliment."

"I look forward to telling my students that we met."

As they rose and headed for the front door, she said, "Do you really suspect Edward Marlowe and Mario Colarossi?"

"Only in theory. Not possible to prove unless they confess."

"If they were behind Renata's and Arthur's murders, then these crimes will go unsolved. Keep looking, but try other theories. Excuse me a moment." She left and returned within seconds with two books written by Mitchell. "Since you're here, please sign these. They may be worth a fortune to my future heirs."

Mitchell chuckled and signed. He returned the books as they headed for the door. Mitchell turned to her.

"Oh, one more subject, Valerie."

"Okay."

"What if Arthur was having an affair and you found out about it? Shattering your perfect marriage. Abusing your loyalty to him. What would you do?"

She didn't flinch or hesitate, and said firmly, "As much as I loved him, I'd definitely leave him for betraying me and the children and my love for him. He'd have crossed the line of no return. A firm decision."

"What about his lover?"

She shrugged. "Irrelevant, once he crossed the line."

"Last questions and probably the hardest to ask."

"Ask."

"Did you kill Arthur?"

She grinned at the boldness. "Right between the eyes. No. As I've said, he was the perfect man for me. Besides, the way he died, I can't handle the boat pulling in and out of the slip and physically unlikely that I could overwhelm and throw him overboard and kill him in such a savage way."

"Maybe you hired someone, or had help."

"I could have, but didn't."

"Did you write that message to the board? Literature is your professional interest."

"No, to that, also."

"I didn't think so on all the above. Now they're questions I'll never ask again."

"You leave no stones unturned, do you?"

"I try not to. I hope I didn't offend you."

"You didn't. Please let me know what you find regarding Arthur. Of the two theoretical suspects, which one do you suspect killed my Arthur?"

"Mario. It's his associates' style of killing. Vanishing corpses. The difference is cement versus chains."

"Say alleged associates. That's a bad rap for Mario. People assume he's Mafia. Just because he's wealthy and is Italian doesn't mean he's involved. I take umbrage to that label, to my heritage. He operates in the open and has created a lot of jobs. He is not an evil man. I know that if you meet him you'll think differently. If only real life was as simple as theory. Josh, thanks for coming here today. Mitchell, it's an honor to meet you and have you in my home. Josh, do you know anyone who wants to buy a good yacht? My club life has also ended. My daughters no longer want to go on *Courtship*—too much of a reminder of their father. I'm sailing off into the sunset, as it were. I'll take any reasonable offer."

"I'll talk to a few dealers for you. Take care of yourself, Valerie. Let me know what else I can do."

Josh and Valerie hugged and touched cheeks.

"Thanks to you both for your concern and your visit."

"And I thank you, Valerie," said Mitchell. "I appreciate your seeing us at this difficult time."

She extended her hand and he took it. "I'm confident that Arthur's killer will be found now that you're involved," Valerie said. "I look forward to seeing you again."

She watched them enter the car and drive away until they disappeared behind the trees. Then she closed the door, turned the lock and rushed to the telephone.

* * *

"WHAT DO you think?" asked Josh. They were passing a day camp on the right and approaching the stop sign at Jericho Turnpike.

"I think she's a complete innocent as far as her husband is concerned. And liked that she was direct and handled the questioning well. Valerie impressed me as the perfect wife and mother, supportive of her husband whom she loved. He must have been an idiot to cheat on her. I believe she never knew about Renata. If she killed her husband, she would have done so on land where he could be found. Thus, she'd have no problem collecting the insurance. If she dumped him in the Sound, there'd be no insurance for years and no assurance that he'd ever be found. No, Valerie didn't kill her husband. Obviously, she holds Marlowe and Colarossi in high regard."

"She believes Mario to be Mafia free," said Josh. "Maybe. No one can prove the allegations. I believe like the authorities. He's *the* man. Only there's no legal proof."

They made a right onto Jericho Turnpike.

"Damn, she's sexy. Why don't you court her, Josh? Let some time pass for the mourning period then make your move. Besides, she's wealthy now. In addition to the insurance, her share of the firm should bring her several more million. She has kids and you'll have an instant family."

"That's a great package, but Valerie and I don't have that chemistry. We're friends and I'll help her where I can."

"Thinking of your interest, old friend. It's time you let a woman in your life. You can buy a bigger boat, have a great house and a wife to be proud of and you both have teaching in common."

"Someday, but not during the boating season." They laughed.

"Tomorrow night, we have dinner with Colarossi. What are you going to say to him?"

"We'll have to handle him a little bit different," said Mitchell. "Maybe we'll ad lib as we go alone."

"He's one of the most social persons in the club. His yacht is practically an open house. Also, it's used for club fund raising functions for the charities in Huntington. On our raft-ups, when boats tie up to each other on a mooring, or anchor, his is the center of activity. He gets along with everyone. And when he hears a member is having business difficulties, he's the first to offer help. Unfortunately, Valerie wasn't available tomorrow. It would have saved you another trip out here."

"Not a problem. Somewhere down the line, we should also talk to Marlowe."

"If we do, are you going to say I observed him leave Renata's boat? I'm absolutely against that."

"If I did, or told anyone else, including the police, you might be dead by the next day."

* * *

VALERIE DRYDEN dialed with impatience, tapping her foot as she heard the fourth ring. The phone was answered.

"It's me," she hastily replied. "Must see you right away. It's urgent, about Arthur. I just had a terrible experience. I'm nearly traumatized and need to be with you."

She hung up, picked up her bag, took out the

car keys, set the house alarm, went out to her red Lexus and drove away.

A person like Mitchell Pappas was dangerous with his speculative probing, theories or not. If the press became aware that Pappas was investigating, the story may take a whole new slant and cast aspersions in an undesired direction. He meant well, but he was a threat, and explosive. He has to be restrained. Josh shouldn't have involved him.

Mitchell Pappas caused her to panic.

She drove with determination and speed to her destination. In twenty minutes, she parked in the landscaped driveway of a large, modern home on the water in Northport. The view from there extended across the Sound to Stamford, Connecticut.

As was habit from many previous visits, she looked around hoping no one had seen her. Her arrival being expected, the front door was ajar. She hurried into the marble foyer into his waiting arms. He had just showered and was wearing a white bathrobe.

Before he could speak, she embraced and kissed him passionately on the mouth. With lips moving over his face, she told him Pappas' theories. His hands unbuttoned her blouse and roamed her braless body. She loosened the robe and her right hand went inside.

"Please tell me everything's fine," she pleaded. "That nothing will happen to you."

His fingers moved, probing, evoking moans. Then she whispered, "My only love, my eternal love. I yearn to always be with you." She pressed hard against him as her mouth found his lips again and her tongue thrust with fervor.

Mario Colarossi savored the passion of the best sexual partner he'd ever known; a secret and passionate relationship that started three years ago on his boat when her husband was playing fourhanded pinochle with Marlowe and others on Marlowe's yacht.

FIVE

Friday.
June 6.

MARIO COLAROSSI was at the festive bar social-
izing with members and wives when Josh and Mitchell
entered. All the tables were occupied. In typical fash-
ion in a social group, Colarossi was the dominant figure with his outgoing personality and stories. His voice
occasionally rose above the chatter. Whether sitting
or standing, he automatically controlled his immediate environment.

Colarossi enthusiastically greeted Josh and
Mitchell. They ordered drinks and joined Colarossi's
group for the next ten minutes before sitting for
dinner, with Colarossi putting his left arm around
Mitchell and expounding his literary prowess as
though they'd been friends for years.

They were seated at a table for four on the south
side of the dining room. Colarossi sat facing the entrance, a procedure he always insisted on. Habit he
called it—a need to know what's going on in the
room and who comes and goes. Josh sat to Colarossi's
left, Mitchell, next to Colarossi. The piano player was

on a cigarette break outside on the metal stairs leading to the pool area.

The skies had darkened from a heavy cloud cover
that threatened rain most of the day. A thin fog was
beginning to settle over the harbor, dimming and
changing distant harbor lights on the southern end
into splashes of diffused color.

Colarossi wasted no time initiating the conversation. "I own a few restaurants, Mitchell, and admit
that I'd rather dine here on weekends. There's something about this place; the feeling of family and
friendship with good food; a secluded haven away
from the public that sets it apart. And the service is
as good as, or better than mine is. The members are
paid strict attention and deservedly so for the dues
they pay. The main thing is, I love boating and the
boating life and these are the people in that world."
His right arm swept the room in an arc. His hands
were animated with emphasis as he talked.

"I'm beginning to sense the familial feeling,
Mario—that family commonality. It grows the more
time I spend here. Actually, this place is good for
me. Some writers and I spend time in isolation to
work and I need to spend more time being with
people, to get out of my mind and thoughts. My wife
would certainly second that motion. I keep hearing
about this club from Josh and how it's a part of his
life-style."

"Become a member. Josh and I will sponsor you.
You don't need a boat. Become a restaurant associate and enjoy most of the benefits. Besides, it'll be
good for the club to include you among its celebrity
members."

"Thanks, but it's far for me to use on a regular
basis. I'll take advantage of Josh when I can."

"Anytime you want with Helene, preferably," replied Josh. "She's also his agent. A good agent is invaluable to a writer. She's one of the best. And she's also my agent."

"Then, Josh, there's hope for you to become a major writer like Mitchell," laughed Colarossi. "I look forward to meeting her some day, Mitchell."

The waitress was prompt, took their drink orders, offered the specialties and menus, and they ordered.

"Mitchell, Josh says you will help find Renata's murderer. I thank you for your involvement because Renata was my family. And whom I adored. Anything you do will be more than appreciated. I want you to know something. I have a philosophy about this place, this refuge. Outside these gates, my business world is hectic and demanding where, like you, I play to win. Mitchell, you do what you must to create and write your product. That's why you ask probing questions.

"After we met, I read one of your books, *Murder by Murder.* I know how detailed you write. And in so doing, you may hurt some people knowingly, or unknowingly." He looked directly into Mitchell's eyes to give advance warning that what he was about to say was important. "My philosophy and code of honor for this place is simple—Never shit where you eat. And the member if it is a member, who killed Renata, laid a huge dump on this place. Same goes for who killed Arthur Dryden." In a slower pacing to underline emphasis, he added, "I would never do anything on these premises to defile my philosophy and environment, or my refuge." The emphasis ended. "And in anticipation of questions I know you'll ask sooner or later tonight, my hands are clean where Renata and Arthur are concerned."

The stare continued to add a bold exclamation point. His eyes shifted to a passing waitress and a social smile returned. He waved, she came over and he asked for the wine list.

Colarossi's opening statement neutralized Mitchell's planned order of questioning. The initiative was effective. Mitchell thought Colarossi as psychic in knowing what he would be asked. "I don't doubt you, Mario. I had you on a possible suspect list and you've erased your name."

Colarossi gave a gracious, but condescending smile. "See what happens when I read your books. Tell me now, how did I make your suspect list? I'm not surprised. Eventually, I wind up on everybody's shit list," he joked.

Mitchell wasn't about to say—By the way Dryden died. Instead, he replied, "Logically, and not by your actions—because of your closeness to Renata. Pure speculation. Sometimes my arrows go astray and sometimes they find the mark. The one with your name definitely went astray. If I continue an investigation, you're a closed issue."

Mario grinned and leaned forward. "I would have bet anything you'd say I made your list because of the way Dryden died. Josh will tell you that label is erroneously pinned on me." He straightened. "I adored Renata, like a sister. And now freely admit for the first time publicly—more than a sister. I just gave you the inside track on that subject. I wouldn't do anything to harm her."

"I believe you, Mario. No reservations in that regard."

"Then I think we three can work as a team to help solve these murders. Josh is a good friend and I respect that he confided in me about seeing someone leaving Renata's boat. That's trust and a compliment. And, Josh, I want to reassure you that I won't repeat your confidence to anyone. I won't jeopardize, or compromise you."

"I know that," replied Josh, relieved that he was correct in confiding in Colarossi. "I'm hoping a combination of you and Mitchell would find solutions. I told Mitchell about Marlowe. Mitchell can function effectively if he knows everything."

"Good. Have you any thoughts about exposing Marlowe without our jeopardizing Josh?" he asked Mitchell.

"Not yet. Josh is in jeopardy here. Marlowe has alibis that give him strength. That makes Josh seeing him a weak case. Who'd believe him? How about you?"

"Let's say I'm quietly working on it. The threat of Italian revenge, real or imagined, which is best when you least expect it, and when its aged a bit often loosens lips because it hangs over you like a dagger. The hand of God, who's Italian, will punish Marlowe." He grinned. "Not me. If he needs help, I do the best I can to provide."

"The Greeks have the same revenge philosophy except that the dagger is the Sword of Damocles. I also believe," added Mitchell, now that Colarossi exempted himself in any killing, "that Marlowe had Dryden assassinated for wanting to tell the police that he covered up. Marlowe went to Renata's boat. Dryden had to know he went there. Dryden could be a dangerous witness."

"A fascinating angle."

"What are your thoughts on Arthur Dryden, Mario," asked Mitchell. "Let me add that he was having an affair with Renata. Did you know that?"

"I assumed so. Josh confirmed. Poor judgment on her part." He shook his head as the wine list came. "California red good for you both?" They agreed. "Good. We'll have a bottle of Sutter Home Cabernet Sauvignon." The waitress left. "Arthur's death is a mystery. An enigma. Although I assumed, I didn't believe he was having an affair with Renata. He and Valerie appeared devoted to each other. In the over-all picture, Marlowe killing him makes sense. He probably shit on this place, on Renata and on Arthur. Edward Marlowe is a short timer. Know what I mean?" He raised his eyebrows. "By being caught by the police, of course."

"You have important contacts in high places, Mario. Should Josh talk to them about his seeing Marlowe, or are the alibis strong?"

"Alibis can be broken. But the authorities won't break Marlowe's. He's now too strong for the system. If Arthur was to betray him, Marlowe had the solu-tion. And the chains."

"What's the answer for now? What posture should be assumed?" asked Mitchell.

"Patience, my dear Mitchell. Patience. Everything comes if a man will only wait. I believe Disraeli said that. It's like having long lasting and drawn out sex. The eventual climax is the capture . . . or the con-quest."

He laughed heartily as he waved to members and Alvin Horatio passing by headed for the rear commodore's table. The room began to fill and the piano player returned to compete with restaurant din. He started his set with *Feelings*.

Commandant Douglas Deever and his wife came by the table, said their greetings then went to their seats. When Colarossi's attention returned within their own circle again, Mitchell said, "You seem to know quotations. Does the cryptic message received by the Board before Arthur was fished out of the Sound mean anything to you? Did you send that message?"

"You are direct and go right for the jugular. Hell, no. It's baffling."

"How can we work together to expose Marlowe?"

"We can work as a team," replied Colarossi buttering his bread. "But we can't work together. Let me explain. I can't go probing, or asking questions of members. But you can. It's not police business, but your line of work. That you're writing about the case. Somewhere there's a fault. Maybe you'll find Arthur's killer as well. But I want Renata's killer desperately. Renata's soul will not rest in peace until her killer is caught and made to pay. Josh convinced me it was Marlowe. With his bodyguards, he's tough to get at. Except in this building when his guards stay outside.

"Again, I don't pollute where I eat, but perhaps we can talk to him later in the evening. He usually flies up from Washington, lands at MacArthur Airport and has dinner over at Alvin's table. Looks like he's running late tonight. You sit and talk to him. But what's he going to say? What can you get him to say? He'll stand behind his alibis. This is not a simple case, Mitchell. Too many private arrangements you don't know anything about. Sometimes, things aren't what they seem. Anyone in the CIA can tell you that."

"You have something on Marlowe?" inquired Josh.

"That's not for publication now. I have friends who know certain things. I may need a trade-off— like his confession that he visited Renata for whatever his reason. So you see, Mitchell, patience and teamwork will topple the house that Edward Marlowe built to protect himself. You hold up your end with your probing because probing arouses curiosity and makes the killer nervous which leads to mistakes. You should do your thing with the police and the press. Keep the killings alive. Just make sure I am never, ever a part of your conversation. When you talk to the press and police, you don't know me. With your type of exterior pressure and my interior pressure, his foundation will crack."

"Telling the press and the police is good strategy," Mitchell said. "I'll do so when the timing is right. Josh, do you agree?"

"That's an intelligent approach. Keep me out of it, also."

"Now, Mitchell, tell me about your next project. What are you working on now?" Colarossi had closed the subject.

For the balance of dinner, Mitchell found Colarossi conversational, intelligent, pleasant and enjoyable company—a perfect socialite among the membership of his secluded haven. He was far removed from the public image associated with organized crime. Here, he was a choirboy, a member of a social group. He and Josh discussed the cost of education on the Island with Colarossi suggesting that one school board for the county would save millions by eliminating the dozens of separate boards. Mitchell participated with his opinions.

When the subject changed to the problems of the yacht club, besides the murders, Mitchell became an observer, a chance to study Colarossi; a difficult study.

Edward Marlowe hadn't arrived at the yacht club

by the time Josh and Mitchell separated from
Colarossi for the evening at eleven o'clock. Josh knew
that meant he'd be arriving tomorrow.

An occasional star peeked behind the cloud cover
that was beginning to separate as Josh and Mitchell
headed for *Coyote* and the north dock.

"Mitchell, I don't know whether to believe Mario,
or not. Whether he has something on Marlowe. Or
was he trying to throw us off the track of his getting
rid of Dryden, or possibly killing Renata."

"He could be lying about Marlowe. I hope he does
have whatever it is on Marlowe. He's a clever guy. He
grabbed the offense immediately and took over the
meeting as if he knew what I was going to ask. And
then his comment of his being a suspect the way
Dryden died. I get a feeling he was alerted. What
are the chances Valerie Dryden told him what we
said to her?"

"None, to slim," said Josh.

"If there is collusion between Colarossi and
Valerie, the situation would change dramatically.
Colarossi then might have motive to kill Dryden and
my mob-hit theory wouldn't be far from wrong. His
domineering personality aside, his suggestions of my
talking to the press and police are good strategy to
keep the pressure on Marlowe. Let's keep moving
forward and see what unfolds."

"Marlowe should be arriving tomorrow around
noon. Shall we talk to him then?"

"Some other time. I promised Helene the day.
Lunch, and then help her at the office. Saturday or
not, this is a busy time for her. Let me know if anything happens. I'll come out Sunday if necessary."

"Let's attend the next board meeting. We'll have

dinner beforehand. I can't imagine anything but fear and chaos being on the agenda."

"You've a date. In the meantime, remain guarded. We had good and informative conversations with Valerie and Colarossi. But it could all be bullshit."

* * *

WITH THE DIRECTOR of the Central Intelligence Agency and his agents on the premises the next day, a Suffolk police boat patrolled the marina and the harbor within a half mile radius of the club and a Huntington Bay squad car stood guard in the club's parking area. The police presence offered security to the membership. The weekend continued normally and uneventfully, leading to beliefs that maybe the killings had finally stopped.

Mitchell spent the balance of Saturday assisting Helene, sharing an early dinner and then a Broadway musical. On Sunday, Helene promised to have her assistant, Alicia, continue to work a good portion of her time researching the cryptic message by first determining who originally wrote the phrase. Since it was an excerpt, maybe the longer text offered the hidden clue to the message.

Calling the college professors and the library this past week proved ineffective, although all promised to continue to seek the answer.

Mitchell continued to make notes of his meetings and observations.

SIX

Sunday afternoon.
June 9.

HE TURNED UNTO Pinelawn Road where a sod
farm on the left and light industry on the right con-
trasted. Continuing south with the weekend traffic,
he crossed the expressway passing the Swiss Air and
Estee Lauder buildings. Approaching Newsday, Long
Island's primary newspaper, the scene on the left
changed to the mind jarring vision of thousands of
white marble gravestones in the Long Island National
Cemetery; a perennial reminder of war in this cen-
tury; that the lessons of war have yet to be learned.

He turned left into the next cemetery in line,
Pinelawn Memorial Park and confirmed that this
beautifully landscaped and maintained park setting
was the perfect and fitting resting-place for his beautiful Renata. He turned left by the Greek columns
to a bend in the road and parked by the colonnade
monument.

Three cars were parked on the road, their owners at gravesites on the opposite side of the road from
Renata. He wore sunglasses and a boating cap to re-

main unrecognized. The grass was damp from the sprinkler system and his footsteps left imprints.

Some grass cuttings and leaves from nearby trees were on her flat metal plaque. He knelt, swept them with his fingers and then touched her name. He also swept the grass that surrounded the plaque while reprimanding himself for not bringing flowers. He rose and said a quiet prayer. The tears didn't come this time, nor was his body a wilted flower like the last trip. He had accepted her death now that he accepted his mission to avenge her murder.

The elimination of Arthur Dryden was the beginning.

The Board of Trustees couldn't decipher the challenging and warning message to tell them Arthur Dryden was next to die. No one was able to warn him, and that was tragic. The warning would have made the revenge daring and challenging, a bit sweeter. The membership present at the meeting and the police must have forgotten their studies in English literature. Next time, he'd send an easier, yet challenging message to the board. A challenge added to the excitement and added fear to the targeted and potential victim in knowing that he was about to die. The victim would lose sleep, be afraid and inflict self-torture by not knowing when the killer would strike. Fear would generate mental punishment before being told why he had to be obliterated from this life, no longer worthy to be among the living. And to be told that he was about to die with his hands tied behind his back, struggling to breathe as he drowned in the cold and dark, dark sea—his final torture.

The finding of the chained body, allowing Dryden the final benefit of a respectful and religious funeral, was cause for frustration because Dryden didn't deserve a dignified burial, no dignity of any kind.

The sounds of a private single engine plane heading northeast from Republic Airport and two memorial park trucks with work crews passing on the nearby road distracted his thoughts. He watched as they moved further away, then returned his thoughts to Renata and envisioned her face.

Focusing on the raised lettering of Renata's name, he offered silent assurances to her that the next body wouldn't be found to have a dignified funeral.

And that the next time he returned to see her, he'd bring flowers.

* * *

Third Wednesday.
June 19.
The monthly Board of Trustees meeting.

MITCHELL AND JOSH had dinner in the club's crowded dining room where conversation at every table revolved around murder, fear and safety. They could feel restlessness and anxiety in the air from anticipation of the upcoming meeting.

The waitresses worked a bit faster than usual knowing the members had to leave by 7:30. At 7:25, Josh and Mitchell went below to the meeting room on the first floor. Mitchell had a yellow pad to take notes.

The large room was filled with nervous chatter as concerned members and wives continued to file in, ready to hear latest news and to demand action. A group was talking about closing the club for the season. The Commodore and all the officers were in the front preparing to sit and start. The Commodore then determined that he'd begin in a few more minutes to allow members more time to attend and the dining room to empty. The atmosphere was thick with tension.

The meeting came to order at 7:45 in a room packed with members, a few guests, the New York City and Long Island media and representatives of the police department; two detectives and two uniformed officers who waited by the entrance. Reporters and television cameras were ready to capture highlights for tonight's late news. Several interviews had already been recorded. Extra folding chairs were brought in by Titus Banks to accommodate the overflowing attendees. The club officers and trustees, in uniform, sat in front of the room behind a long rectangular table, with a white tablecloth, allowing them to face the uneasy audience. The room's tone was loud and disorderly, prompting Commodore Sosnick to bang his gavel again, each time more forcefully. The voices subsided and the rustling ended.

Commodore Sosnick rose to speak on important matters at the club believing that members, especially emotional ones, pay more attention to speakers who stand. This was an important meeting and emotions would run higher.

He was a forceful man, nearly six feet tall, in his early fifties, in his first term of office. In the real world, he was a vice-president for Lehman Brothers, investment bankers. He lifted the microphone from its stand.

"This meeting will come to order. I urge your cooperation at this difficult and incomprehensible time." The audience settled and the last murmur faded. "I am bypassing the regular agenda because of a serious development and more important priorities. I have asked Detective Lieutenant Kenneth Mullins of the Suffolk Homicide Squad to speak to us tonight. A new and alarming development has occurred."

Mullins being here surprised Mitchell, expecting him to be away. He saw him in the back of the room. The Commodore spoke slowly and loud. The audience became more attentive.

"I called Lieutenant Mullins when notified by our office manager, Marie Bailey, that we received another cryptic message which I will read to you." Amidst concerned and frightened murmurs that the message foretold death, he continued in a bit louder voice.

"The original envelope and letter have been turned over for fingerprinting to Lieutenant Mullins. The postscript is from Northport, not the local post office as the previous one."

He adjusted his glasses and read. "Quote—And then there was one. Alas, poor Yorick, I knew him well." He put the note down. "Does that mean anything to anybody?"

"Over here, Commodore." Lorene Grant, President of the Ladies Auxiliary, a small energetic woman in her forties raised her hand and stood in the middle of the audience. Everyone turned towards her, as did the television cameras.

"That's Shakespeare, Commodore, from Hamlet. Yorick was the court jester whose skull was found in a graveyard."

"Good for you, Lorene," responded the Commodore. "Does Shakespeare, Hamlet and Yorick make sense to anyone?" No one responded to stop the murmuring and the puzzled expressions. Lieutenant Mullins, would you come to the front, please?"

A man of average stature, in a blue suit, with salt and pepper hair, a red complexion and in his early fifties, made his way to the front and the podium.

"Thank you, Commodore. I'm going to be direct with you. The note is designed to provoke fear and terror, and to confuse. We don't know what the note's writer wants us to believe. We must believe he will strike again. The lady here," pointing to Lorene, "gave us major clues. Based on those clues, we will immediately begin to warn and protect all members who are writers—Shakespeare was a writer, all members of Danish descent—Hamlet was Danish, and all comedians, professional and amateur since Yorick was a court jester. Is there anyone in this club named Shakespeare, Hamlet or Yorick? How about middle names?"

"No one," replied the Commodore.

"Are there any writer members in the room?" Josh Trimble stood. So did a woman who wrote for Redbook. "Please see me immediately following this meeting. Anyone here of Danish descent?" Four members stood. "See me, also. Is there anyone in comedy, or a clown? Or ever was?" No one stood. "Anyone in the club connected with cemeteries, or graveyards, or makers of headstones? Or funeral homes?" No one stood. "For your safety, we will maintain a police boat and a squad car in the area everyday until this madman is caught.

"Both murder victims had their cars in the club parking lot. It's logical to state that the murderer is using this facility as his or her base of operations. I want to assure that the police and the homicide squad is continuing this priority investigation."

"What is taking so long!" a distraught member shouted. "Our families are afraid to come here."

Lieutenant Mullins pushed on, undeterred.

"Sir, this is not some television drama when the killer is caught in the last five or ten minutes of a show, like *Murder, She Wrote*. Reality doesn't unfold that way. I regret to add that we have no suspects as to who murdered Renata Tredanari, or Arthur Dryden, or know if the murders are connected. You have all been interviewed. I want to stress again if anyone has any ideas, or suspects, or information, no matter how remote, please tell me. We need to question anyone you believe is a suspect. The message connects us to the killer of Arthur Dryden because there was a note before he died.

"The killer seems to be establishing a pattern with the second note, which means he is not a random killer, or an arbitrary serial killer. He pre-meditates his moves and challenges us to stop him before he gets to the next victim. I'm scaring you on purpose. You must be alert and cautious and have a companion, especially at night. No note was sent to the Board prior to Ms. Tredanari's death. Therefore, they may not be connected. The note may also be a hoax by a different person, a prankster or a psycho. We take everything seriously.

"We can't possibly protect all of you on a twenty-four hour basis. Police are on the premises. And those who stood and others in your categories, a squad car will be assigned to your home and to your place of business in Suffolk County. In the back of the room are sheets with my name, address and phone numbers. Take a copy. Also, CIA Director Edward Marlowe will have his agents assist the police when he's on the premises. I spoke to him earlier today."

At the mention of Marlowe, Mitchell looked around the room and noted that Marlowe, Colarossi and Valerie Dryden were absent. He also looked for Matthew DiBiasi and Gina Ferrara. They weren't there. Marlowe was probably in Washington. Where were Valerie and Colarossi to learn the latest on who killed the former members of their families?

"Today," continued Mullins. "I met with the Commodore and your officers and discussed instituting action to be taken for added safety. They will brief you."

Lieutenant Mullins thanked the Commodore for inviting him and returned to the back of the room to hear the balance of the meeting. He did not see Mitchell Pappas.

The rest of the meeting took another hour discussing and arguing matters relative to security at the gate, on boats and with visitors or service personnel. The Commodore used the gavel often. The theme was alertness. The meeting ended with security in place and mental insecurity rampant.

Standing in the rear with the rest of the media, next to Cablevision's News 12, was Adam Farmer, a reporter from Newsday who covered crime and homicide in the Huntington area. He absorbed vital statements, names and noted the room's aura, the cryptic message, and the fear, the concern and defensive actions against a possible criminal assault.

Adam, thirty years old had been with Newsday since being recruited from the School of Journalism at Columbia University. He was five feet eight inches, of average built with glasses and a beard. He had covered Renata and Dryden's murders and his articles of events at the Eastern Shore Yacht Club were

front-page headlines with primary page three stories and pictures.

He published the first cryptic message without
his readers offering answers. He would do the same
with the Yorick message. He had interviewed many
of the members in attendance tonight and was becoming a familiar face.

When circles of conversation began to form,
Adam sought out Josh Trimble and the Commodore.
Josh led the discussion on marina security. Seeing
Josh first, he approached. Josh recognized him and
introduced Mitchell.

"Mitchell, this is Adam Farmer, from Newsday.
He's been covering this story. He did the original
piece on Renata. Adam, Mitchell Pappas." They
shook hands.

"The noose is tightening, Josh," said Adam. "And
terror stalks the yacht club sounds like an appropriate headline, doesn't it?"

"Precautions are mandatory. Better to be safe.
Are you going to be here awhile? I have to see Lieutenant Mullins about my security. The whole world
picks on us writers!"

"See you later, Josh. I have a few questions of you."
Josh left.

"I'm a friend of Josh's and not a member. You
might say an interested observer helping Josh," said
Mitchell. "You need to talk with me."

Adam looked at him curiously. "I do? What
about?"

"I've been doing some investigation and I'd like
to eventually keep you informed." Adam scrutinized
him for a while.

"Are you a cop? A private detective?"

"No, an investigative author."

"Should I know you?"

"No, but get to know me. If you want to be a better writer, read one of my books." Mitchell grinned, as did Adam.

"I know you, Mr. Pappas. I was being a wise ass. We're both alumni of Columbia University. You're standard fare in the alumni news. Should we talk now?"

"No, at Newsday. I want to review your stories in past editions and see them from your perspective."

"That's not a problem. When?"

"At a more propitious time in the near future. I have details to work out. I understand you're not satisfied with the way the police have been handling these cases."

"I say so loud and clear. They're not happy with my criticism. Lieutenant Mullins turns purple when he sees me. I get the feeling there's a power hand on Mullins' shoulders keeping him down. That would be unfortunate because he is one of the Island's best. The whole investigation has a bad odor. Here's my card." Mitchell took the card. Adam looked at him quizzically. "Do you have information the police don't know?"

"I'll tell you what I know before I tell the police, or at the same time. This way, you'll have an exclusive."

Adam perked up. "I look forward to it, Mr. Pappas. It'll be an honor to work with you."

Mitchell was tempted to approach Mullins, to say hello, but Mullins was in discussion with the members who stood during the meeting. He would communicate at another time. He waited for Josh. They edged their way out of the clubhouse into the cool night air that refreshed their crowd-heated skins.

"Mitchell!" Lieutenant Mullins called out. Mitchell and Josh turned. "I thought it was you."

"Hello, Lieutenant. Good to see you again. You were supposed to be away."

"I cut the trip short to be here. I didn't know you were a member. I saw you leaving and wanted to say hello."

"I'm a guest. You were inundated tonight and didn't want to distract you from your work. However, I do need to talk with you. Can I call you tomorrow to discuss the murders?"

"Not at this time, Mitchell. I know we've worked well in the past, but this case is different. Closed for security reasons."

"I understand." Mitchell replied disappointed, but accepting for now.

"Goodnight then, gentlemen. I must be getting back. He tapped Mitchell's left shoulder. "Good to see you again. Say hello to Helene. Let's get together after the murders are solved." Mullins left and returned to the building.

"Well, Josh, so much for my talking to the police about Marlowe."

"Damn!"

On their way to Mitchell's car, Mitchell put his arm around Josh's shoulder.

"Josh, this was a tough night. That message may be meant for you. Be aggressive in self-preservation. Don't count only on the police. And for God's sake, keep that rifle handy. Better yet, get back to the city."

* * *

Friday.
June 21.

MITCHELL SPENT THE following week sorting out research notes on a potential project he considered undertaking regarding a husband and wife lawyer team who were burned to death in a fiery car crash while in the middle of a murder trial they were defending. Six months later, they were seen on a golf course in Blowing Rock, North Carolina and were returned to New York for questioning. The conclusion was still pending. The premise had promise.

He had notes and research on one other possible story, but the deceptive lawyers intrigued him. He wanted to learn why they staged their deaths and who were the two victims in the car. What forces lurked in the background?

He called Josh yesterday to assure he was all right and for the latest news, if any.

"Nothing new regarding the murders." Josh said. National media interest is increasing because Edward Marlowe is a member and Arthur Dryden was his former partner. Why don't you and Helene come out this Saturday? You can talk to some members for additional background."

"Helene can't do anything this weekend. Some kind of seminar she's attending up at Mohonk Mountain. But I can make it on Sunday"

"Sunday's fine, but I'm scheduled for Coast Guard Auxiliary duty. Come along. We patrol the Huntington area waters to aid the Coast Guard on lesser duties like towing boats, assisting in accidents and medical emergencies and discourage speeders. Maybe we can visit with Commandant Deever up at the station. Be here before ten. Any luck on those cryptic messages?"

"Not yet. They're trying another set of professors and literary enthusiasts. The Shakespeare thing they all knew. And from what I read in Newsday, the same for some of Adam Farmer's Newsday readers."

"Since I'm a writer, that damn Shakespeare quote might be a reference to me and I'm nervous. I also teach playwriting. That relates to the stage."

"I said that to you the night of the meeting. Don't tell me there's room in your recalcitrant mind for worry."

"I'm scared shit."

"Then why are you commuting from there?"

"Here, I have police protection. I can be attacked in the city. I can feel safe at night on the boat with a squad car patrolling the grounds. Plus, I have the rifle."

"Helene is confident they'll crack the code soon. I'll call you immediately, then you tell the police and press . . . and alert the possible next victim."

"If Helene finds the answers, she should take the credit. Your name will be mentioned and give added credibility in continuing your investigation. Maybe Lieutenant Mullins will open up to you."

"My only concern is to save your ass. Stay alive until Sunday."

How much did the police know about Renata, Mitchell wondered after finishing the call with Josh? Does Lieutenant Mullins know that Deever, Horatio, Dreyden and Marlowe were more than friends? Did he know the murders were connected? Was he implementing a waiting strategy? Was he the one protecting Marlowe from adverse publicity, which may force his resignation as director of the CIA? Someone was allowing this case to unfold piece meal. Or, maybe it seemed that way. Maybe Mullins didn't know anything about Renata and her drinking buddies. A major door would open to Mullins if he knew that Arthur Dryden and Renata had sex in common.

At noon, an excited Helene called the apartment. He had hardly finished saying, "Hello," when she blurted—

"We got it! Come over for lunch and bring sandwiches. We deciphered the clue in both messages!"

"Outstanding!" He pounded the table. "Tell me now."

"I have to show you the material. Come on, move your overweight body."

"Helene, a man's life might be at stake here. Every minute counts!"

"Then hurry over here and stop the dramatics."

"Two club sandwiches coming up."

Helene was in the office library whose shelves were lined with manuscripts, magazines and books in various languages she had published when Alicia called out to tell her that Mitchell had arrived. She came out, greeted him and they went into her office overlooking Madison Avenue. The rug was shaggy white, the furniture modern red. The wood was rosewood and the drapes a mixture of interwoven whites and reds. The room had a fresh scent, lightly soothed by her cologne. Plants were in every corner and pictures of the authors she represented nearly covered the right wall over the red sofa.

His picture was in the middle, in the largest frame; a three-quarter, smiling profile. Josh Trimble's picture was to the right.

She picked up a folder and two books from her

desk. They sat on the sofa. She placed the material on the coffee table, picked up a large text entitled *English Literature* and flipped it open to a marked page.

"Let me show you how good we are. The first message ordained for Arthur Dryden now becomes obvious. The passage—Secret guilt by silence is betrayed—was written by an English writer of the Restoration Period, the sixteen hundreds, and is included in his book called *The Hind and the Panther*. The hind is the symbol of the Roman Church, persecuted by the panther, being the Anglicans. The writer is named . . . John Dryden."

"I'll be darned." He pulled the book to his side and read the marked section.

"The person who wrote that cryptic message knows their literature," Helene continued. "In this instance, the *name* of the author is the clue."

"That's now obvious. Was the other one just as tough?"

"Yes, and no." She switched books. "We know that Yorick is mentioned in Hamlet and which, as the world knows, was written by Shakespeare. The line, 'Alas, poor Yorick, I knew him well', is a commonly used distortion of the one actually written by Shakespeare. The distortion has been often used over the years and has popular usage. However, in this particular book, in Hamlet, Act Five, Scene One . . ."—she flipped to the proper page—" . . . the line actually reads—Alas, poor Yorick, I knew him, *Horatio*."

Mitchell grabbed and kissed her and rushed to the desk phone to dial Josh, as Helene continued. "This is what Hamlet says in the graveyard to his close friend, Horatio, after being handed the skull of

Yorick, a former court jester. The skull had just been dug up. In this puzzle, the clue *wasn't* the author's name."

The phone rang in Josh's boat without being answered. He hung up and dialed the club's office with impatience. He said it was an emergency and important to reach Josh Trimble. The office manager, Marie Bailey informed him, that Josh was not on the premises and could probably be reached at the university.

He called New York University and was placed on hold until Professor Trimble could be notified of an emergency to come to the phone.

"Helene, you did it!" exclaimed Mitchell, winking at her. "Good for you!"

"Alicia did it. She found Dryden. I uncovered Hamlet."

"To your credit for hiring her. You may have saved Alvin Dean Horatio's life. I'll hold for a few more minutes and then I'll call the police or Horatio directly. It's best the police alert him. How did Alicia find the Dryden piece? The college minds in New York couldn't figure out that Dryden passage. At least, the ones contacted."

"Through shear frustration. As a last resort, she went back to her old high school literature text and there were book excerpts on material John Dryden had written. A gong rang at the name. The similar name made the search simpler and contained."

"Give her a raise. Hello, Josh. Call the police immediately and notify them that Alvin Horatio is the next intended victim. Have Horatio alerted then Helene will explain the solutions. I'm at her office. You have the number handy? Good. I'll be waiting." He hung up.

"Mitchell," Helene said. "Whoever wrote those notes knows English lit. The average person wouldn't know the Yorick misrepresentation or know Dryden's work. Any clues?"

"Yes, Valerie Dryden, high school teacher of American and English Literature. Having the same name, she must have become familiar with his work. She could have written those notes for someone else, someone like Mario Colarossi. But specific knowledge doesn't make her guilty. Is she a suspect to consider? I'd say so. Also, Marlowe is an educated man who could know English literature. It may be a camouflage technique to divert attention from him if he's the killer." He went back to the sofa and bit into the sandwich. "Since you solved the Yorick puzzle, I suspect the media will want to talk to you, along with Alicia. Get all the publicity you can. In your business, publicity will attract new and established authors. Enjoy the benefits since you've done the job. I'll use that publicity to advantage as I help Josh in the investigation."

The phone rang. Mitchell answered the extension on the coffee table. In his excitement about Horatio, he had ignored the extension. "Josh?"

"I told Lieutenant Mullins and they're alerting Horatio and his family as we speak. Let me talk to Helene. I want to thank and congratulate her on spectacular detective work on the solutions. Then I'll call Mullins back and give him the answers."

He handed the phone to Helene, who listened, accepting the accolades. She explained the Dryden and Shakespeare solutions. She passed the receiver to Mitchell.

"I knew by getting you involved," said a joyous Josh, "that something dramatic would happen. I'm

also relieved the killer isn't after me. I can't imagine
Alvin sleeping nights until that lunatic is caught.
Maybe it's time I told the police about Marlowe being with Renata that night. And if he gets Horatio,
then Douglas Deever has got to be next. That will
eliminate the pinochle buddies who covered up for
him."

"Hang him. You may save Horatio's and Deever's
life. But you may also get yourself killed. Just hope
that by Horatio being warned, that whoever is doing
the killing will stop. With Horatio being threatened,
the police may believe you. Two witnesses as victims
should stimulate them. Think on it and we'll talk
some more on Sunday. You should call Deever."

"We'll tell him on Sunday. Rather, you tell him,"
said Josh. "Coming from you would be more credible by telling him your Marlowe theory that he's killing his witnesses and sending the riddles. Maybe he'll
confess about covering up. There's no need to rush
to warn him. The killer will probably precede any
attack on him with a cryptic message, like the others."

"Call Lieutenant Mullins and tell him how the
message was solved and who did it. Make sure you
mention me, also. He may be more agreeable in
meeting with me when I call him. He should know I
was indirectly involved. I need ammunition to get
him to meet with me." Mitchell said goodbye and
hung up.

They continued with lunch while reviewing the
yacht club scenario and various facets. Helene was
excited over uncovering the solutions, adding to the
drama. She became enthused about a possible book.

"Mitchell, do this story. You can do it better than
Josh. It's your kind of subject matter. Or do it jointly

with Josh. If not, promise me you'll help him. Your involvement up front, or behind the scenes will make the book successful."

He moved closer and held her hands.

"My agent, my wife. No, no my darling. As an agent, it makes sense. You know I won't upstage Josh. This is his to claim. As agent, you'll still benefit. As my wife, I'll see that it's right so you can make a lot of money. I'll keep the notes current as we go along."

"My husband, my lover, my star author. You can never do too much for me." She put her arms around him and gave him a passionate kiss with a mouth full of turkey.

* * *

Mitchell returned to the apartment at three o'clock.

Helene left for her seminar directly from the office at four.

At nine o'clock, all hell broke loose.

Josh called in panic to say that Horatio's wife called the police to report him missing.

* * *

The next morning.
Saturday.
June 22.

DOTTIE AND MICHAEL CAMPBELL, school-teachers and avid sailors, begin their vacation the day after schools close in their district—towards the end of the third week in June. They spend the summer hiatus through Labor Day cruising on their thirty-three foot sloop, *Halcyon*—named after the mythical bird that had the power to calm the sea when it rested on its waters. They sailed out of the Eastern Shore Yacht Club where they've been members for six years. Their parents are members.

They looked forward to the casual and meandering life style of living on their boat—especially now, to get away from the murders and terror that was gripping their club.

Reaching Block Island, they picked up a mooring at Great Salt Pond.

They bicycled to Southeast Lighthouse on Mohegan Bluffs and turned right onto the dirt road leading to the bluffs and placed the bicycles in the town provided racks. Four other bicycles were in place. The sound of shuddering surf increased as they reached the edge of the bluffs and admired the spread of the Atlantic Ocean. On this clear day, they could see Montauk, Long Island low in the horizon.

The bluff dropped suddenly one hundred sixty feet to the rocky beach below. They followed the cliff trail down the steep ravine maneuvering cautiously from rock to rock until reaching a shore completely covered with rocks and stones. The sandy beach was further north around the bend. They strolled among the smooth multi-colored stones that the ocean had yielded long ago, piling them up like a collection of rejected children awaiting reclamation.

Dottie and Michael reached the bend where two large boulders stood like sentries thirty yards offshore. Two smaller boulders, side by side, were to the right. The waves burst white around them. The sandy beach, with its promise of a relaxing and fulfilling day, was several yards ahead. They were satisfied being the first bathers there that morning. That's what they liked about this beautiful location—no crowds all day. The steep cliff trail discouraged many. This was their almost private haven.

Some debris floated by the large boulders and something was lodged between the smaller ones.

Dottie saw it first and screamed in horror when she recognized it as a fully clothed body floating face down with hands tied behind its back.

When the authorities arrived and pulled the body out of the water, the shocked Campbells were able to identify the bloated corpse as that of Rear Commodore Alvin Dean Horatio of the Eastern Shore Yacht Club.

SEVEN

THE FINDING OF Horatio's body spread quickly among the media and the club's membership. Josh notified Mitchell Saturday night of the finding and the media was beginning to gather outside the club gate. The Commodore and the police ordered that only club members and guests be allowed to enter the premises. The Coast Guard Auxiliary assignment remained scheduled.

Edward Marlowe, Director of the Central Intelligence Agency was unavailable for comment on Saturday. He left the club upon hearing the news and returned to Washington after making a consoling visit to Horatio's wife and family. From Washington, he'd be able to meet with the media in an orderly manner. This became his personal crisis. He braced for difficult times ahead now that the national media focus was on him and knew the focus would change only when the police had a suspect to snare the spotlight.

His picture and those of his ex-partners, Horatio and Dryden and his boat neighbor, Renata Tredanari were on the Saturday evening news and the major Sunday papers followed with front page photos of Marlowe, and the three member victims.

The CIA director stood at six feet with broad

shoulders on an athletic and trimmed torso. His blond hair and chiseled features were striking, demanding attention when this handsome man walked into a room. In his early fifties and divorced, he has been a club member for fifteen years serving in many officer and committee chairman positions, including commodore. His duties in Washington minimized his attendance.

A graduate of the University of Pennsylvania Law School, he rejected offers from major law firms in favor of establishing his own firm in Huntington—to be part of the political and expanding business activity on Long Island.

He convinced Arthur Dryden and Alvin Dean Horatio to join him as partners. The firm grew to thirty-five employees and moved to luxurious offices in the corporate area of southern Huntington.

He became involved in local government and related politics and won town and county contracts. His involvement with local charities and his contributions to state and federal candidates brought lobbying influence, gaining him entry to state power.

Further, the firm was the primary representative of police officers in Suffolk and Nassau counties in criminal and civil cases. The Policemen's Benevolent Association supported Marlowe.

He was recommended to the administration by state and county leaders and New York members of Congress. The President nominated Marlowe for the position after their initial meeting, fulfilling his political obligation to New York State that gave him an impressing plurality in the presidential election.

In his tenure in office, Edward Marlowe earned the confidence of Congress and the Administration, and was held in high regard.

On Sunday morning, to pacify the media, Marlowe held a heavily attended press conference at his office to denounce and condemn the murders explaining he had no idea why his ex-partners and Mrs. Tredanari were killed. Answering the questions, "Is there some kind of conspiracy against you?" "Is someone after you?" "Are they giving you a message?" Marlowe responded that he had no specifics, but the possibility certainly existed; that he was cooperating with local and county authorities in the continuing investigation and increasing his personal guards.

He planned to return to Long Island on Wednesday to attend Horatio's funeral regardless of risk and planned to meet with the President to have federal agencies help the investigation in the event there is a conspiracy against him and other public officials.

* * *

THE HUNTINGTON BAY police were maintaining traffic order along tree-lined East Shore Road to keep the curious moving and the media in check when Mitchell drove up to the gate. He gave his name as a guest of Josh Trimble.

Adam Farmer of Newsday, sitting in his car, intent on writing notes, looked towards the club and saw Mitchell enter the grounds. He ran along the road to a point near the north dock guessing he was visiting with Josh Trimble. When Mitchell parked and left the car, Adam called his name.

Mitchell turned, saw Adam waving through the greenery, waved back and approached him. Adam was by the guardrail where the road inclined to eight feet above the parking area. Although brush and trees separated them, each had a clear view.

"Good morning, Adam," he said, looking up. "The search for news continues on Sundays. You people are more diligent than the postal service."

"How are you doing, Mr. Pappas?" Adam said, now standing on the guardrail for a better view and leaning with one arm against a tree for balance and support. "Bad news never sleeps. I hear that you and your wife solved those riddles. My compliments."

"My wife, Helene and her assistant did the research. They deserve the credit."

"Can I call them? Your number's unlisted and her office is closed today."

Mitchell gave him his home number. "You'll be the first—a media exclusive. You can also include that she's one of the hottest literary agents around," he smiled while promoting his wife.

"I appreciate the chance to interview her first. What are you doing here? Investigating?"

"Josh has Coast Guard Auxiliary duty and I'm keeping him company and to get some fresh air on this gorgeous day preceded by death and local news."

"I need to speak about what we discussed at the club meeting. When?"

"In a few days. When things settle down a bit and I have more information and time for research. Be patient. I plan to use you as my conduit."

"That's cool. Have you talked to Lieutenant Mullins yet?"

"No. As I've said, I'll talk to you first."

"This story has reached national prominence. So, I'm a bit impatient. I hope you understand. We can use each other for mutual benefit."

"Start with Helene. Tell her you got the number

from me, where and when. I'm running a bit late for Josh right now. I'll call you during the week."

Like any good reporter trying to squeeze the last drop from an opportunity, he asked, "What's your opinion about the latest murder?"

"No opinion yet. I hope the police have some evidence from Horatio's body, or anywhere."

"They have nothing. I've already checked. This new spotlight will make them sweat more, will force them to increase the investigative tempo."

"Call Helene before somebody else traces her down. Go." He started to turn away to leave.

"One more thing," called out Adam. "Horatio's hands were tied behind his back just like Dryden's. Did you know that?"

"I didn't know that," replied Mitchell, turning back to Adam. "That's significant modus operandi."

"May mean that Dryden and Horatio were killed by the same person. Being found in the Block Island area means his body wasn't supposed to be found. Probably meant to be swept out into the Atlantic Ocean."

"Logical deductions," Mitchell confirmed.

"Have you any idea why they were marked for death?"

"If you want to hear fiction, I'll create something. You and I will talk regarding theories, then make what you want of them."

Adam was disappointed, but found room for optimism in the upcoming theories. "Thank you, Mr. Pappas. I appreciate the home number. Have a nice day."

"You too, Adam. Make sure you put your snooping nose only where the sun shines."

Adam laughed and ran to his car to phone

Helene, and knowing he'd receive praise from his
editor for the exclusive.

* * *

MITCHELL WASN'T SURE what miracle or evidence the police would find to avoid Josh from eventually telling Lieutenant Mullins that Josh observed
Marlowe leaving Renata's boat. Josh's statement
would cause a rush to judgment against Marlowe.
The publicity would be relentless. Would Josh be safe
if Marlowe was arrested? Would he be alive to testify
at a trial?

Would Marlowe consent to a DNA test to determine the compatibility of the semen? A positive
match would prove his visit, but not her murder. But
Marlowe wasn't a suspect. If he was, then proved innocent, he may be forced into resignation by media
pressure and distraction to do his important job effectively. Then Marlowe would wind up a victim.

Josh was afraid for his life, and rightfully so.
Mitchell wouldn't jeopardize Josh by telling Adam
Farmer, or Lieutenant Mullins that he knew of a witness. That decision must come from Josh. He'd raise
the subject later in the day now that Horatio was
murdered and hope Josh will change his mind. It
was Josh's best interest to take the initiative to stall
Marlowe, to put this murderer away before someone else was killed—Someone like Deever.

And Josh.

He'd make it a point to visit with Lieutenant
Mullins and probe Marlowe's strength with the Suffolk County police. Adam Farmer was right. The spotlight was on them to find a suspect, or the murderer.

The investigation had to intensify. They needed a suspect. Mullins had to deliver results.

As intense as the pressure would be, would the police listen to Josh if he came forward as a witness? The media would love that and have a field day about an alleged eyewitness, real or imagined. Would they believe him against the remaining witnesses testifying to the contrary? If they conducted an investigation on Marlowe, what other proof was there? If Marlowe was determined innocent, then Josh remained in potential jeopardy. And what exactly was Colarossi holding over Marlowe? What did Colarossi mean by saying he had something on Marlowe? Or was it pompous braggadocio?

Maybe he could convince Commandant Deever to speak up against Marlowe, to say he lied and covered up for him—and in the process, save his life. He'd discuss that thinking with Josh and encourage him to stop at the Coast Guard station sooner, than later.

* * *

ON A NORMAL Sunday morning during summer, the club parking area would be at near capacity. Less than two-dozen cars indicated an abnormality that morning as Mitchell headed towards the ramp to the north dock.

Mitchell liked Adam Farmer. He represented a power medium on Long Island to influence the course and speed in which crimes unfold and suspicions raised. He will need Newsday when the time came to expose Edward Marlowe.

Boats passing the club on their way to the bay

were going a bit slower to gape at the yacht club domi-
nating the news.

The slip next to Josh's was vacant. As Mitchell
approached *Coyote*'s berth, Josh was tying the Coast
Guard Auxiliary banner, printed in bold red letters,
to the starboard beam railing. Also aboard was Titus
Banks, the dock master, wearing the blue Auxiliary
uniform. They greeted and Mitchell boarded. Titus'
uniform gave today's mission an official bearing, supported by the Coast Guard.

"Did you have trouble getting in, Mitchell?" asked
Josh.

"None."

"The Commodore should be arriving soon to
make a statement to help disperse them," said Titus.
"That's who they're waiting for.

Coyote left her berth entering the active channel
at the five-knot speed limit. Patiently, *Coyote* reached
the historical concrete lighthouse and the cloverleaf
shaped waterfront scenery. Josh maintained five
knots and casually patrolled towards the entrance to
Northport and Centerport harbors a mile to the east.

They sat on the top deck beneath the shady blue
awning as they drank coffee while listening with one
ear to the communication chatter on the emergency
channel, ready to immediately respond to any SOS
call.

Titus didn't know much about Mitchell's background, only that he was an investigative author and
friends with Josh.

"We'll have to teach him the ropes today, Titus,"
said Josh. "What we have here is a landlubber with
no sea sense whatsoever."

"Not to worry, Titus," retorted Mitchell. "I'm a

quick learner. And I'll try not to throw up on your uniform after I have one of Josh's cinnamon rolls."

Titus grinned. "If that happens, Mitchell, you go overboard without a life jacket."

Mitchell was pleased Titus was on board and that he had a trace of humor. As dock master, he knows more of what goes on in the marina and is in touch with all members. Mitchell wanted to hear his perspective on the murdering events enfolding the club like a bear hug.

Titus was now behind the wheel. His face expressed his love affair with the sea and being on the sea. The roll of the sea, white foam and the salt scented air and breezes made him a captive to the navy most of his life and migrated him to work that kept him near, or on the water.

He had seen most of the world from San Diego to Perth to Lagos to the major ports in South America and Europe and each new port a new discovery, new excitement and new temporary love affairs.

He left the navy with a flaw in his record when a woman in Perth accused him of rape fifteen years ago. The two sailors with him testified that the woman was lying, drunk and was shaking them down for money. The woman eventually changed her story and all charges were dropped. The blotch on the record remained, noting his innocence and release back to duty.

He had settled into life on land and the yacht club was suited perfectly. His face had been hardened by winds. His eyes had long ago begun to squint naturally to prevent drying, causing 'worry' lines in his receding forehead.

The sea was more than a call, or his mistress. It controlled his life. This motivated him to run an effi-

cient and organized marina and club services. Efficiency was his hold on job security. He stays on duty
on the busy weekend nights until midnight when
launch service to the moorings ends. If tired, he'd
sleep overnight in the clubhouse rather than going
to his house in Northport near the Smithtown bor-
der.

"So, tell me, Titus," began Mitchell's probe. "What
do you make of what's going on at the club? Any
thoughts on who may be killing those people?"

Titus grinned while contemplating his reply. "Let
me tell you a story, Mitchell, so you know where I'm
coming from." Titus was a slow, deliberate speaker.
When you listened, you had to be patient. "I've been
a career navy man most of my adult life. I've seen
men die in Korea and Vietnam, taken orders and
given orders. I did my job, did what I was told and
minded my own business. I never volunteered or created whirlpool type of problems. But in every instance, I protected my own. When my men would
get into non-criminal type of trouble, I'd protect and
side with them and keep them out of harms way. I
was once falsely accused of something I didn't do. I
will never accuse anyone of anything, as a result.

"Protecting my people may not have been right,
but I did. By so doing, I gained the respect of the
men on the ship. And those who committed criminal acts, I went into the background and minded my
own business. The naval authorities did what they
deemed necessary. Although I didn't protect that
type, I never testified against them though I knew
they were guilty.

"Why do I tell you all this?—Because everyone at
the yacht club sails on my ship, so to speak—my shipmates. The tragedies are personally hurtful. If the

murderer or murderers are caught and I am asked to testify for or against him or them . . . I won't.

"There are a lot of social activities at the club, especially love trysts and extra-marital affairs. I know what goes on in most cases, but I keep it to myself. That's part of the social mix of the environment I have to service and part of the job I value. Could I turn on any member? No. Would I tell tales out of school and proliferate rumors? No.

"I liked Renata, Alvin and Arthur. We had good times together, socially or boating. And may who killed them suffer a thousand deaths and excruciating pain. But if more deaths continue, there's nothing I can do about it. I have my responsibilities the police have theirs. What happens happens."

"Sounds cold," said Mitchell.

"It's survival in a cruel and sometimes insensitive world. Josh is the marina chairman this year and is my boss and knows my philosophy. I do what he tells me as far as work goes. Next year, some other member will be my boss, maybe someone I spoke against. Now, by my telling you my philosophy, I am being defensive and neutral, and protecting the future. Should you ever decide to investigate, or do a book on the subject, I won't be able to help you. Better you know now so you won't feel offended later. Being reluctant does not mean I'm withholding something."

"Is that you in a capsule?"

"You got it, exclamation point."

"Thanks for your frankness, Titus, but like I said . . . cold. Disappointing, also. I had hoped you'd provide a clue since I'm not the authority. And you have no idea who could have killed them?"

"No idea."

"Didn't see anything? Any guesses?"

"None. I told the same thing to the police."

"Did you know the relationship among the people who were killed?"

"Like I said, I generally know what goes on around the club."

"Except why they were murdered, or who did it."

"End of subject?—End of interview? Back to patrol?"

"For now, Titus."

Josh laughed. "It's his personality, Titus. He can't stop asking questions. That's how he speaks most of the time."

"No harm in asking questions," replied Titus. "It's the answers that could get you killed or fired."

Mitchell kept coming. "No more questions. But I have some theories I'll lay on the table for you."

"Go ahead.

"In the club, you have two very powerful men— Edward Marlowe and Mario Colarossi. Alvin Horatio and Arthur Dryden were killed gangland style. Both have the resources to carry out the executions."

"I heard rumors about Mario being connected but that doesn't mean he is, or he had anything to do with these incidents."

"On the other end of the spectrum, you have Marlowe. The CIA. He used to be partners with Horatio and Dryden."

"And best friends, I might add," volleyed Titus. "Marlowe's not a killer. He would have to be insane to be involved in this intrigue. Too much to lose."

"Yes, you are protective of your shipmates, guilty, or not. Maybe they had some reason to betray him, say . . . from out of their past that may jeopardize, or compromise his office."

"In the navy, we called that type of theory horseshit, pure and unadulterated. You picked two of the least likely candidates. If I were to make a list of candidates, they'd be at the bottom. Actually, they wouldn't be on the list at all."

"Who's on top?"

Titus chuckled. "That's a question. I have no idea, or concept as to who could have done the killings."

Mitchell gave up. "Titus, you won. Let's change the subject. Being Sunday," said Mitchell, to Josh. "Do you think Commandant Deever is in? Can we take time out to visit with him?"

Josh looked at his watch. "If he's there, we'll go see him, but we have to do it now. We need to be in the lower bay between the lighthouse and the entrance to Northport when boaters begin heading back around six o'clock and we'll troll there."

Mitchell looked forward to visiting the Coast Guard complex with its strategic and expansive view of The Long Island Sound to visit with Commandant Deever.

What would he say to him? Deever advanced the lie about Marlowe being on his boat during the approximate period of Renata's murder. Why lie to protect Marlowe? Did he conclude he might be the next victim?

Or did he help Marlowe get rid of these people?

Mitchell was convinced that Deever was the likely next victim. But he could go along with Josh's timetable in regard to alerting him. With those thoughts, Mitchell felt that Deever has to be frightened.

Josh opened the cabinet to the cellular phone

and called. Commandant Deever was out for the day. He hung up.

"He's not there today, Mitchell. You'll have to see him some other time."

"Are you going to ask him questions, also?" Titus said, winking.

Mitchell decided to be evasive with Titus since he was uncooperative.

"I wanted a tour of the facility. Never been on a Coast Guard station before. But maybe he can shed some light on the murders."

"The police spoke to him. Leads me to believe that he won't be helpful to you."

"Three people are dead and the police don't know why, or who killed them. The reason may be in the past culminating to the present's violence." He wasn't going to reveal to Titus the theories he and Josh formulated as to who committed the murders. Maybe the past *was* involved. He would research that with Adam Farmer hoping some public event may bind them together. He'd try talking to Colarossi again and urge him to reveal the 'something' he had over Marlowe. "What do you think, Titus? Who do you suggest I talk to since you haven't been helpful?"

"You're right, Josh. He talks in questions. That's two more. I would suggest Lieutenant Mullins. At this point, where he has public pressure to solve the crimes, he might be cooperative. He'd be a fool not to accept your help."

"I'll second that," said Josh to Mitchell. "Helping to solve the riddles may be the open door to what he knows. He may confide in you. If you like, I'll go with you when you meet."

* * *

JOSH DROVE back to Manhattan with Mitchell that evening. On Wednesday morning, they would return together in Mitchell's car to attend Alvin Dean Horatio's funeral.

While there, they would alert Commandant Deever. Sooner, if any riddles arrived in between.

EIGHT

The next day.
Monday. June 24.

ADAM FARMER'S exclusive interview with Helene Fisher Pappas included a picture of Helene and Mitchell, obtained from Helene yesterday afternoon. The headlined article also contained photographs of the three victims and Edward Marlowe.

Adam felt accomplished and enthused when he reported to work this morning. Instead of back slaps from his editor and associates, he immediately received another assignment that quashed the stimulating residue of the exclusive with Helene.

An unhappy Adam Farmer left the Newsday building alone, annoyed at his editor for an unexciting assignment outside of Huntington Township. *The yacht club murders are the most important news on Long Island. I need to concentrate on that. It would mean a Pulitzer!*

He entered his car in a parking field surrounded by acres of manicured lawn, sparse trees and singing birds and headed for the exit to Pinelawn Road to cover a commuter plane crash at Republic Airport to the south; three people were injured. *That's peripheral news. I'm above that now!*

The reporter who covered Babylon, Farmingdale and points south was out sick and Adam was available. His editor saw a window of opportunity to use Adam for several hours. Adam was perturbed about the routine assignment, but he was a team player, though privately reluctant in this case. This wasn't the assignment to expose his unhappiness to his boss. He'd save a rebellious attitude for something important. The yacht club story was his to conclusion. He would fight for that.

He stopped at the stop sign at the end of the Newsday property and waited for on-coming cars to pass. Having been at that exit many times before, he had grown immune to the thousands of white gravestones in the national cemetery across the highway. Every now and then, he shook his head when he focused on the white marble landscape. The vision calmed anger at his boss. *It could be worse.*

He waited for the cluster of cars that had amassed at the traffic light around the bend to pass and prepared to enter the highway as soon as the last car, a black Mercedes-Benz, went by.

The driver in the last car caught Adam's eye and Adam recognized Mario Colarossi behind the sunglasses. Colarossi's shocking white hair was unmistakable. The woman passenger looked like Valerie Dryden.

"I'll be damned, damned, damned. That's very interesting. Thank you, dear editor. You might have made my day. There is a God!" He was getting excited. "Go after them, fool! The game's afoot! The plane accident can wait. Nobody died there!"

He promptly followed the Mercedes to chase a

segment of the yacht club maze and changed to the inside lane with the Mercedes. About a quarter of a mile down the road, Colarossi suddenly changed to the outside lane, as if a last second thought occurred, and pulled into the driveway of a floral stand to purchase a bouquet of white and red roses, pink carnations, baby's breath and spray.

Adam, to avoid being seen, turned his face away from the floral stand and kept going past the cemetery and railroad tracks and parked a street further away, and waited. In the rear view mirror, he saw the Mercedes re-enter the highway and before crossing the railroad tracks, made a left into Pinelawn Memorial Park.

"That figures," Adam chastised himself. "I stopped at the wrong place. Shopping for flowers was a clue he was going to the cemetery, moron!"

Adam made a U-turn and as he faced north, the clanging rail crossing gates with red flashing lights began to lower and he stopped at the solid white line. He hit the steering wheel with both palms, annoyed at his inefficient thinking.

He watched the Mercedes head inward as an eastbound Long Island Railroad commuter train crossed in front of him and stopped at the undersized and quaint Pinelawn station, shutting out the view of the cemetery.

The train pulled out slowly, ignoring Adam's impatience. The crossing gates began to rise. Adam again had a clear view of the cemetery entrance across the tracks, but the Mercedes was gone. He became less upset realizing they were contained within the grounds. The Old East Neck Road exit at the other end of the cemetery had been temporarily closed for some time.

He turned right into the park-like cemetery grounds and followed the main road at a slow pace searching for the black Mercedes. When he passed the Greek columns and the colonnade, he saw the parked Mercedes about a football field to the left and Colarossi and the woman standing over a grave.

Adam assumed that grave to be Renata Tredanari's because he attended her funeral as part of his story and that was the approximate location. He stopped his car fifty feet past the crossroad to have a better view of their faces, opened his camera bag and took out the Nikon and a telephoto lens. He slid low in his seat as he connected the lens. The lens confirmed the man as Colarossi, now wearing a boating cap and sunglasses. Then he panned left and recognized Valerie Dryden. There was no mistake. He had interviewed her extensively.

Why were they together? Did he have anything to do with her husband's murder?—A romantic triangle? Was she Colarossi's motive to kill her husband? The thoughts were stimulating, placing him on a road to possibly solving Dryden's murder.

He zoomed back to a two-shot as Colarossi placed the flowers on the plaque then crossed himself. Adam kept taking shots as Valerie and Colarossi talked at the gravesite. Then their body gestures and movement indicated an argument. Colarossi pointed a finger at her face. They soon settled.

Within seconds, Valerie and Colarossi left the area. Adam slid lower when they passed. It was needless to follow them. When the Mercedes disappeared, he drove to Renata's gravesite to confirm it was hers and not Arthur Dryden's. He was buried near here. Adam was unsure where. He moved the flowers and saw Renata's name. What's the story, Renata? Who killed you? What's with your visitors?"

Seeing two main players connected to the yacht club murders became consuming and suspicious. Both were on their yachts the night Renata Tredanari was killed—now her husband. There had to be something going on between them. Were they having a lover's quarrel? What about? Why didn't they visit Valerie's husband's grave?

To make sure, he returned to the entrance and entered the administration office. At the service desk, he asked for Arthur Dryden's grave location.

Following the small map provided to him, he found Dryden's plaque on the other side of the road from Renata's grave.

There were no flowers.

* * *

THE NEXT MORNING, a photo of Colarossi and Valerie standing solemnly by Renata's grave appeared on page three of Newsday unaccompanied by a story. The picture was a stand-alone identifying them as family members of the club murder victims visiting to deliver fresh flowers to Renata Tredanari.

This is the posturing Adam insisted on with his editor. Here is where he took a stand, a time for rebellion and firmness. The story can always follow. Adam wanted to see what impact the photo would make, who could be surprised by their being together . . . and who would call him with information and the all important lead.

He was optimistic his bait would lure someone.

After the paper was put to bed, he had misgivings about the photo that he selected. Maybe he should have used one where they were arguing.

* * *

WHEN Josh Trimble saw the photo, he immediately sent a fax of the photo to Mitchell with a note, "What now?"

* * *

THE PHOTO BEGAN a domino effect of telephone gossip among the club members and had a profound effect on a desperate Lieutenant Kenneth Mullins of the Suffolk Homicide Squad whose suspicions were aroused. He had Colarossi and Valerie come in for further questioning regarding the murder of Arthur Dryden.

Valerie and Colarossi, calm and collected and with an attorney from her husband's former firm, maintained that they, being long time acquaintances and fiends, were visiting the graves of their family members as victims of two tragedies who went to pay respects to the dead. Colarossi stated that Valerie asked him to accompany her to the cemetery because she couldn't bear to visit her husband's grave alone, that her daughters weren't at home. She needed support and he was available—a friend in need.

The attorney reminded Mullins, who was unable to dispute their reasoning, that he had no legal reason to hold them further. Mullins thanked them for their time and cooperation and authorized their release.

He noted their interview for the official record

with his personal notation of no obvious conspiracy between Colarossi and Valerie Dryden; a misleading photograph with no legal basis.

* * *

TO ADAM's disappointment, no one called Newsday, or him with more information.

* * *

THE PHOTO WASN'T surprising to Mitchell Pappas. The photo confirmed his new theory of their collusion. Was Valerie writing the riddles? Did she tell Colarossi he and Josh met with her, and the discussion? If factual, then the threat to Josh increased. He called Josh. Josh preferred theory. No, he insisted, the only killer is Edward Marlowe who killed the beautiful Renata and two eyewitnesses and was probably plotting the murder of the third.

Mitchell couldn't ignore this series of murders. He had to get involved to save Josh's life.

He kept updating the notes.

The time was ripening to begin his offense.

Let it begin at the Horatio funeral.

NINE

The next day—
Tuesday. June 25.

THE WIND GUST in the harbor and sailboat halyards began chiming haphazardly across the marina as a symphony orchestra warming up prior to the start of a concert.

The persistent metallic chatter began to irritate Titus Banks, stirring the persistent uneasiness that began when he entered the club grounds at eight o'clock this morning. Three cups of coffee since then heightened tension and tightened the internal knot; a feeling he experienced prior to going into combat—not knowing what lay in waiting.

Determined to quiet the pronounced irritation and to quiet his day, he left the dock office for the south dock to search for the culprit halyards protesting the increase in wind velocity. He found the four noisy boats and tied the aluminum and rope halyards away from the aluminum masts, ending the metallic concerto.

The club was sedate during the week—a time for routine activity to prepare for the coming weekend in the usual manner prior to the murders when

the club was teeming with members and guests. A
fruit and vegetable truck made a weekly delivery to
the restaurant. A Texaco fuel truck was pumping
diesel into the fiberglass holding tanks beneath the
parking field. The pool area was being cleaned and
a dock assistant on a motor sweeper cleaned the parking area in preparation for a water hosing.

The tennis courts were unused—a blessing to
Titus. He lacked patience for that annoying thump,
thump noise of bounces and racquet hitting yellow
balls again and again. If he ever lived in a house with
a tennis court in the neighbor's yard, he'd move.

The undetermined cause of restlessness continued, rejecting that he return to his office. Instead,
he fidgeted with several docking lines, re-tying where
necessary, dressed dock lines and curled the excess
line in an orderly manner. His docks were orderly to
military neatness. He walked by the pool area to the
machine and tool shop where two dock assistants
were refurbishing moorings; changing lines and
chains and applying paint.

After checking their work, he went to converse
with the fuel delivery driver. After the delivery was
completed and the truck began to leave, he went to
the squad car by the gate and chatted with the two
now familiar policemen for five minutes.

He meandered to the new dock under construction and watched the pile driver at work. He was
drawn to the north dock, and walked to the end
where Mario Colarossi's 72-foot Broward, *Mario-nette*,
was berthed. No one was aboard, as was the case of
all the boats berthed at the north dock.

The Suffolk County Police boat was coasting towards the southern end of their patrol boundary
before turning north again in a continuing cycle to

protect the club. Titus waved to them. The two officers waved back.

He began to head back and stopped between *Coyote* and *Champagne Lady*. If Josh Trimble were on the premises today, he'd knock on the door and have a beer with him. He liked Josh and enjoyed talking and having a beer with him. Of all the members, he respected Josh the most. He knew Josh wasn't the reason he stopped, finally accepting and admitting to himself the reason for his unsettled state.

He was drawn to the north dock by the uneasiness caused by Renata Tredanari. What shrouded him with her presence? What brought her to life . . . and why today?

He fingered the yellow police tape that blocked the finger to *Champagne Lady's* boarding ladder, knowing that the tape would be removed by tomorrow, Saturday the latest. The police had everything they needed for evidence. The tape deterrent had little value.

He had straightened and organized Renata's stateroom with police permission. Who else was there to do it? He felt obligated to help since Renata was alone. When Josh learned that Titus was working on Renata's yacht, he helped.

He stood on the dock thinking about Renata and a prevailing urge prompted his departure.

He returned to the dock office for *Champagne Lady's* key.

When he walked down the ramp again to the north dock, he looked around suspiciously for a presence on the dock. Who would be watching him? He looked into every aft cabin to assure that he was alone. Seeing no one, he ducked under the yellow tape and boarded *Champagne Lady*. Having second thoughts, in case he was seen by the police, or by office, restaurant or marina personnel, he walked around the yacht checking docking lines as a routine mission on an ownerless craft and was assuming responsibility for its well-being. He checked the squad car. No one was coming to inquire why he was there, to remind him that the yacht technically remained as evidence and was off limits.

Titus turned the key and opened the door. He walked through the cabin, his fingers touching anything that was nearby: the counter, the vase, the bulkhead, a door, a doorknob—anything that was once in Renata's presence. He went below to the stateroom area and checked the closets, guest room and engine room and then entered Renata's room.

The air seemed stale. He went to the bureau and sprayed cologne to make the aura feminine; to bring Renata back. He picked up her photograph at the base of the mirror and looked at her endearingly. He opened drawers and closets, touching her clothes.

Titus could feel the tremor within as his fingers brushed the material that once caressed her body. He took a silk slip and wrapped it around his neck like a towel. Then he rubbed his face with Renata's softness. He closed his eyes and breathed hard, consuming her cologne and extracting Renata from the silk.

The need that came urged him to sit at the bed's edge, to lower the slip to his lap, to make love to the imaginary Renata.

Now I gotcha, bitch!

TEN

Wednesday.
June 25.

DIRECTOR EDWARD MARLOWE'S announcement this past Sunday that he would be attending Alvin Horatio's funeral today, brought the local and national media to the funeral service and added to the funeral procession and attendance already in excess of two hundred.

The funeral procession entered Covington Hill Cemetery in Huntington and proceeded up the hill to the gravesite and the mounds of dirt covered with artificial grass.

Mitchell and Josh missed the church service, but arrived in time to join the funeral procession leaving the church grounds in Cold Spring Harbor with three squad cars as escorts; positioned in the front, middle and rear with lights flashing. Mitchell turned on the headlights.

"Too nice a day for a funeral," said Josh, looking at the cloudless sky scarred by an increasing white line from an unseen jetliner. "Funerals should be rainy and overcast and gloomy to complement the mourners. The weather should be dreary and dolorous!"

"There are no good days when you bury a loved one, but in New Orleans there's music and the Irish party—whatever works. By the size of this procession, you'd think a head of state died. William Cullen Bryant in his poem *Thanatopsis* approached death different—Approach thy grave like one that wraps the drapery of his couch about him and lies down to pleasant dreams."

"How come you memorized something like that? That's weird," said Josh."

"I once did a paper on death and death rituals. Way back."

"Know any more?"

"Strange, that's the only one I remember. Seems to have stuck with me. I know Robert Louis Stevenson wrote *Requiem* and Tennyson wrote *Crossing the Bar* and *In Memoriam,* but I no longer remember excerpts, among others."

"I know some of Tennyson. Let's see if I get it right. He's my favorite of all poets. Remember, you know what happens to memory as you get older."

"I know the feeling well."

"Sunset and evening star, and one clear call for me and may there be no moaning of the bar when I put out to sea."

Mitchell said, "That sounds appropriate for any lawyer . . . of the bar. Horatio was a lawyer."

"Appropriate topics for such a day. What isn't appropriate is that Marlowe remains free."

Standing by their car, they watched as the casket, draped with the American flag, was solemnly carried to the gravesite and the voluminous flower arrangements.

Edward Marlowe rode in the family limousine with Mrs. Horatio. He helped her out and escorted her to the gravesite, holding her left elbow. The other cars emptied and the casket area became encircled as the mourners arrived. Reverend Thomas Needham waited with an open bible to begin the service; waiting for Mrs. Horatio's preparedness. She nodded assent. The service began.

In addition to the family friends and relatives, local political dignitaries, business associates, a military honor guard and the officers of the Eastern Shore Yacht Club, in uniforms, were in the front. Yacht club tradition warrants that officers attend the funeral of any member. Commandant Douglas Deever, in uniform, was behind Edward Marlowe. Marlowe, with head bowed, held Mrs. Horatio's elbow. The media waited on the perimeter. Several video cameramen, with shoulder SONY digital video cameras walked around taking random shots.

Lieutenant Ken Mullins, another detective, six uniformed officers and Marlowe's four bodyguards were spread out behind the mourners. Mitchell and Josh were towards the rear.

Mario Colarossi and Valerie Dryden did not attend.

Mitchell noticed and turned to Josh, in a hushed tone, "Isn't it strange, Professor, that Valerie Dryden isn't here? You'd think she'd attend her husband's partner's funeral."

"The Drydens and Horatios were close," whispered Josh. "Wives included. Valerie must have a good reason for staying away, or could be out of town. Her daughters are here. This is her last week before schools close. Probably couldn't take the day off."

"She took time off to go to Pinelawn with Colarossi this past Monday. You sound like Titus defending his wayward troops."

"I'm sure she would have been here if possible. Deever's here, but I don't see his wife," said Josh. "I'll go talk to him after the service and warn him."

. . . and a time for every purpose under heaven. The Reverend's voice was dominant.

Adam Farmer nudged Mitchell. He stood next to him, hands held in front in a respectful gesture to the deceased.

"Hello, Mr. Pappas," he said, quietly.

Mitchell nodded and winked.

Earth to earth, ashes to ashes, dust to dust; in sure and certain hope of the Resurrection unto eternal life.

Within five minutes and a brief eulogy, the service ended amidst sobs and volleys from the military honor guard in recognition of Horatio's military service in Vietnam. The mourners passed by the casket, picked up and placed flowers on the casket as their expression of farewell forever. The sobs grew louder as the casket began to lower and sway slightly on the lowering gray straps.

Josh, Mitchell and Adam joined the irregular line and filed by the grave. Each dropped a pink carnation. They continued on and stopped at the edge of the road.

"Mitchell, I'll go talk to Deever. Be right back." Josh left.

"Adam, that was a good piece on Helene. Thanks. You're a good writer. Not much room for improvement."

"No, *thank you!* And I accept the compliment gladly from an alumnus."

"Are you working, or paying your respects?"

"Both. I have a photographer here. I also took

that photo of Valerie Dryden and Mario Colarossi at Renata Tredanari's grave. Did you see it?"

"I did."

"Maybe my follow-up angle would be that she and Mario are absent at this funeral. They should be here. My guess is that they're involved in all the murders."

"Including Renata's?"

"Yes."

"I don't think so. Be careful what you write. Stay with the facts and don't create news. You don't want him as an enemy."

"A columnist can print his opinions. As a reporter, I have to deal in facts. Noting they were absent today is a fact. The intrigue in me got aroused when I saw them together."

Mitchell searched for Josh and saw him standing near a tree, talking to Commandant Deever.

"Don't be a hero, Adam, and don't get carried away in the undertow of your intrigue. Save your arousal for your favorite woman. I met Colarossi and Valerie. I didn't sense a romantic link, or a conspiracy."

"No need to protect me. We'll exchange thoughts on those two."

"Every road leads to somewhere, Adam, even though Valerie Dryden is as innocent as a lamb. Colarossi and Josh confirm she's incapable of such subterfuge. Mario is capable. We'll get together soon."

"Then you're definitely getting involved?"

"I'm approaching the starting line."

"Great!" Adam left to join his photographer.

Josh continued to talk to Deever. Mitchell turned towards the gravesite where the crowd had thinned. Mrs. Horatio hesitated to leave as she wept. The loss was difficult. As a final gesture, she picked up a handful of dirt and tossed it over the casket. Marlowe emulated her. Marlowe was now talking to her, encouraging her to return to the limousine. Reluctantly, she turned away as Marlowe embraced her as they walked slowly away. She held the folded flag with her right hand. The cameras were on, and clicking.

Most of the nation's newspapers would show that photograph of the CIA director comforting the widow of his ex-partner. It positioned Marlowe in a better public relations light, which he desperately needed.

Mitchell saw Deever and Josh shake hands and then Josh heading towards him. The crowd was dispersing to cars. Josh returned.

"Deever doesn't believe he's in danger from anyone. But thanked me for the warning and concern. Nothing more we can do."

"We tried. His fate is in his own hands."

Mitchell and Josh waited for Mrs. Horatio to enter the limousine then headed for their car. They stopped when hearing their names called.

Lieutenant Ken Mullins was approaching with an extended right hand. He wore a black tie.

"Gentlemen, may I have a word." They shook hands. "Mitchell, I want to thank you and your wife for solving those riddles. Great job. Your initiative is appreciated. Now, if you can find me the killer . . ."

"Unfortunately for Alvin Horatio, not in time."

"Lieutenant Mullins," said Josh. "I asked Mitchell to get involved. Maybe write a book on these events. That's why he knows about the riddles."

"I'm glad you did."

Said Mitchell, "I have some theories that may prove valuable. I might find the killer with your help."

"Theories won't cut it with these murders. I have theories plus more theories from dozens of interviews and interrogations that lead to nowhere. I have a long list of suspects, especially those who slept on their boats on the north dock when Renata Tredanari was murdered. But which one crept out in the middle of the night? We've worked well in the past, but have to exclude you this time."

"I know I can help."

"Not this time," Mullins said firmly.

"We should exchange theories," said Mitchell, disappointed that an old friend was rejecting him. "We may be able to make substance."

Mullins appeared impatient. "I can meet all you want after these murders are solved. Solving them is all consuming. I'm all ears should you have information that leads to solutions. You have my phone number."

Mitchell remained persistent. "You know my investigative experience. I would like to be current in your investigation and to function as an observer."

Mullins pondered, as Mitchell waited, hoping he was convinced. "Mitchell, I must exempt you on this case. Don't get me wrong. I want your thinking, but it has to be on my terms."

"I appreciate that," responded Mitchell, forging forward. "But three unsolved cases? Aren't you being pressured to solve them? You have nothing to lose. Maybe an occasional cup of coffee, no fees, no expenses."

Mullins absorbed the logic offered. "That may become a likelihood and I appreciate your concern about my pressure. But in the meantime, proceed with what you're doing. The solutions to the riddles helped by formulating a pattern. See you around."

Disappointed, they watched him leave to join the detective by two uniformed officers.

"He was almost agreeable, Mitchell", said Josh. "Not bad for a serious, stiff-upper-lip cop."

"That was a cold reception, unlike him. He'll come around, Professor. He needs help. He doesn't like living under a public microscope and not succeeding. He needs a push for him to extend a hand to me."

"What if he doesn't?"

"The journey's harder. All uphill. And we don't know if he's protecting Edward Marlowe."

* * *

MITCHELL WAS DISAPPOINTED with Mullins' attitude and rejection of an offer to help in a difficult case, leading him to believe that Josh's and Adam Farmer's objections that the police were dragging their feet had validity. Mullins had to be pressured from higher up.

Of all the people the police questioned, Mullins had no indictable suspects. Weren't there rumors around the club about Renata Tredanari's cavorting? If members knew, why didn't they tell the police? Or did they? Maybe no one knew about her affairs— except Josh. And Colarossi knew because Josh told him.

Titus mentioned knowing about the love trysts in the club. Did he know about Renata? But he had his distorted ethics of life and loyalty. Or was he afraid to mention the rumors? Was he afraid for his job, or his life? Were Marlowe's agents telling the truth that they couldn't see part of the north dock? Did they see Marlowe and lied to protect him?

Three people are dead and no one seems to care!

* * *

MITCHELL DROVE JOSH to the club and they discussed Mullins, Adam Farmer, Marlowe, the meetings with Colarossi and Valerie Dryden, and the three victims. Once again, Mitchell urged Josh to tell Mullins what he saw. Josh didn't trust Mullins. He stood firm that Colarossi or Mitchell would find another way to expose Marlowe.

"Realistically, there's nothing I can do without Mullins' help," said Mitchell.

"Keep looking," Josh urged. "You'll find a way. I know you will."

They had lunch at the club before Mitchell returned to Manhattan.

Mitchell reviewed the murders, the riddles and possible suspects. With Mullins closing the door to involvement at the police level, his only way out of the dark, the only match he could light was Adam Farmer. He would be of little value to Adam, unable to reveal what Josh told him.

Adam would be helpful in providing him with all the articles since Renata's death and everything else he could find on the victims, Colarossi, and Marlowe. He needed to round out his research.

Maybe he could find something from the past that would give Mullins a new motive, a new angle to justify questioning Marlowe again. Maybe the old newspaper articles might divulge what Colarossi held over Marlowe's head. Colarossi did business with his law firm.

A shot in the dark.

What else was there besides Josh, the eyewitness?

ELEVEN

Two days later.
Friday. June 28.

MARIE BAILEY, the office manager for the Eastern Shore Yacht Club for the past twelve years, opened the club office a few minutes before 8:00AM, Monday to Friday, a habit she developed to prepare for the day and to have breakfast before her three office staff members arrive at 9:00AM. The office is closed on the weekends and holidays.

She loved her job and environment. Her member bosses came and went each year and she usually advised and guided them into making the right decisions in regard to office matters. She was close to being her own boss, and was respected.

She waved to the two officers in the squad car and pulled into her private parking space by the bulkhead between the north and south docks. She savored the lovely morning and fresh breeze from the southwest knowing that by late morning, the day would turn overcast and the wind would increase to over twenty knots.

Now in her fifties, she had a husband of thirty years, an electronics engineer and three children in their twenties; one daughter still in college, and two sons who graduated. She had one more year of college expenses to go. Thank goodness! With education expenses on the rise, she worried how her grandchildren would be able to attend college. The problem worried her. Why was education so expensive? Was that to be the prelude to the dumbing of America?

Office dress was casual and comfortable. That environment enabled her to wear support sneakers to ease the burden on her legs. She was a bit overweight and the cushioned footwear helped. She was content with everything in life except the murders that destroyed people she knew, agonized and frightened the others and tarnished the club's environment; once a happy place, a little corner of Disneyland, a private enclave away from the outside world.

For the first time, she felt unsafe coming here. The police at the gate and in the channel allayed most of the fear. She looked out over the marina and breathed a deep inhale before opening the office door, which was unlocked today. This meant that Titus was in early. She carried a small package. She returned the keys to her pocketbook and entered.

Titus Banks was in the office pouring coffee in a mug. "Morning, Titus. I brought coffee crumb cake today."

"Perfect. You read my mind again—one of my favorites. Shall I pour?"

"Pour. Black, no sugar."

"I know. No need to tell me all the time."

"Bad habit."

Titus poured. "Here you are, my sweet. One custom designed brew. Hello and goodbye. We're having problems with mooring number fifty-seven, so we're going to get it done before the weather changes."

"What's wrong?"

"It's drifting out of our zone. The last thing we need is to have encroachment problems with Baldwin Marina again. They've been a pain in the ass since we legally expanded our mooring zone southward two years ago."

"Expansion forever! The power of affluence."

"See ya later. But first, the crumb cake." He cut a piece, stuffed half in his mouth, wiped the powdered sugar from his lips, garbled a goodbye and left.

Marie placed her pocketbook in the lower left hand desk draw in her office, turned on the computers, and opened the blinds on the picture windows to add light and scenery.

In addition to handling the club's finances, payables and receivables, member's needs and questions, she and Titus remained the only continuous employees with management responsibilities. They made the club operate. The members came and went in shifting assignments and politics, but the club ran efficiently because of Marie Bailey and Titus Banks. They were stability and continuity.

The mail arrived. She undid the rubber bands and sorted the mail in three categories—member mail, bills and checks, and general. She was quick in determining which letter belonged where. The next letter stalled her flow.

"Oh, my God! Blessed Jesus!" she murmured.

She opened the regular size white envelope addressed to the Board of Trustees, unfolded the single sheet of paper with trepidation then read the contents and closed the door to her office so her three assistants wouldn't hear her talking to the commodore.

Bernard Sosnick was called out of a meeting at his investment firm to answer the emergency phone call.

"Sosnick, here."

"Bernie, this is Marie. We just got another letter." She nearly began to cry. "Shall I call the police, or would you rather?"

"You call, Marie. I have an out-of-town client in a meeting I must be in. Call Lieutenant Mullins and I'll call you back as soon as I can. Read it to me. What does it say? I can't believe it!"

Upset and nervous, she said, "First, it's postmarked Northport, like the others. It could be the same person. Here's what it says. 'To the Board of Trustees—Try harder and read carefully. This one's easy—They've taken of his buttons off an' cut his stripes away. An' they're hanging _____ in the mornin'.

Yours truly, RK'. That's it . . .and another thing Bernie. It's postmarked four days ago. This is a late delivery. I hope we're not too late getting it solved. Should have been delivered at least two days ago."

TWELVE

The same day.

MITCHELL WAS ENGROSSED at his computer when the phone rang at 3:25PM. Intent on his work, he reached for the phone.

"Yes?" he uttered, barely audible.

"This is Lieutenant Mullins." Mitchell perked up. "The club received another riddle and I need your help again. Do you have a fax?" A tinge of urgency was in his voice.

The unexpected call now had Mitchell's full attention.

"Are there obvious clues?"

"None obvious to me." Mitchell gave him the number. "Please do what you can. The message appears urgent."

"I'll get on it immediately, Lieutenant."

"I'm releasing this riddle to the media. Should be on the early evening news. We'll probably have the solution tonight, if the riddle is easy. Can you meet with me Monday morning? I now agree. I can use help and you can observe all you want. Are you free?"

"It's what I've asked for. Where?"

"At eleven o'clock at the Second Precinct. Do you know how to get there?"

"I'll find the place."

Mullins gave him directions. "See you then. I'm sending the fax now."

Mitchell hung up saying to no one, "All right!" He had broken through the invisible wall. He called Helene upon receiving the fax and faxed a copy to her. She and Alicia would start making calls immediately to their college professor contacts.

He called New York University and got through to Josh. Mitchell faxed a copy to him.

"Listen, Professor. I don't know what this riddle means. You and I know it's for Commandant Deever. You've got to warn him. The word 'stripes' could mean a military man, or another club officer. Anybody with a service background."

"If not Deever, then our theories are useless. Hold on. I'll call his office on the other line to save time." Josh placed Mitchell on hold and Mitchell listened to Mozart's Piano Sonata Number 17 in D Major KV 576. Josh returned. The music ended. "Deever's not there. I left word to call you at home and me at my boat tonight when they find him. His wife's been out of town this week visiting her mother in Columbus, Ohio. It's possible he left for the long weekend to be with her. They don't know. They'll call Ohio, also. Here we go again. I'm leaving here in another half-hour. I'll call you if I hear anything from the club."

"Mullins now agrees to meet with me Monday morning at eleven. Still want to go?"

"The semester ended today, so I'm free. Where?"

"The Second Precinct. I'll meet you in the parking lot. Be there a little earlier, please. I don't want to be late. Get ready, Professor. The roller coaster is about to start and we're in the first car."

* * *

TEN MINUTES LATER, Mitchell deemed it neg-
ligence not to tell Mullins that the riddle might be
intended for Commandant Deever based on the word
'stripe' and remind him that the last two victims were
on Marlowe's boat the night Renata was murdered.
Since Deever was also there, he may be the connection to the puzzle. The other club officers may also
be threatened. He called Mullins.

"That's good news. Your stripes deduction sounds
reasonable. We'll promptly notify the Commandant
and the other club officers and give them protection. You said Mr. Trimble already called the Coast
Guard station and Deever wasn't there?"

"Correct. His people are now trying to locate him.
According to Josh Trimble, his wife went to Columbus, Ohio. The Commandant may be on his way to
see her. If he drove, he may not have arrived yet."

"I hope you're right about the stripes because
we can respond to that. But please solve that riddle
and then we'll know for sure. We have to prevent
this murder or the killer wins again. If that happens,
we'll have more media up our backs then we can
count."

"I've already begun the research."

"Good. I've been thinking about you. Something
tells me you're going to find the killer for me."

* * *

THE THIRD RIDDLE hit the newscasts like a star
burst, placing the Eastern Shore Yacht Club in the
national spotlight again.

Dozens of correct solutions to the riddle were

called in to the 800 number provided by the Suffolk County Police within the first half-hour of broadcast beginning at 5:00PM.

But Lieutenant Mullins was told the answer just prior to the first newscast when a familiar member of the Eastern Shore Yacht Club called him directly with the solution.

The caller said, "The blank space in the line 'An they're hangin blank in the mornin' is filled by the name Danny Deever, written by Rudyard Kipling, which may stand for the RK initials in the signature. It's a piece from *Departmental Ditties and Barrack Room Ballads* entitled *Danny Deever.*"

By the end of the news hour, the solution was announced nationally with "And the police and Coast Guard are now trying to reach Commandant Deever."

The caller with the solution was Valerie Dryden.

* * *

HELENE AND MITCHELL learned the riddle's solution by watching the evening news. Josh called to say he'd just heard the solution on television and wondered if they watched the news.

"Let's hope the police find Commandant Deever in time to protect him. We warned him. I told him at the cemetery to be careful. I should have tried harder, been more convincing."

"You can't scrub your conscience, Professor. You took your stand when you refused to turn in Marlowe. Let me also remind you that you resented that Deever lied to defend Marlowe. Tell Mullins you saw Marlowe leave Renata's boat."

"No, I can't do that."

"Then clear your mind—too late for a conscience,

or guilt trips. I'm sure Mullins' team will find and warn him on time. If you hear anything new, call me."

"I have a call in to the Commodore. If he calls me with news, I'll call you back. I'll see you at the precinct."

Mitchell listened to the ten o'clock and eleven o'clock news, mainly replicas of the evening news. Deever hadn't been reached yet and the police continue to seek his whereabouts.

The Commodore didn't call Josh.

When Mitchell awakened just before seven on Sunday morning, he went to the door for the delivered Sunday New York Times. The story was front page.

No mention in the news of Deever being notified.

THIRTEEN

Sunday. 10:00AM.

VISIBILITY WAS LIMITED to two miles on the Sound and the rain fell with sufficient force for the drum beat drops to create thin mushroom geysers when hitting the dull gray water.

As the rain's force began to wane to normal rainfall, the two-man Coast Guard patrol boat came out of the Eaton's Neck boathouse and the cove with sirens and lights flashing. Guided by radar and GPS system, they headed at high speed for the buoy off Stamford.

The crews of the fourteen sailboats, die-hard racers, watched the patrol boat disappear into the mist, curious of its mission. Their radios were tuned to the pre-arranged race channel and they hadn't heard the emergency call. Seventeen other boats, scheduled to race, dropped out due to the inclement weather.

Three local yacht clubs sponsored the race for their members. The Eastern Shore Yacht Club participated.

Commodore Bernard Sosnick, on the race Committee Boat that controlled the race, along with representatives of the other clubs, Russell Durham and Cliff Lincoln, agreed to hold the race unofficially because of the desire of the fourteen boats and crews to race in spite of the weather. The crews wore rain slickers, mainly yellow.

The Committee Boat would launch the race, now separated into two divisions with handicaps in place and remain anchored until the last boat finished, approximately four hours later. The starting line then becomes the finish line; an imaginary line between the boat and Buoy "R8" by Target Rock.

Bernard Sosnick was a recognized racing sailor in the area and was an acknowledged authority on racing rules.

As the race was about to begin, the rain changed to drizzle. The rain would end in another five minutes.

Bernard hoisted the blue preparatory signal and Russell Durham fired a gun indicating that precisely five minutes are left before race start. After nearly five minutes, Bernard hoisted a red signal and Russell fired the gun simultaneously to mark the start of the first division. The maneuvering sailboats of the first division, which had been jibing and tacking for position with all sails up, raced to cross the line. The red flag now served as a five-minute warning for the next group.

With the starting procedures over, the crew of three on the Committee Boat settled in to await the finishers and log their time.

"Those who sit and wait, also serve," voiced Russell, recalling the World War II slogan.

Bernard wasn't listening. He was uncomfortable with the way Buoy "R8" was leaning. Maybe it was his imagination. Maybe that's the way it always leaned.

He turned to Russell Durham, fleet captain of Shore Cove Sailing Club out of Lloyd Harbor.

"Hey, Russ. Isn't the buoy leaning the wrong way?"

"How could it be leaning the wrong way?" asked Russ, removing his yellow slicker and looking in the direction of the red buoy at the other end of the imaginary finish line.

"It's leaning southwest instead of northeast. The wind is out of the southwest and the tide is going out. The wind and tide combination should lean it towards the northeast."

"Son of a gun. You're right. The chain probably snagged on a previous low tide. The slack could cause it."

"We should report it to the Coast Guard since they control the buoys. This is a vital buoy in a busy bay to have a problem. It's bad enough that the lobstermen are now dropping traps in the bay instead of concentrating in the middle of the Sound and the Connecticut side as they've done for years."

"Let's flag down that Coast Guard patrol boat when it returns. Have them take a look at it."

Cliff Lincoln, from the Halesite Yacht Club, came on deck with towels to dry the topsides. He tossed one to Bernard and one to Russell. He agreed that there was definitely something wrong with the buoy. He stroked his damp beard as he spoke.

They sat in the now dry cockpit, opened sandwiches and beers.

"Bernie, what's the latest at your place? Did anyone find Commandant Deever yet?" inquired Cliff, holding Newsday and pointing to the headline with Commandant Deever's picture—Riddler Continues to Stalk Yacht Club. Adam Farmer had given a name to the yacht club killer.

"Not yet. The police called all the places provided
to them by the Coast Guard where the Commandant might be, but no contact as of this morning. He
could be on the road to Ohio to meet his wife."

"What a horror show," said Russell Durham. "A
nightmare."

"That's exactly what it is. I've talked to a few members of the Board of Trustees. They're for shutting
down for the season if Deever isn't found and protected. The membership is scared not knowing who
could be next after Deever. And next weekend, the
July Fourth weekend, we may close. I'll fight against
it. That's one of the busiest weekends for boating. If
we don't, we'll probably only get a handful of boats
for the traditional July Fourth raft-up and fireworks
in Lloyd Harbor where we usually get four to five
dozen boats. Our club cruise to Newport may have
to be cancelled.

"The media was all over me this morning when I
came to the club. The weather doesn't bother them.
Thank goodness we had a race today and don't have
to go back for a while. Don't be surprised if they come
out here after me. These are not good times, gentlemen. I wish I had answers."

Connecticut remained hidden from view when
Cliff Lincoln saw the Coast Guard patrol boat when
it came out of the mist, its wide red stripe standing
out against the gray background.

"There she is. I'll flag her down."

He went below and reached them on the emergency channel. The patrol boat changed course and
headed for the Committee Boat two miles away.

The crew of the Committee Boat was waiting as
the patrol boat came close and shifted to idle.

"Good morning, Commodore Sosnick. Bosun's

Mate First Class Jimmy Nelson at your service. How can we help you, sir?" He had seen Bernard at the base when he attended a meeting on pollution control on local waters.

"Can you please check out the buoy? Looks like it snagged cause it's leaning the wrong way."

Jimmy looked at the buoy and quickly checked out the elements.

"It certainly is. We'll look at it immediately. Oh, sir. Any word about the Commandant?"

"No, Jimmy. I'm certain he'll turn up. The police are still looking."

Jimmy looked disappointed. "So is the Coast Guard. Thanks. We're keeping our fingers crossed."

"He'll be found. I'm confident of that," reassured Bernard.

Jimmy turned the bow, headed for the buoy and slowed to approach. Technician Third Class Kevin Morales went to the bow for a better look.

"Jimmy, there's a rope tied on the other side pulling it down. Looks like a lobster pot. Incredible." Kevin came aft, took a boat hook and returned to the bow. "What idiot would tie a lobster pot to a buoy." He extended the pole and pulled. "Jesus, it's heavier than I thought. Must be full of lobsters. Lobstermen use winches to do this. I'm going to need a hand on this, Jimmy. I'd like to find who owns this pot and give him a summons. I know we have lobster pot wars around here, but this is ridiculous."

"Hold on so we don't drift," Jimmy called out. He came forward after shifting to neutral and got behind Kevin. "I got it, Kev."

They pulled enough of the rope out of the water for each to get a good two-handed grip. The rope yielded further. They pulled hand over hand until they saw the cause of the problem and recognized the familiar weight when it broke water.

He was there in civilian clothes.

They had found Commandant Deever with the rope around his neck and hands tied behind his back.

FOURTEEN

AT TWO O'CLOCK, Josh called Mitchell from the club to inform him that Deever's body had been found, describing how discovered and killed, fulfilling the riddle's prophecy. He also said that Valerie Dryden was the first person to solve the riddle. Mitchell thought—Was it possible she solved the riddle she may have sent?

"Any comments about Valerie?" asked Josh.

"Interesting for now. Tell me more about Deever."

"The police were here again interrogating members. The difference is that Dryden's and Horatio's cars were found in the club parking lot. Deever's car wasn't at the club, but at a public parking lot abutting Northport Harbor. The police believe he boarded a boat at the Northport pier. They're interviewing people there, looking for eyewitnesses. Through the media, they'll be requesting that anyone with information call a special number in Suffolk."

"Probably Northport because of the increased security at your club," surmised Mitchell. "Professor, you have to end all this. Tomorrow, you must tell Mullins what you know."

Josh hesitated. "I'm more scared. But since Marlowe had Dryden, Horatio and Deever killed, the killing will stop now. He has eliminated his witnesses. But if he finds out I saw him, I'm a dead man. I'll never make it to trial, if it goes that far."

"The police will protect you. You've got to talk. We've got to get him off the streets."

"If one of your theories is true," Josh retorted, "than Colarossi may also have killed those three to avenge Renata for lying to protect Marlowe, plus the added motive that she was having affairs with them."

"You're a dead man then, Professor, if you don't speak up. I beseech you. It's too late for the others. Please, please tell Mullins. He'll protect you."

"Not if he's protecting Marlowe. Mitchell, let's face reality. You can't run from the CIA, or the Mafia. When will it end? Does it ever? I'll take my chances that I'm safe from both. I trust Colarossi, and if he's responsible for killing those three liars, I sing his praises. By lying, they're as guilty as Marlowe is. The hell with them!"

"Somebody already sent them. What you're saying is that I should continue the charade with Lieutenant Mullins tomorrow."

Josh faltered. "Well, maybe not. I'm making you an accessory. I hope you're not in legal trouble because of it. Maybe I'll change my mind tomorrow."

"I hope you do. I love you, Professor, but I'm a hair's breadth away from telling Mullins in order to protect you from yourself. He *has* to protect you. The case is public."

"Amen, on all that, Mitchell. I'll see you tomorrow."

Mitchell felt confident that Josh would come

around after a good night's sleep. He updated his notes.

* * *

THE REST OF the day, Josh, Colarossi and Marlowe and various possibilities preyed on Mitchell's thoughts again bolstered by the news flashes and the evening news on Deever, the yacht club and the other murders.

He watched an uncomfortable Lieutenant Mullins face dozens of microphones, unable to pacify the reporters why no one was arrested for four murders, all club members. Mullins had no satisfactory answers. Mullins added that as of Monday, he'd be operating out of the Second Precinct on Park Avenue in order to be nearer the club as opposed to the Suffolk Homicide Squad headquarters out in Yaphank. He gave out the phone numbers in the event the media, or the public needed to reach him. He'd be there seven days a week, twelve hours a day until the killer was apprehended.

The County Executive, the District Attorney and the Chief of Police were with him to lend support and to assure the public that all resources were involved in the matter.

The District Attorney praised Mullins and the police efforts in investigating by adding that hundreds have been interrogated and felt confident of results shortly. The County Executive announced the county was offering $50,000 for information to the killer's arrest and conviction.

Mitchell turned off the television and rehashed the entire scenario with Helene, hoping her thinking may open a door wider, or a new door.

"Try looking at the least obvious place," Helene said. "Something you're not taking serious yet."

"Like where and what?"

"The unexpected, like the Crawford case in Baltimore. You mentioned that Marlowe or Colarossi might have gotten rid of Horatio, Deever and Dryden because of the past. We'll call them the trio."

"How about Renata?"

"She was murdered. Period. I don't think they did business in the past. Sex is her connection. Maybe her death and the trio's aren't connected. The trio killer used her death to cover up the real reason. An appropriate time to get rid of them when the opportunity didn't exist before; tying it to a serial killer, or mass murderer haunting the yacht club. Then you have a killer cleverly using English literature with the wherewithal to kill or have someone kill the trio. Marlowe most likely was in Washington and can account for his time. He therefore, wouldn't be directly involved. Does Colarossi have alibis?

"If you were writing a book on this subject, you would pursue that direction because it's another option to explore. However, finding evidence would be extremely difficult."

Mitchell digested her comments. "That's sound thinking, Helene. That would be unexpected. Josh will turn in Marlowe tomorrow and chaos will reign. Then my theories will be history. And if Marlowe didn't kill Renata and the trio, we'll have a new set of rules."

FIFTEEN

EDWARD MARLOWE SOUGHT refuge in his office on Sunday afternoon to avoid the media, and now sat behind his desk staring at the sunset sky comparing the evaporating daylight to his career; slowly fading.

He needed to be away today from the constant pressure and publicity over the four murders at the club. The execution style killings of his two former law partners was fodder on the evening news and the "dirty tricks" segment of the opposing political party to embarrass the Administration by focusing the killing around Marlowe's environment; to taint him with a continuing negative press. That's how politics played in Washington; undermine and discredit the current administration, he complained; win the White House back anyway possible; all's fair in American politics. A terrible example of ideals and ethics, and getting worse! They have become the new ugly Americans. Will he be called one?

He wouldn't have gone to Renata's yacht that night if she hadn't called. *Damn that call!*

It was important, she had said. For just a minute, or two. He told her he was in the middle of a card game, an inopportune time. Was it an emergency?

She repeated it was important and need was in her voice. Please come, she had said.

He was a fool to hide his visit. That could have been explained. Now, everything was getting out of control. He felt like Nixon during Watergate.

The pinochle players took a break and he went next door scanning the marina to assure he wasn't seen boarding the widow's yacht at that hour. The hour was close to two o'clock in the morning. When he boarded *Champagne Lady*, the door was open and the salon was dark.

"Over here," she whispered.

Renata was standing by the galley, naked, holding a glass of champagne, the bottle nearby. She had a bit much to drink. He could see her nakedness as she moved into the dim cast from the dock lights. He closed the door and went to her, knowing the emergency. The scene had played before. She hugged him and whispered in his ear, "I felt like someone and you're it." She tongue kissed him, devouring his mouth until his excitement was obvious as his hands roamed her body.

She took out the erected muscle, poured champagne over it and then went to her knees.

Emotionally charged, the act didn't last long. When satisfied, and when Marlowe began to recede, she rose, and tongue kissed him again, saying, "Thank you, Mr. CIA man. You were better than last time. Bye bye." She filled the champagne glass to the top, wiggled her fingers and cautiously went below to her stateroom.

Smiling and satisfied with the unexpected passion, he followed her down the carpeted stairs and entered the head to wash and use the toilet. He straightened his clothes, brushed his hair with his hands and returned to his boat. From the salon, he looked around the dock and saw no one before exiting *Champagne Lady.*

His career would be finished in the world knew that he had an encounter with Renata that night.

It didn't matter that he didn't kill her.

He was there!

He had lied!

He should have been a man of integrity, owning up to his action, rather than hiding facts and convincing Dryden, Horatio and Deever to cover-up for him, to protect him. Dryden and Horatio had no hesitation in protecting their ex-partner and the good name of their firm. Deever hesitated, advising Marlowe to admit the visit and maintain his innocence. He had sex. So what? They were unmarried and it wasn't a scandal. Deever did protect him. Marlowe now wished he had listened to Deever.

He couldn't run away from the club, or stay away. He must continue to brave the crisis. He always spent the July Fourth weekend at the club. He would do so again this year with Clair Roseman, his female companion and lawyer. He now thought of marrying her. That would ease the negative publicity in the event it came out that he visited Renata on the fateful night. He believed the public and the media would react better if he was a settled and married man; that the past could be forgiven.

How could he protect himself? Deever and his ex-partners were dead. They couldn't tell anyone now that they lied to protect him. As long as he kept quiet, he might weather the storm that should ease *if the goddamn police would only find Renata's killers!*

He knew his three pinochle companions were

the only ones to know he visited Renata. That was controlled now.

What he didn't know was that he was seen leaving Renata's boat by Josh Trimble.

And by others.

SIXTEEN

Monday.
Early hours.

AT THREE IN the morning, Titus Banks awakened on the couch in his clubhouse office responding to nature's call. After shutting the dock and launch services at midnight, he had gone to the bar and joined the discussion on the Deever riddle and the murders until two in the morning with several members and Warren Moss, the bartender. An excessive consumption of beer forced his awakening.

Other nights recently, the awakening cause was panic.

He sat at the couch's edge and held his head to silence the numbing hum within. He rose and staggered to the door, his body unprepared for movement. In the dark, he groped to the men's room in the lobby, nearly bumping into the display case of yacht club paraphernalia. The restaurant was closed and no one else was in the darkened building. As he stood before the urinal, his head filled with familiar panic. He became alert, straining to listen for any sound indicating danger.

None. He heaved a sigh, telling himself he was

perfectly safe. He had to keep what he knew to himself. The police outside would protect him tonight.
Their presence was re-assuring. *But they didn't protect the others, did they?*

He returned to the couch with an over-active
mind opposed to sudden return to sleep. With fear
expelled, he rose and dressed after deciding to walk
along the bulkhead by the south dock and fuel dock.
He needed fresh air to expunge his negative thinking and to push out the aftereffects of liquor.

The night was clear, starry, windless and quiet,
and he listened to the hush of the nautical evening
as hundreds of boats from one end of the harbor to
the other nested at their moorings. Most of the commercial harbor lights to the south had already
turned off leaving the area clearly outlined by the
sweeping arc of the halogen street lamps. To the
north, the Suffolk Police boat had tied to the outer
slip on the north dock, standing guard. The two
marine policemen, plus the two at the gate added
to his security.

He watched a pair of headlights heading north
on West Shore Road until the road curved west and
the car disappeared over the hill.

To occupy his thoughts, he reviewed the work to
be done for the long July Fourth weekend. The
Fourth fell on Thursday this year. He was sure most
members would stay away. His efficiency profile demanded he be prepared for the maximum. That's
what his staff would do.

He walked down the ramp to the fuel dock and
re-checked that the launch was securely tied. A splash
behind him was startling. He turned suddenly and
saw nothing obvious. He shrugged the splash off as a

fish breaking water. He walked to the south dock and went up the ramp to the dock house.

He checked the locked door. He changed his mind, unlocked the door and went in without turning on the lights. He looked out towards the entrance gate. A police officer was approaching. He quickly went out to identify himself. The officer, recognizing Titus, returned to his car. Titus apologized for forgetting to check with him first before walking on the half-darkened property. Titus returned to the dock house and looked out the window towards the north dock.

He began to see past visions.

Sudden fear returned. The longer the visions and the longer he kept quiet the worse the symptoms.

Titus Banks was scared to a level bordering shaking; no longer the brave young man in the navy.

With the entire killing, he had reason to be. Some nights, he'd sit on the floor at home in Northport and roll into a fetal position to calm himself. The finding of Commandant Deever's body added burden. How safe was he on this killing ground, the place he loved? Police or no, he could become a victim. The shaking started again.

Knowing much caused the restlessness. Had anyone seen him? No. He was positive. The dock house was dark that night, like tonight.

He attempted ignoring the sensations, hoping the shroud would go away by shoving it aside.

After all, no one had seen him that night.

No one knew what he knew.

No one knew he couldn't sleep that evening and was looking out the window of the darkened dock house.

No one knew he was a witness to the activity

around Renata Tredanari's yacht the night she was murdered.

And no one knew that he knew who killed Renata Tredanari.

SEVENTEEN

MITCHELL ARRIVED AT the Second Precinct at 10:50AM. He parked in the visitor's area and looked for Josh, who hadn't arrived yet. Dozens of cars were in the parking lot where officers on duty left their civilian vehicles.

This was a community action precinct with community watch programs, lectures with civic associations, churches, temples, PTA's, senior citizen groups and school programs to answer questions and lead discussions on criminal matters and how to avoid becoming a victim.

Restless and desirous of being early for his first meeting with Mullins, Mitchell called *Coyote*. Mitchell considered promptness a common courtesy. Arriving late can be aggravating to some people. Why begin on the wrong foot with Mullins if lateness bothered him?

Josh's hello was an irritant.

"What are you still doing there? I drove in from the city and I'm on time," scolded Mitchell.

"I'm sorry, Mitchell, I'm sorry. I can't do it. I thought hard, but I got cold feet."

"Dammit, Professor. You just castrated me. I could have sworn you'd come forward." Exasperated, he added, "I'm unhappy with your decision. People are dying all around you and you're sitting on a wall like Humpty Dumpty."

"I can't, Mitchell. I can't overcome my weakness."

"I'll call you later, Professor." Annoyed, disappointed and resigned to his desertion, he forcefully pressed the car phone's END button. Checking his watch, he hurried and entered the precinct expecting the chaos of a New York City station. The subdued and lack of chaos was reminder he was in the suburbs, and less crime. He asked the desk sergeant for Lieutenant Mullins; he had an appointment for eleven. The attractive sergeant checked with Lieutenant Mullins, and then waved another officer over.

"Harry, please show this gentleman to Lieutenant Mullins' office."

She returned her attention to Mitchell. "Sir, I need you to sign my register." She offered a pen, and he signed. Harry escorted to the building's east wing, to an open doorway with the sign CONFERENCE ROOM on the door.

Mullins, working at the far end of the long conference table, stood when Mitchell entered. Computer lists of the club members were on the walls, those that were suspects, newspaper articles and a blackboard with names that were familiar and unfamiliar to Mitchell. Unopened boxes were stacked in a corner—the signature of a new tenant.

"As you can see, this has become my new strategy room, the command center for the yacht club murders. How are you?" he added, extending his right hand while moving towards him. "Happy to see you and thanks for coming. Have a seat." He pointed to a chair opposite the blackboard. "Can I get you a soda? Coffee?"

"No, thank you. I'm fine."

Mitchell shook his hand and sat. Mullins went to the entrance and closed the door.

"You had quite a weekend, Lieutenant. You don't look bad on television."

"The worst of my professional life. When it gets to the point that the county is offering a reward, it means the war isn't going well." He stood by the blackboard. "It'll get worse. Because of Deever and Marlowe, government agents will be arriving this afternoon to get involved. They won't be as sensitive as our people to press for arrests, hard evidence, or no. What I'm going to do, Mitchell, is provide you with an overview, an overview mind you, of what we know to date. Then you can tell me your thoughts and theories. Everything I tell you is confidential. Agreed?"

"Yes."

"And don't take notes."

"Fine."

"How's your memory?"

"I have enough gigabytes in there to hold what you put in."

"Let's begin then. I'll start with Renata Tredanari." He placed a check after her name. A section on the blackboard was for Renata. He pointed to the word, KNIFE. "The knife was a common steak knife with serrated edges that usually come in a set of six, and not a part of Renata's set on her boat. Whoever killed her pre-meditated doing so with their own knife. There were no fingerprints on the knife, or useful prints for that matter. Mostly smudges on her body. We do have prints from the room that we can't identify." Mitchell listened studiously.

"She may have known her assailant. No forced

entry to the boat and no signs of a struggle in her stateroom. A spilled champagne glass was next to her. The small amount of champagne on the sheets indicates most was ingested. Her blood alcohol level was pretty high.

"I'll let you in on a secret if you're to help besides solving riddles. Not one hundred percent, maybe ninety-five." He grinned. "Pertinent facts to help your deductions. Like you said at the cemetery, I have nothing to lose."

"Your confidence may be overstated."

"Modesty doesn't fly here." Mullins returned to the professorial posture. "What we know and the public and media, does not, is that *two* men, were involved in Renata Tredanari's death."

That stunned Mitchell. *Two men! Josh was only half-right!*

He suddenly had a serious problem. Promising secrecy to Mullins, he couldn't tell Josh about two killer's on Renata's boat. What if Colarossi was the second one? How could Josh protect himself? *He had to tell him!*

"Again, the information is for your eyes only for now."

Mitchell was surprised and perplexed. "Then why not say you're looking for two killers, Lieutenant? Maybe one will panic and make a deal."

"I know. For now, we're withholding that as an ace card for when we have evidence on one. The second may then come running fearing the other will turn him in and make a deal. There is no one way that's correct and variables to consider. Our call is to wait. Actually, the decision was made by the District Attorney and the Chief of Police."

Involvement by the higher ups made Mitchell

believe Marlowe *was* being protected. He asked, "Could they be protecting Marlowe? Two men involved may increase Marlowe's odds of being one of the men."

"No, Marlowe isn't a suspect at all. I agree with the strategy. If they are defending him, I am not."

Mullins moved his finger to DNA. "The semen specimens differ in the mouth and vagina. Two men, but which two?" He pointed to a computer list. "To begin with, here are the primary suspects—those who slept on their boats that night and had access to the north dock. CIA Director Edward Marlowe is on the list. His bodyguards reported they saw no one on the dock and importantly, saw no one leave. Therefore, the killer returned to a boat on the north dock. The other three victims, Deever, Dryden and Horatio were on Marlowe's boat playing pinochle. We have signed statements and all verified none left the game, or the boat. There's no reason to suspect Marlowe. His alibis are solid.

"The others you may, or may not know. Mario Colarossi, entrepreneur, Valerie Dryden and her two daughters, teacher and recent widow, Wallace and Lorene Grant, President of the Ladies Auxiliary, Josh Trimble, Dr. and Mrs. Charles Chu, cardiologists at St. Francis Hospital. Also included are Mr. and Mrs. Preston Robinson, owners of an advertising agency and Matthew DiBiasi, private investor. The Dryden girls were also interviewed.

"Motive to kill? Renata had no enemies. Why would anyone want her dead? What warranted sacrificing her life? Did those two men rape and then killed her to be quiet?" He shrugged his shoulders. "They had a knife. The plan was to kill her, making

it pre-meditated murder. It wasn't spontaneous com-
bustion, so to speak.

"You could help me by spending time at the club.
By inquiring in your capacity as author people may
open up to you. People want lawyers around when
they speak to me and lawyers won't let them speak.
By finding Renata's murderers, we may learn why
Deever, Dryden and Horatio were killed if there's a
connection to the deaths. Another option is that she
had sex with one guy and he left after getting his
jollies off. The second guy showed up afterwards and
had sex with her, or raped her and then killed her.
In this instance, the first guy could be innocent of
murder—innocent of everything except having con-
senting sex with her; thus, no crime. These are the
variables.

"The so called Riddler who pre-saged the other
murders appears to be an educated person with
knowledge of English literature. He, or she followed
a pattern, serial like, of throwing the victims overboard alive and hands tied behind their back.
Dryden's body was to vanish. A rare fluke by some
kid fishing with a magnet upset the killer's strategy."

He paced periodically as he talked, his body alive
with thoughts and movements. "Renata's body was
left in place. Therefore, the person, or persons who
killed Renata and the person, or persons who killed
Dryden may not be the same." He pointed to
HORATIO, listed under VICTIMS on the blackboard.
"Horatio's body didn't disappear. He was taken out
east to Block Island Sound and dumped overboard.
The tides turned up his body on Block Island instead
of swallowed by the Atlantic Ocean; another quirk of
fate. Again, to disappear without a trace." He pointed
to Deever's name. "Deever was hung and meant to

be found. Yet, he also was thrown overboard when alive and with hands tied behind his back. The killer, or killers deviated from a pattern.

"What does that lead me to conclude? The killer, or killers, let's say killer, is methodical, intelligent, knows what he's doing and doesn't belong to a psychiatric profile of the obvious serial killers whose names leave an acrid taste in my mouth and won't mention them. I'm sure you heard of the garbage.

"Is our assassin doing this for vengeance? What's the motive?—lots of dead ends. The key is to find Renata's murderer and perhaps the rest of the dominoes will topple."

"Sounds like reasonable strategy," Mitchell said, following intently.

"Let's now talk about some of the people on my suspect list. Ironically, two of the most influential people on Long Island were on the north dock that night—CIA Director Edward Marlowe and Mario Colarossi. Most anyone would make them likely suspects especially the way Deever, Horatio and Dryden died. Both have the power and authority to clandestinely authorize their deaths. Why would they do that? I'll explain later. Keep the thought up front. Should I arrest them? No. Do I question them? Yes. And I did.

"Take Marlowe. He had witnesses and his card partners never left the game the night Renata was killed. Why would Marlowe then kill his witnesses and two former partners? Doesn't figure by present day facts. I'm not about to arrest the CIA director because he knew all the victims. That certainly isn't a crime. I have no evidence on Marlowe, other than to keep an eye on him.

"I've been accused by the Long Island press of

dragging my feet in arresting someone. Do I arrest someone just to pacify the inhumane Roman arena mentality? I'm not about to destroy anyone's career, or reputation on hearsay, or innuendo. I'll pursue every lead as I'm currently endeavoring to do.

"I called in Colarossi and Valerie Dryden again when I saw their photo in Newsday at Renata's gravesite—why together? I found no legal reason to hold them, as their lawyer graciously advised me. Do you know Mario Colarossi?"

"Enough to know his influence," replied Mitchell.

"Let me tell you about the gracious Mario. We know his businesses, how they interact and with whom he does business. He has the best lawyers on the Island and everything he does on the surface is legal. Marlowe used to be his lawyer. Did you know that?"

"Josh Trimble filled me in on some background."

"What he is, Mitchell is a powerful Mafia figure." Mullins looked for a reaction. "You don't look surprised."

"I was told the godfather of Long Island."

"Correct, except he's connected to the Brooklyn and Queens families. He's the Long Island representative. My driving ambition is to put him away for good. I'm privately hoping he's involved with the yacht club tragedies so I can nail him. His lily white image and facade with his millions to charity make me puke."

Mitchell instantly thought of Josh telling Colarossi that he saw Marlowe. "Do you believe Colarossi *is* the killer?" he inquired.

"It's a wish. I need you on this. You're close to Josh Trimble and see him often. Even did Coast Guard Auxiliary duty with him. I saw the list. I can get Josh to help me, but he's on the suspect list by being on his boat that Renata night.

"I thought about asking for semen, or DNA samples from all the male suspects although the request would be futile. That will identify the killers. But their collected lawyers would rise in protest. Their constitutional rights protect them if I don't have sufficient evidence.

"I need an arrest, anything to obtain an indictment. We're continuing to interrogate and protect those that need protection, including the suspects. Have the killings stopped? Who knows? How many more victims and who?"

"Can I ask you a direct question, Lieutenant?"

"Go ahead."

"Are you protecting Marlowe? Do you have any information that ties him to Renata?"

"I said I wasn't and there's no connection to Renata. What's wrong with your gigabytes?"

"I know he's popular with the police and is a hometown hero type. It's hard to believe the higher authorities won't go out of their way to keep the favorite son clear."

"I have no problem hanging him if he's guilty. I'm reticent, as is the DA, to act without evidence against him. If you find something, I assure you, I'll arrest him. Any other questions?"

"I now believe the killings have ended," stated Mitchell.

"You do?" Surprised, Mullins went to his chair and sat. "What leads you to that conclusion."

"My theories were based on one killer, not two. I have to re-think the entire situation. You mentioned the Marlowe and Colarossi connection and the Marlowe, Dryden and Horatio connection. Some connection to the past may have caused Colarossi or Marlowe to get rid of Horatio, Dryden and Deever using Renata's Tredanari's murder as an excuse and blaming a serial killer."

"You think there is no connection to *all* the murders?"

"Only the last three; no relation to Renata. Is there any history among those people? Something where the Coast Guard may have been involved with the law firm and Colarossi companies.

There must be."

Mullins thought hard, and nodded, and grinned. "Very clever of you to tie-in the Coast Guard to the past. You are another dimension. I'm glad I called you. That information isn't posted on the wall yet. There *is* a history. I recently reviewed the file since it contained activities by our list of players. I couldn't find legal substance to blame the past for today's murders. Renata's death could be camouflage. I'll get the file. Maybe you'll find it worthwhile to pursue certain aspects."

"I'll include that. I plan to meet with Adam Farmer of Newsday to review some history and catch up on his articles on the subject."

"Adam Farmer," Mullins sighed. "Remember, everything I said to you is confidential. That pain in the ass has been a pain in the ass. He's made my situation tougher."

"Don't call him a pain. Call him a stimulator. You have my assurance."

"Good. I'll get the file. I'm still getting used to this temporary set-up and not sure where everything is. Have some coffee. I'll be right back." He rose and left the room.

Mitchell was pleased with Mullins' openness. The

meeting was going well, better than expected. He stood and read the various material and data on the walls. Other than Mullins' revelation of two separate semens in Renata, everything else was secondary knowledge. That was shocking, a cause to re-evaluate theories.

A list of club members and employees with police notations was included; a long paragraph on each; years at club, connection to victims, north dock or south dock or moorings and an interrogators opinion on possible guilt or innocence. Next to it was a layout of the yacht club marina indicating boat slip number and name of boat and owner. A red dot was placed on the victims' slips; a blue dot on the primary suspects' slips.

The names of all members living in Northport were underlined in red. Mitchell knew that the Riddler's letters were postmarked in Northport. That's also where Deever boarded a boat to his doom. Mario Colarossi and Titus Banks were among the names underlined in red.

Mullins returned holding a green file, closed the door, sat in his chair and said, "I'll put this data up later." He shuffled the file's contents in sequence.

"An investigation, several years ago, had an obvious connection to Colarossi and Marlowe—where Marlowe, Dryden and Horatio represented the Colarossi companies. Federal law makes each state responsible for the proper and safe disposal of low-level radioactive waste: materials like equipment, and clothing exposed to radiation from places like hospitals and research institutions. Add nuclear power plants to the category.

"Such low-level wastes used to be shipped to Barnwell, South Carolina. That year, that legal dump-

ing ground was closed for six months and affected
such waste from Long Island. This opened a six
month window of opportunity for unscrupulous cart-
ers to by-pass the law and dump illegally. New York
State to this date doesn't have a legal site anywhere
in the state. We're talking tons of waste and millions
of dollars.

"The word radiation frightens people. No one
wants a radiation dumpsite in his backyard. The problem is so bad that some states are willing to pay millions of dollars to any community that accepts the
radioactive waste. It continues a tough sell.

"What happened to the accumulation of the
waste during the six months? Colarossi's carting company was accused of dumping the radioactive waste
in the middle of The Long Island Sound at a point
near Stamford, Connecticut, then the old Army
dumping ground, now no longer in use as part of
the Sound clean-up program. Fishermen had reported huge fish kills in the area. The fish also littered Huntington beaches.

"Colarossi also owns barges. The charge was that
his barges were off-loading the radioactive waste at
night. Some believed that his barges where filled by
his garbage trucks at his oil depot marinas.

"Colarossi and his battery of lawyers vehemently
denied all insinuations. Two of his barge employees
died mysteriously. The Coast Guard got involved in
the investigation. Based on the Coast Guard field report, a very comprehensive and detailed evaluation,
the Coast Guard determined that the fish kill may
have been due to an increase in nitrogen in the water. This condition existed in the western part of the
Sound at the time because of excess pollution by the
heavily populated towns on the Sound.

"The Coast Guard found no evidence of radioactive articles though the fish had radioactive traces. The radiation couldn't be traced to anything near Stamford. Because of the Coast Guard report, the Grand Jury failed to indict. Rumors started that Colarossi and his lawyers influenced the Coast Guard report—again, no proof.

"Witnesses saw the company barges in the area. Saw the company names. They didn't see dumping. That's because the barges only came out in moonless nights, or in inclement weather. The dumpsite in South Carolina re-opened after the six months and business for Colarossi went on as usual.

"From this, a conjecture I can make to connect the past to the present is that the lawyers knew Colarossi was lying and helped him to cover-up by offering advice to evade the law. How do I prove that? I can't.

"And a fact that makes a strong tie is that the person in charge of the Coast Guard investigation was then a *Captain* Douglas Deever."

EIGHTEEN

MULLINS TURNED THE file around and showed Mitchell Deever's signature. Mitchell saw the name.

"That may explain," said Mitchell, "why Deever rose in the ranks to become commandant of the Eaton's Neck station. Maybe Marlowe helped to move him nearby and why they were so friendly. The friendship assuring that the past remained closed. What we're saying here is that its likely Colarossi, or Marlowe killed those people." Those were his original theories.

"But I can't prove it without a confession," replied Mullins. "Whatever you can come up with would be a home run."

"The first thing is to use Adam Farmer—the power of the press. Your vociferous opponent who can be a weapon for our side."

"There's that nemesis again. Please tell him that I'm not an enemy of the people."

"He's a young man. Maybe he doesn't know about the Colarossi, Marlowe, Deever history. Exempt this from secrecy. Let me bring it to his attention. To do a story, to revive the past and put some pressure on the guilty."

"That can only help. Put him on the team."

"Can I get a copy of the file?"

"No. Farmer has what he'll need in his library. Newsday covered the story at the time—old, but public. He can put any slant to the story using the true and tried 'informed sources say'."

"I will play the spy. I'll spend the July fourth weekend with Josh and involve myself at the club."

* * *

Mitchell left the meeting with mixed feelings. He was now on Mullins' team as an observer, with an open line to him with any new information. He received important data about two persons possibly killing Renata and confirmed his theory about the trio dying because of the past. There *did* exist a history.

It seemed logical that Deever was bribed and lured with promises, probably by Marlowe who advanced his career when he became director of the CIA.

Two of Colarossi's employees on the barges had died mysteriously. Those deaths Mitchell attributed to Colarossi's thugs. Did Colarossi kill Dryden, Horatio and Deever using Renata's death as the environment? Was he the Riddler?

The remaining major player in the low-level radioactive waste dispute was Marlowe. Would Colarossi now have Marlowe killed so that history wouldn't come back to indict him? Is he that daring and stupid to kill the Director of the Central Intelligence Agency?

Was Josh in jeopardy from Colarossi?

He started his car and called *Coyote*. Josh answered.

"Professor, I have to see you later."

"I'll be here all day. How'd it go with Mullins?"

"You'll be briefed when I see you. First, I have to see Adam Farmer. Afterwards, I'll come to the club. See you later."

He hung up, pulled out of the driveway, headed south towards the expressway and called Adam Farmer.

"Nice surprise, Mr. Pappas. How are you?"

"Fine, Adam. I have some information for you. I just came from a meeting with Lieutenant Mullins. I had to change our program to see him first. I know you'll be glad I did. I can be there in about twenty minutes, okay?"

"Terrific, park in the Pinelawn Road parking area. See you then."

Something wasn't right based on what Mullins told him and annoyance began to fester as he passed Wolf Hill Road. Everything in his mind spun in separate categories like spaces on the wheel of fortune. When the wheel stopped spinning, the last click landed on a frightening category.

He was approaching the exit to Pinelawn Road and Route 110 on the expressway. His mind fixed on the wheel's revelation as he exited. *Tell me I'm wrong! Re-spin the wheel!*

He had to see Josh.

He called Adam, saying that he'd see him towards the end of the day instead. Something important had come up. He took Pinelawn Road north to Route 110-New York Avenue and followed that north to Huntington, passing the Walt Whitman Mall, named after the famous poet who lived in the area. There was no room in his head to think of his literature. He was growing impatient to reach the club as he crossed Main Street in Huntington and continued along the harbor in Halesite to East Shore Road and the club. He parked by the north dock and proceeded down the ramp. The tide was high and the ramp was level. The marina was subdued on this first day of the workweek. The pile driver by the new dock was installing the few remaining pilings before the project was completed.

Approaching *Coyote,* he kept hoping he was wrong. He tried to remain calm and coherent although his blood was racing. *It wasn't possible!*

Josh wasn't on the main deck, or topsides. Mitchell entered the salon and called out for Josh. Josh came up from below with a clean rag, wiping his hands.

"There you are, Mitchell. Grab a seat while I wash up. I've been doing my usual routine of checking and tightening hoses. Some time ago in Newport, my toilets were clogged. I had somebody in to fix them and he forgot to fasten a hose clamp. The next morning, I had two inches of water in the stateroom. All the carpeting had to be replaced. That's why I try to be self-sufficient. Lunch? I have some cold cuts."

"No, I lost my appetite today."

"Bad hair day, huh? How about something to drink? Was Mullins that bad of an experience?"

"No, to both."

"Are you still pissed at me about this morning?"

"That's no longer important."

"What happened with Mullins?" He finished wiping his hands, tossed the rag on the galley counter and sat opposite Mitchell. "So, talk to me."

"When you saw Marlowe leave Renata's yacht, you were only half-right."

"What do you mean? How can I be half-right?"

"What I'm about to tell you violates my secrecy

oath to Mullins, but I must to save your ass if it's sav-
able. Don't utter a word to anyone. The police have
evidence of semen from two men." He raised two
fingers. "Two, Professor. Therefore, sometime before
Marlowe, or after Marlowe, Renata had another visitor who killed her with a steak knife."

"I'll be a son of a . . ." His eyes widened as the
voice trailed off.

"If that other person was Colarossi, you're in jeopardy. You said you went below shortly after Marlowe
left."

"Correct."

"If Marlowe was the last to leave, then Marlowe
killed her. If Colarossi went to Renata *after* Marlowe
left, then Colarossi killed her. And if that's so, you're
dead. You shouldn't stay here."

"Wait a minute, Mitchell," Josh protested, holding up his hands. "As I told you once, Colarossi would
kill *for* her, *do* for her, *not* kill her. He loved her too
much to harm her. The second guy was probably
Dryden, or Horatio, or Deever most likely. Marlowe
probably told them that he got a little action and
one of them went there for his share. My belief in
Colarossi is solid, no deviation. Mario wouldn't do
that. He can commit atrocities in his world, but he
wouldn't harm Renata."

"You won't testify against Marlowe and you refuse
to believe that Colarossi could kill you if he believed
you may have seen him, also. You're becoming pre-
posterous."

"I know I'm right in my positions."

Mitchell gave up the argument. "A theory I was
able to verify was the history of Marlowe, Colarossi
and Deever." He told Josh his discussion with Mullins
on the 1988 incident. "I concluded that Renata's

death was unrelated to theirs and that Deever, Horatio and Dryden were probably killed by your saint, Colarossi, or Marlowe as an excuse to wipe out history. So their secrets remain secrets. Then there's the remotest possibility that Marlowe and Colarossi are co-conspirators."

Josh leaned back digesting the statement. "That's a powerful combo. Marlowe and Colarossi killing them could apply. My premise that Marlowe killed his witnesses, or Colarossi possibly exacting revenge for their lying for Marlowe still apply. Now there are *three* possible reasons for deep-sixing those three."

"After I leave you," said Mitchell. "I'm going to meet with Adam Farmer and have him rekindle this history and infer it to the murders. That should boil the tempest in the pot."

"If anything, the publicity of the added material should heighten the tension. See? Aren't you glad you went to see Mullins without me? I think you're well on your way to getting Marlowe. You didn't need me there, after all. And no need for me to admit to being a witness."

Mitchell shifted in his seat, uncomfortable with what he had to say next; that space on the wheel of fortune that deferred Adam Farmer's meeting in order to meet Josh. He had extended the conversation as long as he could to avoid this.

He wet his lips, took a deep breath and leaned towards Josh.

"After you saw Marlowe leave, didn't it bother you that he and others were having sex with her and you weren't? Did you really go below to sleep and leave the scene? Or did you go to *Champagne Lady?* Were you the second man, Professor? Did you rape and kill Renata?"

NINETEEN

JOSH STOOD WITHOUT looking at Mitchell and headed for the galley. He didn't return to face Mitchell immediately. Mitchell wondered if his delay was a guilty sign. Josh meandered to the refrigerator, opened the freezer for a cold beer that he usually kept there for about twenty minutes, flipped the top of the Coors Gold and before closing the door asked, "Sure you don't want one?" Mitchell shook his head and waved him off. Josh continued his delay. He opened a cabinet, took a tall plastic glass, wiped the insides with a paper towel, filled it with beer and placed the empty can in the re-cycle bin. He sipped and returned, holding the glass.

Mitchell followed the movements and fixed on Josh's eyes when he sat. A contemplative Josh took another sip then placed the glass on the coffee table. He adjusted to sit at the edge of the seat and looked Mitchell in the eyes to underline his response to the accusations.

"Josh!" The voice calling from the dock belonged to Titus Banks. "Josh, you in there?"

With the last second reprieve from the piercing sound of his name, Josh slowly rose without expression and went to the aft deck. Mitchell slammed his fist into the couch cushioning at this horribly timed interruption. Josh slid the door.

"Titus, give me a few minutes. Don't leave. I have to finish a meeting with Mitchell."

"Righto. No problem."

Josh closed the door.

The tension caused by the questioning had eased with the interruption and delay in a response. Josh returned to his seat.

Mitchell braced for the answer. Josh looked less tense.

"I swear by all I hold sacred that I told you the truth. I went below. Like Colarossi, I also loved Renata. I wouldn't hurt her, much less rape and kill her. If I killed Renata, I wouldn't have asked you to get involved to expose her killer. I take no offense to your questions because I'm not completely surprised. I figured it would be a matter of time before you closed any loophole you found." Finished, he sat back.

Mitchell digested his friend's statement.

"I accept," he responded, relieved. "Sorry, Professor. I had to ask, to close the loophole. Sometimes my imagination and theories run away from me and I spare no one . . . and trust no one. I needed to eliminate you as a suspect before I could continue or I'd be running in a circle chasing my tail."

"And can you continue?"

"I'm going ahead to meet with Adam Farmer. Titus is waiting. How would you like to have me as your guest for the Fourth weekend. It'll give me a chance to probe a bit more around here."

"Perfect. I'd love it. How about Helene?"

"I'm sure she'll agree. I'll ask her tonight and call you to confirm."

Josh slid the aft door. "Okay, Titus, come aboard. All clear."

Titus boarded and entered the salon with a broad grin.

"How're you doing, Mr. Question Man? Happy to see you."

"Hello, Titus," said Mitchell, shaking hands with him.

"Thanks for waiting. I'm on my way to another meeting and can't stay."

"Still asking all those questions?"

"Titus, help yourself to a beer," said Josh, interrupting Titus' humor. "I'm going to walk Mitchell to his car. There are also cold cuts in the fridge. Be right back."

"So long, Titus," said Mitchell. "Keep the flag flying."

"All the time, Mitchell, all the time. Long may it wave. Have a good meeting."

Mitchell interrupted his departure and turned to Titus.

"Titus, I need to ask you some questions even though I know your philosophy. You should know that Lieutenant Mullins has asked me to help by asking questions. How about it?"

"I don't know how I can help, but proceed. I'll make an exception this time. We'll call it a weak moment."

"Great. On the night Renata was killed, did you work up to midnight?"

"Yes. I closed the dock facilities."

"Then what?"

"Like I told the police, I went to the bar for a few beers. Had one too many and decided to sleep in my office rather than drive home."

"On your way to the bar, or back, did you see any activity on the docks?"

"Friday's a busy night and quiet after midnight. There were people in the parking area leaving the restaurant, nothing unusual. If your next question is did I see anyone around *Champagne* Lady up to closing, the answer is no."

"You know more about what goes on here than anyone else, especially in the evenings. Who might have killed her?"

Titus puckered his lips and shook his head. "Can't even fathom a guess. When I'm working, I have no time to notice the usual. Obviously, nothing unusual occurred, or I'd have noticed, or been notified. The night of the murder had no significance at the time, nothing to watch for. The next day, that night proved to be significant. I liked Renata a lot, but don't know who killed her. I wish I knew."

"Okay," said Mitchell. "You surprised me by saying so much. You're not as tight lipped as you claim. I appreciate the courtesy of your response. Keep your ears open and notify me if you hear anything that would help. For the hell of it, if you did see someone, a club member, around *Champagne Lady* after midnight, would you tell anyone?"

"No."

"I didn't think so."

Mitchell and Josh left and headed towards the ramp.

"Professor, think on who else I can talk to this weekend."

"The two people around here involved with most of the members are Titus—and he's a clam— and Warren Moss, the bartender. Warren's a talker. He may be productive. They talk to a lot of members, especially Warren. We'll talk with him for a while in the evening. You never know. Also, the others who were on their boats on the north dock the night Renata died. Mullins mentioned the Chus, the Grants, the Robinsons and Matt DiBiasi."

"If they're here, I'll introduce you. You've already met Matt and Gina. It's a major step that Mullins accepted you. You're on your way to Marlowe's demise. And Mitchell, one more thing."

"What is that?"

"I don't own steak knives."

* * *

Ken Mullins, whom close friends and associates nicknamed, Moon, after the comic strip character, Moon Mullins, closed the door to his makeshift command post to digest Mitchell Pappas' visit.

Allowing Mitchell to be involved was the right decision, he concluded. He could be a major weapon in this war of good versus evil, which is how he looked at every crime committed in his jurisdiction; a war he must win at all costs, down to the last round of ammunition. Last year, Suffolk County had thirty-two homicides and only four remained unsolved, and two were about to be. That was a good record by other's standards; not his. He wanted and strove for a perfect record this year. He had that up until the yacht club murders.

Would Mitchell do a book on the yacht club murders? He recalled Josh Trimble mentioning something about a book at the cemetery.

Ken Mullins was a proud and dedicated man who hated to lose. His team was losing the war with the Riddler and Renata's killer. Mitchell had experience working with law enforcement officials and procedures. He considered Mitchell to be a detective. The major difference is that he wrote books instead of getting his hands dirty with society's scum, made a healthy income and didn't have a day-to-day job that devoured his nerves and stomach and deprived him of sleep. After nearly thirty years on the job, he had no solution to mental and bodily peace. As he progressed through the ranks, he thought they would ease. They got worse.

He was born and raised on Long Island, attended the Half Hollow Hills School system in the southern part of Huntington, went to Hofstra University, married his college sweetheart, moved to Commack and had three children, now in their twenties.

His four grandchildren, whom he sees often and serve as medicine, prove to him there is good and beauty in the world and on Long Island . . . and human beings that make you feel good.

Added pressure was being applied now that government agents would be involved. He removed items from the green file and designated them to a section of the wall by the blackboard. He'd be ready for his presentation to his new guests when they arrive later this afternoon—most likely at the end of the day. They would be added weapons, but weapons he wouldn't be able to control. Perhaps Mitchell Pappas' suggestion was now timely; that an announcement be made that two men were involved in Renata's killing. It was time to change the strategy. The delay could be attributed to verification of evidence. It may not bring in the killer, but would show the world and the hounding media and politicians—who were using every opportunity to get before a microphone and get free publicity—that we have strategy and direction in the effort to solve these crimes.

The more he deliberated the juicier the thought. Better yet, he now wanted an announcement before the Feds arrived and before the evening news— his own politics of one-upmanship. *Thank you Mitchell Pappas for the motivation!*

He wanted to neutralize any impressions that the Feds were called in because the Suffolk police weren't doing their job, or weren't able to catch the killer. *No one is better than my team!*

He called his chief.

* * *

MITCHELL BELIEVED JOSH'S proclamation of innocence and remained convinced that Deever, Horatio and Dryden were killed because of their past to the radioactive waste incident. Josh continued to believe Marlowe killed Renata. The two options—that Marlowe killed the trio to eliminate the witnesses to his visit to Renata, and Colarossi killed them to avenge Renata—took second and third place in probability.

Three categories on his spinning wheel of fortune of the many that remained unanswered were— Why was Renata killed? Who was the second man? And is he alive?

He agreed with Josh that Colarossi wouldn't harm Renata. Absent of Marlowe confessing and Josh admitting he saw Marlowe, he had to exert pressure on Marlowe, who was at the crime scene. The implementation of this pressure would emanate from Adam Farmer; to use the press in its worse form— news by innuendo, probability and assumption of facts.

Adam Farmer wouldn't go along with irresponsible journalism.

Neither would the high standards of Newsday. A columnist might. Adam would report the facts; a columnist's opinion is his opinion. Then he considered his journalism attitude irresponsible because he indicted Marlowe on the initial assumption that he killed Renata.

Maybe he should tell Adam about the past, his Marlowe theories and put pressure on the powerful man. Maybe the pressure would force him to admit that he visited Renata, but didn't kill her. That he didn't commit a crime.

He decided to present the past to Adam and let Adam decide how to best utilize the background material. That would be proper.

If only there was another witness.

TWENTY

TITUS BANKS, with a can of beer, watched Mitchell and Josh from his seat on *Coyote's* aft deck expecting them to head for Mitchell's car—probably parked near the north dock, he surmised. He had come by to share a beer with Josh whom he admired. Every now and then, he'd bring a six-pack to replenish Josh's stock. That was the fair thing to do.

Titus became friendly with Josh because of their close working association in the design and construction of the third dock. Josh treated him with respect and accepted him as a friend. They also boated together occasionally and shared many evenings at the club bar with other members, including Renata. His working and private world revolved around the yacht club. The balance of his spare time went to maintaining his home in Northport.

"Titus is tight lipped and the protective type and didn't tell the police anything. But between us, he lied," Josh said to Mitchell. "I now believe that. He knew Renata was having affairs. One night at the bar he offered to walk her to her yacht, probably thinking he could get into her pants, and she politely refused. He had a bit to drink and the rejection brought the ugly comment when she left—'The way she's going, she'll eventually screw everyone around here. She's already starting from the top on down.' Now, that could mean the Commodore, or Marlowe. And in my book, it's Marlowe. I thought he was going to punch Warren Moss, the bartender, when Warren said—'You won't be one of them.' Men do get ugly when they get together to drink. I had already offered to escort her, but she wanted to go alone and meander back since it was a pleasant evening. There are times Titus acts a bit strange though he's a good sort. I like him. But he lied."

TWENTY-ONE

MITCHELL LEFT THE club parking lot made a right at the gate and headed south along the water on scenic East Shore Road.

The hour neared three o'clock when he phoned Adam Farmer to inform him he was on his way and that he'll arrive within the half-hour.

"I was about to leave a note for you with the receptionist," Adam explained. "I have to cancel today. We just received notification that Lieutenant Mullins is having an important press conference over at the Second Precinct. By the time I return with the story and put it to bed, it'll be late. Do you know why Mullins called the conference?"

"He didn't say. It's a surprise to me."

"Could it be what you wanted to tell me?"

"I don't think so, Adam. I'll tell you what I know about Deever, Dryden, Horatio, Marlowe and Colarossi and the past in the event the news conference deals with another subject. Then you could attach it to today's conference, or do a separate story."

"Good idea. Go ahead."

Mitchell explained the radioactive waste story, those involved and roles, and suggested he review the Newsday library. Mitchell could hear him using the computer keyboard.

"Outstanding, Mr. Pappas. Outstanding!"

"How ever you slant the story, the background correlation's to the murders will have to raise eyebrows. Your updated story should make Marlowe and Colarossi extremely uncomfortable."

"I love it! I think Colarossi had something to do with Dryden's murder to get his wife."

Mitchell chuckled at the various theories that could be developed. "I don't think so, Adam."

"Where are you going to be later?"

"At home. You still have the number?"

"Engraved in stone. Anything else I can use? Anything new?"

"Yes, but not at this time. Mullins may inform you today of what I know. It's major news if he does."

"I can't wait." The excitement in his voice continued. "I'll call you as soon as I get back to my desk. Thanks a lot, Mr. Pappas. I owe you."

"Adam?"

"Yes. Still here."

"I want to say something off the record."

"Confirmed. Off the record."

"Lieutenant Mullins has officially asked me to get involved. Recruited me, you might say."

"Excellent!"

"Keep it to yourself, however. I don't want the media hounding me. I'll give you an exclusive when I can. Remember, I'm off the record."

"I'm a reporter, not a fool. Don't look a gift horse in the mouth and don't bite the hand that feeds you. Ancient codes I live by."

Mitchell entered his apartment at 4:55. He immediately turned on the television set, switched channels to his preferred newscast, changed clothes and hurried back to the living room in time to hear a station teaser ad, "New evidence in the yacht club murder mystery. Coming up next," the lady newscaster said with a faint smile. That annoyed Mitchell and he changed channels. *Why do they smile at tragedy? More concerned with how they look than what they're saying!*

Mitchell knew that Mullins would announce that two men were involved in Renata's murder. *Good thinking!*

A lot had happened. He went to the computer and added notes, including his attack on the newscaster.

✻ ✻ ✻

"MITCHELL, I'm calling to see if you saw Mullin's announcement," said Josh, who called while Helene and Mitchell were having dinner.

"Yes, I did. I wonder how Marlowe reacted to the news."

"I hope he confesses to killing her. If he doesn't, we haven't advanced because Titus will remain tight-lipped. After you left, and one hour and three beers later, Titus refused to admit that he knew Renata was having an affair with anyone. He mentioned a few other extra-maritals, but avoided Renata. Why?"

"We'll talk to him again."

"I'll wait a day. If the new evidence doesn't stimulate Marlowe and Titus to act, then I will."

"You're coming to your senses, at long last."

"I promise to have a definite answer before the weekend's end. If I do it now, the weekend will be shot with cops and media. This weekend, the weather forecast is perfect. I've waited this long, a few more days won't matter, I guess."

"Then Monday, you'll go to Mullins' office?"

"That would be the best thing."

"Hallelujah. The awakening of Josh Trimble."

"A good book title. What about this weekend? Have you talked to Helene?"

"We'll be there late Wednesday. After dinner and after the Long Island holiday traffic has waned."

"I'll plan the activities."

"One stop has to be Port Jefferson for Helene."

"That and more. See you then, Professor."

Mitchell terminated the line.

"And the gist of the conversation was . . ." asked Helene.

"He's happy about the weekend and he'll confess to being a witness on Monday."

"You better go with him, don't you think? He's wavered before."

"I definitely will to prevent cold feet. I believe he's going ahead this time."

* * *

Same day.

DIRECTOR EDWARD MARLOWE had established a procedure with his executive assistant, Betsy Hobart of no interruptions during meetings with members of his senior staff. The exceptions were by the President and his chief of staff, the Director of the National Security Council, the Director of the Federal Bureau of Investigation, the Secretary of State, the Committee Chairman of the Senate Intelligence Committee and matter related to the murders at the Eastern Shore Yacht Club.

A meeting had begun at four o'clock on operations in middle Africa, a thriving den of corruption, disease, murder and unstable governments. Recently discovered oil from the east to West Coast was creating new economic factors and changing policies. With Marlowe were his director of African affairs and his second in command. An opened map of Africa was on the desk. At 5:08, Betsy, a career CIA employee in her forties, used the intercom.

"Yes, Betsy."

"Director Marlowe. There's something you have to see. It's important."

"All right, Betsy. Bring it in."

"It's best you come out."

Marlowe excused himself and went to the outer office. When Betsy said important, it was. Another procedure was that Betsy would tape the evening newscasts in the event anything pertaining to the CIA was mentioned and he'd view it later. She had taped the opening of the news broadcast, stopped the machine when the subject changed and pressed rewind. She was standing and holding the tape when he came out.

"We'd better go in here." She led him to his conference room. She went to the VCR and he closed the door.

"What's the subject, Betsy?"

"Your club."

The words were distressing. She inserted the tape; turned on the thirty-five inch television set and hit PLAY.

He listened to Mullins' announcement with riveted concentration. The story had become

Washington's priority news with his picture. Betsy sadly watched her boss, knowing how sensitive the subject was since the death of his ex-partners. The segment ended.

"Again?" asked Betsy.

"Not necessary. Erase and then go home. No need for you to stay. This meeting will be awhile."

Absorbed in thought, Marlowe left the conference room. The newscast had stirred the Renata problem, placed on a back burner temporarily, as the execution of his responsibilities became dominant. Now the Renata problem became dominant, haunting his security.

How long after he left Renata did the second guy enter *Champagne Lady*? Did she invite him? Did she want more passion? Why would anyone want to kill Renata?

He tried to rationalize his role that fateful evening with the public and the President. Would they now believe he killed her if he came forward? That he masterminded a cover up with witnesses now dead? That he wasn't forthright? Would capturing the second man dim the spotlight on him?

He had grown friendly with the President, becoming a regular golfing partner and occasional visitor to Camp David. He was strong and respected on Capitol Hill. His leadership had made an impact in the CIA's re-organization to conform to a changing world. Nevertheless, he was standing on an ice floe headed towards hot weather; and eventually, he might drown.

He hesitated opening the door to his office as Renata's death blanketed his mind. He had to think Africa to implement the new strategies, to help protect America's interests and policies.

The continent of Africa lost to Renata. He went into his office and cancelled the meeting, sick to his stomach. The ice floe continued moving.

In the loneliness of the office, a dominant thought kept returning.

Who the hell is the second man?

TWENTY=TWO

Tuesday.
July 2.

THE NEXT DAY belonged to the media and
Newsday. The second man revelation was Adam's
headline story. The prime third page was all yacht
club, continued on another page. The radioactive
waste aspects began on the last column and continued to another full page replete with photos of the
murdered, Marlowe and Colarossi, while highlight-
ing the role of the involved yacht club members.

Adam treated the stories fairly, presenting the
history and facts. He also added that the Senate had
reviewed Edward Marlowe's involvement and found
no cause. That toned down the sensationalism of the
past, to some degree. Adam unfolded the news in a
professional, journalistic manner.

They all read the articles.

Bravo, thought Mitchell Pappas. Well done.

One-upmanship beamed Lieutenant Mullins.

Hold on; hold on, braced Edward Marlowe. It'll
pass.

Excellent story said Josh Trimble.

It's getting worse, shook Titus Banks.

The Commodore buried his head in his hands, murmuring a Hebrew prayer.

F——! Cried Mario Colarossi.

* * *

ALTHOUGH HE HAD prepared for maximum activity for the July Fourth weekend, Titus knew it was more of a drill than reality. The majority of the members will be staying away, or disappear on their boats for three to four days in some other harbor for a mini-vacation. Their vacated slips would remain empty, and unavailable for rent. The club was reject ing reservations from other clubs whose members would have stayed for the weekend to enjoy the pool, tennis courts, and restaurant and nearby Huntington Village. The club had a lot to offer. The place should be a virtual ghost town, he concluded.

The loss of revenue from slip and mooring rentals, fuel sales and the restaurant for the long weekend would have a negative economic impact. Member dues may have to be increased next year to offset the continuing seasonal losses and the need to subsidize the restaurant deficit. He was already considering laying off two, or three of his assistants, college students who were hired to handle the increased summer volume. He would have to tell them at the end of the weekend. They, too, would become victims of the dismal and arcane club environment. He wasn't pleased with that impending action. They were a part of his crew and felt a need to protect them.

* * *

LIEUTENANT MULLINS scheduled another press conference for four o'clock. He will announce that Suffolk officials have invited representatives of the CIA and the FBI to assist in the search of the killers of Commandant Deever and the others, to assure that Director Marlowe was additionally protected, and to provide investigative and scientific access to federal resources.

He added that since the President had offered federal assistance, the County Executive accepted his offer. The priority was to catch a killer.

At the conference, he would introduce the two agents who will offer additional re-assurance that local and federal authorities would be working hand in hand to resolve the case.

Once again, Lieutenant Mullins had taken the image initiative.

One-upmanship!

* * *

MARIO COLAROSSI was an early riser out of habit. Sleep was unproductive to him. A necessity he couldn't control. He lived with the premise that life is not about sleeping. He normally retired late, after midnight, hated for the day to end, endured four or five hours of sleep and occasionally supplemented his bodily requirement with an afternoon nap, business permitting. His favorite cruising time was in the evening when he seemed to be wide-awake.

He had heard about the second man and Renata on the evening news. That was troublesome, but not as stiffening and chaotic as when he retrieved the delivered Newsday at 6:00AM.

His eyes flared upon seeing the accompanying article about the past. He began to read the histori-cal article as he headed back to the house overrid-ing the read with numerous expletives that best de-scribed his concern, including ones he hadn't used in years.

The readers would probably blame him for the murders of Deever, Horatio and Dryden because of that re-awakened article, he concluded.

Not good, he muttered to himself as he closed the front door behind him. *No damn good!*

With the added publicity of the revised past, his associates would want to know—"Who killed these people? Who used these killing methods?"

The business and charitable images were re-quired—the prevailing attitudes for those in the fore-front. Bad publicity was unacceptable, to a point.

How the f—— do I explain this one?

* * *

VALERIE DRYDEN was up early waiting by the screen door and listening to the morning birds voic-ing their presence. Hearing about the second man on the late news after returning from a local theater with her two daughters, she waited for Newsday to be delivered.

That was their new arrangement. At least once a week, they'd go to a theater, locally or in New York City, go to dinner, or both. The daughter's boyfriends dominated their young lives and Valerie wanted at least one night with them on a social activity away from the house and basic routines. Such an evening was deemed special.

She saw the brown van approaching her property. A plastic wrapped, folded newspaper flew out of the open passenger side window to land on her driveway. She picked up the bundle, went to the kitchen, poured a second cup of coffee, removed the plastic wrap, unfolded the paper and read the headline.

She read the articles and became upset on seeing Mario's photograph alongside Arthur's. There was no story, or substance in the past here, she concluded. Newsday was reaching. Arthur had told her Mario was innocent. He should know. He was one of the lawyers at the time. Now, Mario, her precious Mario, her lover of three years was next to her dead Arthur.

She knew Mario's image would survive the unfounded publicity of the past.

Her curiosity began to stir. Was one of Renata's visitors her Arthur? Was he disloyal? Was she wrong about him?

She closed and held the paper, picked up the plastic wrap, rose from the table and threw the wrap in the garbage container under the sink. She went to the laundry room, opened the blue recycle container and pensively stared into it as if mesmerized.

Her thoughts complete, she dropped the paper face down into the bin as a gesture of burying the article. But the probability that Arthur might have cheated on her was bothersome.

She didn't consider herself cheating on Arthur. She didn't have a cheap, meaningless love affair, a sidebar, with assorted men. Mario was an extension of a passion and love that was beyond what Arthur could give her. Arthur was comfortable and provided a comfortable life and she wanted her daughters to have a good family life as a foundation for their future.

She replaced the lid to cover yesterday's news— to put it out of her new and reconstructed life.

TWENTY＝THREE

Same day.
Morning.

COLAROSSI'S BLACK MERCEDES entered the club's parking lot, made a right and parked by the entrance to the north dock. The police in the squad car recognized him and waved him through. He exited carrying a bag of groceries and headed for *Marionette* to spend the day, to get away from Adam Farmer and Newsday and the rest of the media needing to talk to him. He came to his refuge for privacy.

His fully equipped mini-office on the boat would suffice to conduct his daily affairs. Only his secretary knew where he could be reached. If the media found him, the squad car would stop them at the gate. Today was perfect for the statement—Members Only.

Titus Banks was on the other side of the clubhouse and didn't see his arrival. He was talking with the pool service representative who rendered weekly pool maintenance.

At noon, Titus strolled towards the north dock to visit with Josh Trimble, to have a beer, or invite him to lunch at the club restaurant. The black Mercedes indicated that Colarossi was on the premises. Josh's car was gone. Maybe he was on his boat, anyway.

Reaching *Coyote,* he called his name. The doors were closed. He climbed the boarding stairs and tried the locked door. He returned to the dock, hoping he wouldn't run into Colarossi to avoid conversing with him.

After lunch, he headed for the new dock to talk to and be with three of his assistants who were laying the final run of water lines. The docks and fingers were completed, the electric and cable lines, in. By the end of the day, the project would be completed. Starting this Friday, members assigned to the new dock would move in; mostly sailboats moved from the moorings.

The slip assignments were prepared with Josh and approved by the Commodore, in the absence of the Rear Commodore. The Board decided to fill the officer positions held by Arthur Dryden and Alvin Horatio after the killer was caught; a memorial gesture.

At four o'clock, looking across to the north dock and the parking lot to the right, he saw the Mercedes and Josh's car. He'll stop by and see Josh later for a final review of the assignments. First, he had work to do in the machine shop.

Champagne Lady, the Dryden's *Courtship,* and the Horatio's *Courtside* would remain in their present slips until further disposition. *Courtship* and *Courtside* were for sale. The boating life had ended for those families. Early next week, Renata's family would move *Champagne Lady* to Florida.

At five o'clock, Titus returned to the dock house for the slip assignments and prepared to visit Josh. Looking towards the north dock, he saw Colarossi exit *Mario-nette* holding files under his arm and head for the ramp. Titus decided to wait, not wanting to run into him.

Just as Colarossi was approaching *Coyote,* the aft deck door opened and Josh came out to read a book.

"Working on the boat, Mario?" Colarossi stopped by the stern.

"Hi, Josh. It was impossible at home and the office with that Newsday story, so I came down here."

"I could imagine. Your high visibility and achievement make you news. You shouldn't be so popular."

"I'm going to drop these files off at the car, have dinner and then spend a quiet evening watching television. The Yankees have a night game against Cleveland." He reacted to a sudden idea. "Why don't you join me for dinner at the club and then watch the game. Better yet, let's take a ride to Norwalk, have dinner then take an extended night cruise."

Josh replied enthusiastically, "Great idea. I'll go in and change."

"Come over when you're ready."

"I shouldn't be long."

Going to Norwalk and other ports together for lunch and dinner wasn't new. They visited Norwalk numerous times over the years.

Titus watched as Josh went inside and Colarossi to his car to open the trunk and deposit the files. Titus watched him as he returned and passed *Coyote* and board *Mario-nette.* Soon, he saw Josh, wearing a blue sports blazer and tan slacks, leave *Coyote,* head for *Mario-nette* and board.

Titus panicked.

He mustn't go with him!

TWENTY-FOUR

TITUS CALLED TWO assistants standing by the fuel dock and told them to release *Mario-nette*. They jogged to arrive at the farthest slip in reasonable time. They arrived and released the stern line, passing it to Josh who had uncoupled the water, cable and electric lines. Josh went forward to receive the lines, then the forward spring line. The other spring line remained on the dock, awaiting their return. *Mario-nette* began to ease out of her berth.

The alarms were now going full blast in Titus' head.

The *Mario-nette* made her turn, gave the required blast of the horn to announce her exiting the marina and entering the channel and swung into the channel at five knots.

Titus was in a quandary. What could he do? Where were they going—Northport, Norwalk, Greenwich? Norwalk was his guess; ample docking space. At fifteen knots speed, they would be in the waterfront restaurant in about fifty minutes.

What could he do? How can he get Josh to come back? What reason could he give that was credible? That wouldn't expose him?

He had to save Josh's life!

* * *

"MARIONETTE, Marionette, Marionette. This is the Eastern Shore Yacht Club," said Titus, calling on the club's communication channel.

Colarossi replied. "I hear you, Titus. What's up?"

"I need to speak to Josh. There's an emergency."

"Hold on."

"What is it, Titus," Josh asked.

"Josh, a hose loosened on one of your head intake lines and we're working on it now. It'll be okay, but maybe you should come back. It made a real mess."

Silence. Titus held his breath hoping for a favorable response. "We're now by Eaton's Neck and on the way back," Josh replied.

Shortly, Marionette was making the turn by the green buoy. Titus could see Josh putting out the fenders. He called his other assistants on his portable radio and they came running and stood by *Marionette's* slip.

"It's under control," Titus called out to Josh before *Marion-nette* entered the slip. "I'll be there." He left.

Colarossi docked, an assistant boarded to take the lines as Josh rushed to *Coyote* and entered the flood area. Two dock assistants were scooping water.

"Which head?" he hollered.

"The guest."

"Damn, Titus. I tightened this hose the other day. Not tight enough, I guess."

"I was on the dock and I noticed your bilge pumps were on. I took it upon myself to check."

Josh changed clothes. In his shorts and shirt, he began to use and wring the towels.

Colarossi came down, stood on the last step and shook his head.

"You under control, Josh?"

"Mario," said Josh. "Don't come down. The worst is over."

"Let's have dinner at the club then. Come over when you're done."

"I'll be another hour at least. See you then."

With their efforts completed and the dock assistants gone, Josh was dismayed.

"I'm positive I tightened that hose, Titus. I can't explain why it happened. I owe you my thanks."

They were in the salon. "Where were you and Mario headed?"

"To Norwalk and to hang out on the Sound."

"Josh, you're not going to like this. I wasn't going to tell you . . . but I loosened the hose."

"What? Why would you do that?"

"I had to stop you from going with Mario. It would be night when you returned, and the Sound has few other boaters at night during the week."

"What does that have . . ." The answer came. "Are you saying that you thought Mario is the killer and that I was to be his next drowning victim?"

"I believe that," Titus said, firmly.

"I can't believe it." He was flabbergasted. "Was it the story in Newsday?"

"That helped. I've always believed he had something to do with Deever, Alvin and Arthur. The way they died."

Josh was at a loss for words. "Titus, sit." He did. Josh sat opposite. "Look, thank you for the effort to save my life. But I wasn't in danger. Mario's a dear friend. Your guess is that it's Mario. My guess is someone else."

"Who? Or are you saying that in defense of Mario?"

"Marlowe—for the same reason you applied Mario. The past. We're guessing. Listen to me, Titus. The killer acts only if certain there were no witnesses to identify him. Then he'd do his savagery. That's logical. Besides, there's no reason for Colarossi to kill me. I'm not a part of his past, which is your basis for judgment."

Titus evaluated the statement. "He could have knocked you out, thrown you overboard and report it to the Coast Guard as an accident. It was dark, you tripped and if he added weights, they'll never find you. You won't be another Dryden found with a magnet."

"Not likely. And there's no riddle to solve. A riddle precedes the murder and again, he has no reason."

"You're right. I'm terribly sorry, Josh. I was emotionally involved to save you that I wasn't thinking properly. I'll help pay for the damage."

"No, unacceptable. Your concern for me is appreciated and valued. I thank you. It's a gesture of a true friend. Let's go. I have to meet Mario."

With all the fans in place, they left.

Titus went to the dock house to lock his office and then go home. The terror symptoms returned, knowing that he couldn't say anything to anyone that he had the cap securely tight on emotions that were like an oil well ready to gush.

Titus knew he would be mentally free if he confessed.

But he will tell, in due time . . . in his own way.

He'll expose them all.

And then the world will know that Mario Colarossi was the second man.

TWENTY-FIVE

Wednesday. July 3.
The next day.

KEN MULLINS left his home in Commack at 8:15AM to arrive at the Second Precinct by 8:30. His attitude was clear and bright as this summer day. If only crime would go on vacation to make it a perfect day.

He needed to get some sun, to spend time outdoors. But not until these cases were solved. At times, he thought he'd never see the sun again.

His press conferences established the Suffolk police firmly in control—who had invited investigator guests from Washington. He hadn't given his presentation to the Feds on Monday due to their late arrival after the conference, and did so yesterday morning.

He related to them, introduced them at the press conference, then took them to dinner at a local Italian restaurant at his personal expense. The Suffolk Homicide Squad didn't have a budget for entertainment. He wanted to make them feel welcomed, that he wasn't an adversary.

He didn't want the Feds being in his conference

room office as their base of operations. Too distract-
ing. He arranged to have the two adjoining offices
vacated. They were professional, courteous and experienced. Both agents were in their late thirties and
had worked together as a team before several years
back when the CIA and FBI had a rare joint mission.

Driving to the precinct, he decided to spend
more time with them, to take advantage of their train-
ing and knowledge. He stopped at a bakery and bought
a dozen assorted pastries for them and himself.

His priority this morning was to review the thousands of transcripts of interviews with suspects, club
members, club staff and family members of the victims. He virtually memorized the synopsis of each
interviewee. He needed to reassure himself that he
didn't overlook anything no matter how trivial before the analytical Federal talent found it first. He
had to stay on top of the heap.

He knew, upon reaching the precinct, that his
first act would be to call his chief who called every
morning since Renata Tredanari's death to ask—
"What's new?" The call always ended with the chief
saying—"Call me first if anything breaks." He called,
the routine followed.

He respected his chief and understood he also
wanted to give the public impression that he was on
top of the heap.

He liked Mitchell Pappas' idea of exposing the
past to Adam Farmer, who he thought did an excellent job on yesterday's articles. He was pleased with
his decision to bring Mitchell aboard—something he
didn't tell the Feds—and decided to accept Farmer
as an ally rather than a critic. He needed help; no
longer the time to be all knowing.

Today was the day before the Fourth when businesses close early to allow their employees' added time to travel and a week when most people take vacation leave. He hoped the precinct had a similar lethargic day.

He had coffee and pastries with the Feds and chatted until ten o'clock when he headed back to his office to begin his review of the yacht club data, to roll up his sleeves and dig in.

When he reached his office, the wished for lethargic day exploded in his face.

An express mail envelope from the U.S. Postal Service was on his desk. The overnight package was addressed to Kenneth Mullins, no title, and the street address. The Second Precinct was excluded. The postmark was Hicksville, one of the busiest post offices on the Island.

He was curious why anyone would send a costly overnight letter to him. He opened the envelope. A single sheet of white paper was inside. He pulled the sheet out and read the correspondence—'The scourge of God must die . . . in a tavern at the age of 29 . . .The solution will arrive on Friday.'

Mullins was skeptical acknowledging the riddle was from the Riddler because of two obvious variations; the postmark wasn't Northport like the others, and the other riddles were sent to the club's trustees. Was this a new tactic? If so, why? Was it a prankster?

It could be a crank letter, but he couldn't be complacent. He had to assume the Riddler was striking again and had already selected his next victim.

He immediately set his wheels in motion to find the answer. He'd release the riddle to the media, call a press conference, call the Commodore, Mitchell Pappas, Valerie Dryden and the Feds to

get Washington involved with a solution, make a
special call to Adam Farmer and call his chief who
in turn would notify the District Attorney and the
County Executive.

He hoped the public response would be as broad
as the Deever solution. He needed one caller with
the solution to save the scourge of God whoever that
may be.

Why direct the letter to me? He had no answer.
He had answers for the Hicksville postmark and the
absence of his title and the Second Precinct on the
address.

A regular letter can be placed in a mailbox and
take a few days to deliver, sender unknown and unseen. An overnight letter requires the sender to go
to the post office counter. To address it to a lieutenant and a police precinct may have called attention
to the sender. Since Hicksville is an active post office
and distribution center, another overnight letter was
part of the day's volume. The sender minimized the
possibility of a postal clerk remembering the mailer.
The sender probably wore a disguise; glasses, wig,
beard, mustache, colored lenses, cap, or any combination.

He assigned one of his men to Hicksville to check
the post office. Within the hour, Mullins was called
and told that no one there could make a connection
to the sender.

The next two days of waiting until the Riddler
sends the solution will seem like a month if a solution isn't found. The overnight letter suggested to
Mullins that the decision to send him the letter was
either made yesterday, or the day before.

He must have the answer today, or someone may
die before the day is out.

TWENTY⧸SIX

July 3.
Same day.

MULLINS CALLED MITCHELL to inform him of the latest note and that he was calling Adam Farmer to compliment him on his fine articles.

When he called, Adam notified Mullins that Valerie Dryden called him as a follow-up to the historical article. At the time, her husband, Arthur, adamantly believed that Mario Colarossi was innocent of any alleged charges and the attack on him and his companies were unjustified and unfounded, and she wanted to testify that his feelings were genuine and to please let her husband rest in peace. Adam assured Mrs. Dryden that her comments of Mr. Colarossi's innocence would be included in the next article relating to the yacht club.

When she hung up, Adam was convinced something was going on between the widow and Colarossi. The call confirmed his belief that one of them, or both killed Dryden.

* * *

HELENE AND MITCHELL arrived at the yacht club after nine o'clock at night—Helene to start a mini-vacation, Mitchell, to continue investigating.

Josh told him about the flooding incident and apologized if there was a remnant of dampness, though the rugs had dried. He had seven fans going day and night.

The itinerary for the Fourth was Port Jefferson, return and investigate; then on Friday, a cruise to the Battery, the Statue of Liberty and around Manhattan, and return. Departure on Friday would be at 7:00AM to allow Mitchell to probe in the evening.

Saturday and Sunday, an overnight in Sag Harbor with trips to the Hamptons via taxis, or car rental.

Josh mentioned that Mario Colarossi would be staying in Montauk at the Montauk Yacht Club and Mario wondered if they can get together on Sunday for brunch. His daughter had a summer home in East Hampton. He had a car and he'd pick them up. Helene and Mitchell agreed.

* * *

EDWARD MARLOWE arrived from Washington with his entourage at ten o'clock and slept on *Legal Tender* with Clair Roseman.

* * *

July Fourth.

HELENE AND MITCHELL awakened before Josh, decided to rise and Mitchell would make breakfast. Helene came out on the aft deck and absorbed the surrounding scenery and nautical air. She looked at *Champagne Lady* and *Legal Tender* and thought of the murder victim within and the intrigue surrounding her and Marlowe.

She decided on a walk, notified Mitchell and left. She turned right towards the channel and looked out over the peaceful harbor. Several sea gulls perched on the pilings. One piling had a plastic owl nailed to its top to scare away the sea gulls. The owl wasn't helping today. At seven o'clock, three boaters were carrying supplies, preparing to leave to their destined ports for the weekend. She had a final look of the harbor, turned and headed towards the ramp. She saw the Dryden yacht *Courtship* and, just opposite, Horatio's *Courtside*. Four yachts, three murders.

She went up the ramp and studied the hillside homes overlooking the harbor and the club, and tried to determine from which one a sniper could shoot Josh.

She noticed only three-dozen cars in the huge parking lot. Last July Fourth, when they came out for the day, she and Mitchell couldn't find a space and left the keys with valet parking by the clubhouse. Valet parking was canceled this year.

She finished her circuit on the new dock; the empty tennis courts, the pool area and fuel dock, and overlooked the sailing fleet on the south dock.

When she returned, Josh and Mitchell were finishing preparing breakfast; scrambled eggs, orange juice, fresh fruit, Canadian bacon, coffee and Belgian waffles. The table was neatly dressed on the aft deck.

"What's wrong with you two? There are only three

of us, not six. How come when you two get together common sense leaves the room?"

"Enjoy it today for tomorrow you may wind up with cinnamon rolls. That's all I got last time," retorted Mitchell.

Breakfast was served on the aft deck while the weather remained cool. The high today will reach eighty-five. The air conditioner was on inside *Coyote*.

"Nearly forgot with all the cooking, Professor," said Mitchell. "What you said about Titus crept back in the middle of the night."

Helene was looking at the houses on the hillside. In one, two people were on their veranda lounges reading newspapers, having breakfast. She erased the sniper thoughts for now.

"About Colarossi?" replied Josh.

"Yes. Titus was convinced Colarossi was going to kill you, that you were the next victim. Why would he think that? He nearly scuttled the boat to have you return. He knows something. He reacted in desperation and with knowledge. We have to break him by Sunday night. After that, you'll be confessing to Mullins. Right?"

"Absolutely, one hundred percent. That's what I promised."

"Happy to hear that," said Mitchell. "I called Lieutenant Mullins last night before we left and no one called in with a solution to the riddle."

"It looks tough," added Josh. "Insufficient substance."

Helene jumped in. "Let me tell you something, Josh," said Helene. Mitchell knew the stern facial gestures. The mother agent lecture was coming. "You better get your act together and do what you must before somebody does assassinate you. Have you ever heard me curse?"

"No. You're too much of a lady," Josh answered.

"Have you ever seen me angry?"

"No, and I don't want to."

"If you don't commit to Monday, I will personally come out here with a cleaver and cut your f——— balls off!"

Mitchell began clapping and laughing. "Brava, brava!" Helene wasn't smiling.

Josh went to her chair and kissed her head.

"I don't have any. That's why I haven't gone yet. And I love you."

They left for Port Jefferson at nine o'clock.

* * *

HOLIDAY, OR NO, Lieutenant Mullins was at his office at 8:30AM. His crisis was on going. Police precincts never sleep, or vacation. He couldn't believe no one called after the late news. Where the hell were the literary experts—on vacation? So what if academia was in recess. The literature experts still watch television and read the papers. If the Riddler could find an appropriate passage, why couldn't they determine his source?

This is taking long he bemoaned. Something has to break. Maybe they'd have an answer today. We must get a solution before the Riddler strikes.

* * *

COYOTE RETURNED to the Eastern Shore Yacht Club a few minutes after 6:00 for Mitchell to talk to primary suspects and leave by 8:15 to join the raft-up in Lloyd Harbor to watch the fireworks display at 9:00. The local towns sponsored the program for the first time. National pride had finally won over political bickering.

Helene's body and face had reddened as she sun bathed on the forward deck to and from Port Jefferson. The wind contributed to the burn. She remained on *Coyote* to take a nap as Mitchell and Josh left to seek prospects. The *Legal Tender* had left its berth. "Maybe Marlowe's at the raft-up," guessed Josh.

The Grant slip was vacant. The Robinsons and Chus weren't boating today. Matthew DiBiasi was on his 44-foot Searay, *Bull n' Bare* berthed next to the Grants.

"You met Matt at the club, remember? He was with Colarossi."

"I remember him and his fiancée, Gina Ferrara. I wrote their names in my notes." The sleek and spacious luxury sports craft impressed Mitchell.

Matthew was in the process of cleaning the water tanks and replacing the water. Water poured out of two seacocks.

"Hi, Matt," called out Josh. "What's doing?"

Matt turned, saw them and came towards the stern and dock.

"Josh, Happy Fourth. How are you? Mitchell, good to see you again." He extended his hand to Mitchell.

"And it's good to see you. All I see of people who own boats is work. Always repairing something," mocked Mitchell.

"That's all part of the love of boating, Mitchell," Matt replied. "That old nemesis, Josh, the rotten egg odor in the water. Haven't had that in years."

"Don't forget to add a drop, or two of Clorox."

"I won't. We don't drink the tap water, anyway. That's the least of my problems today. The starboard engine refuses to behave. We were supposed to leave yesterday and couldn't get a mechanic. I'm stuck until tomorrow. A guy's coming at seven in the morning. And I was looking forward to these four days. They were to be my vacation for the year. Every now and then, Mitchell, it gets exasperating, usually before a long trip. Boats can be ungrateful at the wrong time."

Matthew DiBiasi was a long-term member of the club, sociable, outgoing and liked. He declined serving on any committee due to his business demands and travel. He participated in as many social events as time permitted and was closest to Mario Colarossi at the club. They boated together often.

"Matt, Mitchell is helping out with everything going on around here. May he ask you a few questions?"

"Come aboard. Josh, turn the water off for me." Josh turned the water valve alongside the dock. They sat in the leather cushions in the wide and open cockpit. "Are you doing work for the police, or prosecution?"

"No. I know you've been through that already. I'm being myself, as an investigative author. Josh thought I could help by doing some evaluations. My questions are brief and basic and," he smiled, "you won't be needing a lawyer. Or should I say you won't be needing Gina."

"Not a problem," Matt replied.

"Where were you going?" asked Josh. "We just came in from Port Jeff."

"Montauk. I was to leave yesterday with Mario. My upset Gina left to go home. She'll be back later in about an hour for dinner. She's also disappointed about missing the fireworks as an option. I am not winning with her at all this weekend."

"Come with us," Josh offered. "We're going out about eight-thirty. That would make Gina happy and Helene, Mitchell's wife, will have someone to talk with besides us."

"Great. That will also make me happy."

"Did Mario go by himself?" asked Josh.

"You know, Mario. Single-handing is no problem and he enjoys night cruising. No sun, less traffic, obvious landmarks and the drunks are already in port. He left about seven o'clock last night." The conversation was good, thought Mitchell. Perhaps Matt will be friendlier and open up to his questions. "I have a reservation alongside Mario that I'm paying for," continued Matt. With the fireworks thrown in, I don't feel so bad. I can consider that as a form of rebate."

"We've plans to meet with Mario in Sag Harbor on Sunday for brunch. Why not join us?" said Josh.

"Done. Mitchell, what would you like to know?"

"You were on your boat the night Renata was killed."

"Correct. I fell asleep during the Tonight Show and missed Jimmy Buffett's appearance. I also missed anything happening on the dock. The TV shut off automatically at one."

"How well did you know Renata?"

"Pretty well. I've socialized with her up at the bar occasionally with and without Gina."

"You're a handsome guy. She ever come on to you?"

"Not once. I couldn't understand that," he laughed. "We weren't friends, exactly. More like social acquaintances. You know, club type of closeness where everyone acts like one happy family."

"Any idea why anyone would want her dead?"

"Zero."

"How about the others? Any idea why Alvin Horatio, Arthur Dryden or Commandant Deever were killed?"

"Triple zero. Newsday insinuated some connection to the past. Other than that," he shrugged. "I wasn't social with them. The only lawyer I hang out with is Gina."

"How about suspects? Do you have any?"

"None. I can't imagine Renata having an enemy, or who'd kill her. She was too nice for that ending."

Mitchell didn't expect any revelations, but was disappointed.

"I like your boat's name," said Mitchell.

"Some people think I'm a stock broker. I'm not. I invest in various things, including stocks and commodities. And I am a bull and usually bare. Gina could confirm that." They laughed.

"Thanks, Matt, sorry for the interruption. We'll leave you to your problem. I should say, problems," added Mitchell.

"We'll see you later," said Josh. "Oh, would you like me to look at your engine?"

"Thanks, but don't bother. The mechanic's already hired."

Mitchell shook hands with Matt and left *Bull n' Bare*. Josh turned the water valve. Josh and Mitchell walked towards the ramp.

"Him, I like," said Mitchell. "I'm glad you asked him along tonight."

"Let's try the bar, the restaurant and the pool area," Josh said.

The tennis courts were unused. The pool was active with families taking advantage of a hot day,

the bar had two couples having dinner and the restaurant was empty. Warren Moss, the bartender, was
off today. Three waitresses were by the entrance looking concerned at their lack of tips.

"Want to talk to Titus," asked Josh.

"Let's get him tomorrow night at the bar. Let's
go back."

Helene awakened from her mat on the bow as
they were boarding and asked Josh, "Where are your
binoculars?"

"On top. Right hand cabinet."

"Thank you, sir." She left.

Helene found the binoculars and focused them
on the hillside homes across from the club looking
for locations for her imagined sniper.

TWENTY=SEVEN

Same day.

LIEUTENANT KEN MULLINS stayed at the Second Precinct till midnight. He had a terrible Fourth. No one called with the solution. He took time out to watch the televised Macy's fireworks display along the East River. His last stand, the late news at eleven, was lost.

Several involved people called during the day to inquire if a solution were offered, including Mitchell and Adam Farmer.

He left, accepting that the killer now had two days on him. Remaining was for the Riddler to provide the solution tomorrow and hope the potential victim was alive.

Would it be an after-the-fact riddle . . . like Deever's?

* * *

MITCHELL SPOKE to the Grant's and the Commodore at the raft-up after the fireworks display and after the boat horns minimized their celebration in the crowded harbor.

Matthew DiBiasi and fiancée, Gina Ferrara added to the evening with their pleasant and social personalities. Helene enjoyed their company. Gina was energetic in a social scene and stimulated her environment.

Gina, a partner with a Nassau County law firm in Garden City, specialized in criminal law and mentioned the frustrations of a defense attorney. Helene mentioned that she had edited and published two novels written by former defense attorneys who now wrote novels full time.

"I don't have a creative bone in my body," said Gina. "Law's it for me. I love every aspect of it, including the frustrations."

The *Legal Tender* was at the raft-up; a total of seventeen boats, motor and sail. In deference to Josh, they didn't visit, or socialize with Marlowe and guests.

Mitchell had no gain from his interviews.

Only Titus remained.

* * *

Friday. July 5.

THE DREADED morning came.

Although the mail didn't arrive until after nine o'clock, Ken Mullins was at the Second Precinct at 7:30. The Feds arrived at 8:30, concerned and anxious. Mullins assured them he'd call immediately when the mail arrived.

The *Coyote* left for her Manhattan cruise at 7:10 to catch the favorable southwest ebb current at the East River. The river had a treacherous current that flowed to 4.0 knots at high water and 5.2 knots at low water. Proper seamanship was to go with the flow in either direction.

Bull n' Bare left for Montauk at 8:40 with fresh water and a repaired engine. Matt Dibiasi untied and collected the lines and Gina captained the Searay out of the marina and into the channel. Matt had taught her well. Matt took in the lines for docking at Montauk. He called Colarossi to say the engine was repaired, were on their way and should arrive in three to four hours. Mario said he'd wait for lunch, delighted they were able to make repairs.

* * *

AT 9;15, THE MAIL hadn't arrived. Mullins was pacing, nervous as a father in a birthing room. At 9:25, a rushing officer instructed to do that when the mailman came brought the mail to his office.

He closed the door to his office and read the address on the envelope. Again, his title and the Second Precinct were excluded. This time, the postmark was from the Long Island City post office in Queens, another major post office. *He figured we'd check the Hicksville post office, be waiting for him.* His men were waiting.

He heaved a deep breath and uttered, "All right, let's see what you have to say, you clever swine." He pulled out the single sheet of white paper and hurried to read the typed words: 'The writer of the quotation—The scourge of God must die—was the first, great Elizabethan writer of tragedy in the fifteen hundreds. The quotation is from *Tamburlane the Great.* The writer died at the age of twenty-nine in a tavern duel. He also did secret service duty for the government. His name was Christopher Marlowe.'

Mullins then immediately called CIA agent Charlie Messina.

The *Legal Tender* had spent the night in Lloyd Harbor on the club mooring. Marlowe was reached by radiophone by Agent Messina, who knew his schedule and *Legal Tender* immediately headed back to its berth at the club where police would be waiting to provide additional protection. His bodyguards were relieved Marlowe was returning. Protecting the Director on the water was security wise, uncomfortable and disadvantageous.

* * *

COYOTE CRUISED. The problems at the yacht club were far away. They cruised the Battery and the lower bay to the Verrazano Bridge, the Wall Street and financial area then dropped an anchor by the Statue of Liberty for lunch. They enjoyed one of the best views of Manhattan.

They proceeded up the Hudson River and picked up the slack current down the Harlem River and into the northwest flood current back up the East River. A casual two-hour cruise along the Connecticut shore and across the Sound to Huntington Bay would follow. For Helene, it was a lovely, casual day— medicine for the soul.

Mitchell called Ken Mullins as the return trip began. Mullins read the solution offered and stated that additional police protection would be provided to Marlowe. Mitchell copied the solution.

"Mitchell, Marlowe may be the fourth marked member of the radioactive waste scandal. Looks like Colarossi may be the hit man. The only one left."

"Very plausible, Lieutenant. Finding a way to prove it, isn't."

"That's going to be tough."

Mitchell also suggested he call Adam Farmer to add spice to a better relationship between them.

Mitchell repeated the message to Helene and Josh.

"You'll be happy to know that I'm rooting for the Riddler," said Josh.

"Don't be harsh on Marlowe, Professor. Remember that there is a second man. Don't wish him death, yet. We'll see what happens Monday when he's confronted that you saw him. If he killed Renata, the death penalty may apply. Harbor your anger for now."

"That's pretty nautical, Mitchell. The salt air has taken effect. Beautiful, beautiful day, isn't it? The prelude to the fall of the house of Marlowe."

* * *

THE *BULL N' BARE* traveled at a cruising speed of twenty-five knots and went through The Race, a body of water at the eastern end of Long Island's islands and Fishers Island where The Long Island Sound becomes Block Island Sound. She steered a direct line to Montauk, which was visible at the horizon.

Gina and Matt entered the inlet and steered to port at the head of Star Island and the Coast Guard station, to the Montauk Yacht Club on Lake Montauk and to a slip next to *Mario-nette*. Colarossi saw them arriving as he, his daughter, son-in-law and two children were sunning on the top deck.

He waited for them and the dock assistants to finish docking and he boarded. He kissed Gina and hugged Matt. During the conversation, and before they went to the *Mario-nette* and then lunch at the restaurant, he told them that Valerie Dryden would be coming out tomorrow for the day. She couldn't stay over because of her daughters; it was soon to appear in public with another man, never mind doing an overnight.

Gina and Matt were aware of Colarossi's and Valerie's friendship. Colarossi trusted them both, as did Valerie when she got to know them. Gina and Valerie were friends.

* * *

THE TWO FEDS and Lieutenant Mullins drove to the yacht club to meet with Edward Marlowe, to show him a copy of the Riddler's solution and discuss safety precautions if he remained in the area. The Feds remained at the club grounds and Mullins returned to the Second Precinct to arrange for a press conference for this afternoon, knowing that the media's potential headlines would emulate, 'Yacht Club Killer Threatens CIA Chief.' 'Riddler Announces Next Victim.' 'Riddler Takes on the CIA.' 'Marlowe Threatened.'

Driving back, Mullins called Adam Farmer to inform him on the substance of the note and that Marlowe was at the Eastern Shore Yacht Club under expanded protection. Adam thanked him, said he'd make the conference then took off immediately with a photographer and a long lens and headed for the yacht club.

Another first!

* * *

COYOTE'S PASSENGERS viewed the press conference on television while passing the waterfront amusement park in Rye.

The Suffolk police boat was tied to one of the north docks outside slips when *Coyote* approached the club at 6:00.

Two suited men were by the police boat and another two at the top of the ramp. An additional squad car was in the parking lot. A man at the top of the ramp began scanning the hillside homes with his binoculars.

"Look at that activity, Josh," said Mitchell.

Josh was seething. "He's too damn stupid to get out of here and go back to Washington," he said, beginning his docking procedures to enter stern first. "He's ruining what's left of this place. He must be with his girl friend."

"Calm down, Josh. Get angry after you dock safely."

Josh reversed cautiously. Titus was on the dock telling an agent that *Coyote* belonged here and knew the people on board. The agent left.

The activity on the dock caused a slow-down in the channel. The police presence was being rubbernecked. The even-tempered Josh began to unravel, angry that Marlowe was the cause of disruption. Mitchell failed to tone him down. Then Helene tried. The mother agent failed. Josh's anger was impregnable.

"I've got to get out of here before they shoot me for strangling him." He jumped off *Coyote* and jogged to the ramp.

Josh didn't go far. At the top of the ramp, he

went left to the new dock then walked to the end
and back again. He did some stretching exercises to
ease tension. Mitchell kept an eye on him. Josh
seemed calmer and the crazed look was gone when
he returned.

Helene had a cold beer waiting for him. "Better?"

"Like a million. I don't want to sit out here and
look over there. Let's go inside."

They did and Mitchell closed the aft door, shutting out the Marlowe scene.

Within forty-five minutes, after they changed for
dinner in town at a restaurant at the foot of the harbor, Josh started again on the aft deck with Mitchell
as they waited for Helene.

"Look at that. He killed Renata and now the CIA
and the police are protecting the son-of-a-bitch! The
whole thing's a decoy created by him to focus attention away from him as the real killer. The note and
solution are a scam. And he's going to win!"

"Josh, there was a second man."

"I don't care. The other guy could have been
the first visitor and he's the second man, the killer.
He probably killed the others. It's a scam, I tell you.
It grates the hell out of me." His eyes were distant.

"Don't do this, Josh. Don't torment yourself or
self-destruct. Go and wait by the car. The more you
look at his boat and his lurking men, the worse you'll
become. I'll lock up."

Josh breathed deeply. "Sorry, Mitchell. I promise
to be good company at dinner. I won't spoil Helene's
day. No Renata, no Marlowe."

"Mother Helene would appreciate that. She's
had a perfect day, don't upset her, or the both of us
will beat up on you. She usually doesn't lose."

They returned to *Coyote* at eleven o'clock. The police boat patrolled the perimeter; squad cars were in place and the gate closed. The two agents at the ramp greeted them with a good evening and cordial smiles.

In the *Coyote's* salon, Helene announced, "Perfect day, gentlemen, with two of my favorite men. Thank you and goodnight." She went below.

"What time do you think Titus will finish tonight?" asked Mitchell. "It's quiet out there. Can he get off before midnight? We have to break him tonight."

Josh began to pace and went to stare at *Champagne Lady* and *Legal Tender*. He looked morose, saddened.

"I did a lot of thinking tonight. Titus is no longer important."

"Why not?" Mitchell replied to the strange statement. "I thought we agreed he was key."

"No, I'm key, the only sure key that fits the lock. Let's call Mario in the morning and tell him we're canceling Sag Harbor."

"That will disappoint Helene. She called and made plans to meet friends there. I'm sure Mario will also be disappointed."

"The only person that will be disappointed is Marlowe. Tomorrow, I want you to go with me. I'm turning him in."

TWENTY-EIGHT

UNABLE TO SLEEP at the good news that Josh would finally confess, the conflict within Mitchell struggled against the bad news that Josh could expose himself to danger. Once Josh admitted being an eyewitness, Marlowe may have difficulty surviving the publicity and his office. Would Marlowe be arrested? He had three witnesses and probably the two agents. Who would the police believe—six people, or Josh?

If Marlowe killed Renata and his former associates, he could be a continuing threat. If Colarossi was the second man and believes Josh saw him as well, than Josh had two adversaries.

It wasn't a simple matter of walking into the precinct, bearing witness and saying—Sorry I took so long then sit back and watch the drama unfold. Critics could make him a punching bag.

Regardless of the numerous reasons Mitchell could offer regarding Josh's disadvantages, the overriding need was that Josh come forward to initiate a closure to Renata's unsolved mystery. Who killed the others was another mystery. Beginning the process with Renata may lead to solving the other murders and the identification of the Riddler.

For Mitchell, the decision for Josh to come forward came with mixed blessings.

Mitchell came upstairs to the aft deck and sat. Marlowe's security force was in place; the police boat, two squad cars and agents on the premises. No one was on the dock. The lights were out in *Legal Tender*—a serene atmosphere in the quiet. The boats were motionless on this windless night and the insects weaved undisturbed around the lights.

Mitchell evaluated the dock's ample, but demure lighting. Sufficient light was cast from the light poles for anyone to see activity near the stern and by the dock around *Champagne Lady,* or any other boat. Mitchell had no doubt that Josh could easily identify the person leaving Renata. The district attorney's office would accept there was adequate lighting to make the positive identification.

Josh would be questioned, scrutinized, and maybe discredited. Marlowe was a popular native son and others corroborated his statement.

He looked across to the south dock, the restaurant and balcony and dock house. A person there at the time would have clearly seen and identified the 'prowler' on the north dock, especially if the viewer knew the person.

The western shore across the harbor was far for anyone to see clearly from there. Was there a passing boat in the channel? Then he looked to the left at the darkened hillside homes. A positive identification from there would be difficult. Was someone sitting on one of the porches or verandas and saw how many visitors Renata had that night? He was confident the police had talked to the homeowners and searched for possible boats near the club that night.

Then his attention reverted back to the south

dock and the clubhouse area. Titus had acted suspiciously. He wondered if Titus witnessed what went on from over there.

Josh had seen Marlowe. Did Titus see the second man? Is that why he thought Colarossi was going to kill Josh?

* * *

Saturday. July 6.

JOSH AND MITCHELL left the yacht club at 8:30 and headed for the Second Precinct, ten minutes away. Josh wasn't talkative; his mood, funereal. Mitchell didn't wish to distract his thoughts by talking. Josh had come to a difficult decision. Mitchell was hoping Josh wouldn't change his mind.

Halfway to the precinct, Josh ended the silence. "Should we call Mullins that we're coming?"

"If we do, a reception team may be awaiting your arrival. They might get over anxious to have a witness, at long last. Would you prefer that, or just go to his office, close the door and let him take it from there. The media may be outside waiting as part of the reception." Mitchell knew Josh was still sensitive to his decision to meet with Mullins. Josh should make the choice.

"No chaos. Let's tell him privately. I'm ready for whatever comes." His answer heartened Mitchell.

They pulled into the precinct parking lot. A television van was in a visitor's parking space. Its passengers were outside talking to reporters and photographers from local papers.

Seeing them, Mitchell said, "You made the right decision, Professor."

"Every now and then, I do that."

Mitchell turned into the officers parking area to give the impression they were officers.

They entered, were announced and escorted to Mullins' office. So far so good, thought Mitchell. Josh wasn't getting cold feet.

Mullins was pleased to see them. "Nice surprise. Have a seat. What's the occasion?"

"I think we'd better close the door," said Mitchell. He did. "Josh, sit there." Mitchell pointed to the chair nearest Mullins. Mitchell sat next to Josh, who looked determined.

Mullins was perplexed by the preparation. "What's up? What's so private? Why is everybody so gloomy and serious?"

"Josh will tell you," Mitchell replied.

Josh began. "On the night that Renata Tredanari was killed, I was in a darkened area of my yacht, which is directly opposite hers, and at around two o'clock in the morning, I saw Edward Marlowe leaving her yacht."

The statement hit Mullins like a slap to the forehead, stunning for a few seconds. He looked at Mitchell with skepticism. "Is this true?"

Mitchell nodded. "Josh saw Marlowe. I'm convinced, or I wouldn't have brought him here."

Mullins trusted Mitchell to validate the first major break in the case. "You can state unequivocally to me that he is a sound and creditable individual?"

"Yes, no compunctions. I've known him for years and he's a professor at New York University."

Mullins rose and began to pace then looked at Josh. "Are you aware that Marlowe had witnesses? It's your word against theirs?"

"Yes. I told you the truth. They are his ex-partners and lied to protect him."

"Unfortunately, they're dead. All I can only go by their affidavits which remain valid and make a strong argument for Marlowe's innocence."

"I don't care what they make. I swear to what actually happened," retorted Josh.

Mullins, accepting what he heard, began heading for the door.

"Wait here, please. I'll be right back."

"We'll be here," replied Josh. "It took me a long time to get here. I'm not leaving." Mullins left. Having a witness excited him.

"I'm proud of you, Josh," said Mitchell. "He believes you. It's a good start. Brace yourself and do what he says." He patted his forearm to indicate support and approval. Josh took his time perusing the yacht club data on the walls. The riddles were enlarged and mounted on the back wall.

Within minutes, Mullins returned with the Feds, Agents Charlie Messina and Kelvin Jackson, a tape recorder and closed the door. Mullins didn't tell the Feds what Josh said. He wanted them to hear it directly to avoid appearing prejudiced for, or against Marlowe, or the witness.

"Mr. Trimble. Mr. Pappas. This is Agent Charlie Messina of the CIA and Agent Kelvin Jackson of the FBI." The Feds gestured hello and sat opposite Josh and Mitchell and acted official, representing the federal government and their professional affiliations.

Mullins connected and turned on the tape recorder and pressed the Record button. Mullins spoke into the microphone, mentioned the names of those in the room and what Mr. Trimble would say was of his own free will and without coercion—date and time.

"Mr. Trimble, would you please repeat what you told me." The Feds were intent on listening.

Josh leaned towards the microphone and repeated the statement, word for word, as if memorized.

The Feds had the wind knocked out of them.

Mullins let the machine record the silence, then said, "Mr. Trimble, is what you said the absolute truth?"

"I saw Edward Marlowe."

"The director of the Central Intelligence Agency?" asked Mullins for verification.

"Yes, the director of the CIA."

"Mr. Pappas, do you stand up for Mr. Trimble, that he is a responsible individual?"

"Yes, I do. Completely."

Mullins turned off the recorder and set it aside.

"What I'm about to ask you, Mr. Trimble, is something you can say no to. We can proceed without you as part of normal police procedures. I will ask because of Director Marlowe's position and impact on our government by your statement. I add that so it's not misconstrued as favoritism, or doubt what you said. I reiterate Marlowe had witnesses to validate his side. Would you be willing to confront Edward Marlowe with your statement? Again, it's not necessary for you to be in that position."

"I want to. I know what I saw."

Mullins looked at the Feds and shrugged a silent 'That's it'.

The Feds looked at each other. They nodded to accept the testimony.

"Charlie," said Mullins. "Call ahead. Make sure he's on his boat. We'll give the courtesy and go to him."

CIA Agent Messina went to the phone and dialed an agent's portable phone. "Sam, is the direc-

tor on his boat? Okay, delay him until I get there . . .
Tell him it's an urgent matter." He hung up. "He's
getting ready to return to Washington."

* * *

MULLINS HAD THE statement transcribed un-
der strict security to a document that Josh signed.
Mullins rode with Mitchell and Josh to the yacht club.
The Feds followed in an unmarked car.

Agent Charlie Messina was driving distressed. "I
cannot accept what I heard, Kelvin. I'm having difficulty with it," he said.

"You'd better start believing, Charlie. Trimble
seemed like a solid citizen. It doesn't mean your boss
killed the woman. Maybe he's not the second man.
He could be innocent of murder."

"If this guy, Trimble, turns out to be a decent,
responsible citizen, the media and political opposi-
tion will be leeches on The Director."

"We'll see how he responds when Trimble con-
fronts him," said Kelvin. "Remember, we have signed
statements from Deever, Horatio, Dryden and then
there's the two agents. Trimble has that against him.
Three are dead. They can't change their story. The
question is, will The Director? If he doesn't, then it's
Trimble versus Marlowe for the truth."

"The best option is that Trimble is lying," said
Charlie "and that The Director told the truth."

"Under the circumstances," said Kelvin. "A good
lawyer could easily overcome Trimble's sole statement."

"I'm sure The Director knows plenty of those."

* * *

Lake Montauk.

VALERIE DRYDEN arrived at the Montauk Yacht Club at 9:20AM to spend the day with her Mario, knowing that in another month, or two, her daughters will have accepted her dating other men, that she had to go on with her own needs. She was confident they'd come around and accept a mature outlook. Then she'd introduce Mario to them and they'll love him and accept him as someone their mother can date, and some day marry; not a stranger completely, but a former friend and client of their father's. That would make everyone happy.

She could see *Mario-nette* from the parking lot, headed for it and passed *Bull n' Bare*. Gina and Matt weren't aboard.

Mario was on the main deck, watching her approach with a look of admiration and lust. He loved how she walked; very feminine.

"Val," he called. He went to meet her at the boarding ladder. She heard him, waved and quickened her pace. She boarded, they touched cheeks in public, went inside and closed the door. Alone, he hugged and kissed her tenderly.

"I missed you, darling. I couldn't wait to see you." They kissed again.

"And I couldn't wait to see you, my love," she replied.

He clasped her hand and led her to the stateroom where they nestled in each other's arms for most of the morning, savoring togetherness.

* * *

"MR. TRIMBLE," said Mullins. "You've just done a brave and noble deed and have your reasons for waiting this long. Understand that I believe you. It comes down to you against Marlowe and witnesses who disagree with you. Your long delay is a disadvantage. Maybe Marlowe will finally admit the truth, especially if he didn't kill her. Now that there's a witness, he may own up to the truth. I must add that if he rejects your statement, I can't arrest him. He can go back to Washington. What we can do is review the investigation with him as the leading suspect."

"Lieutenant, if he doesn't confess, you may be looking for my body in the Sound."

"You believe he's the Riddler?"

"Absolutely. He was part of that waste incident. The dead can't testify against him for the past, and they can't change their testimony that he didn't visit Renata."

"Then we'll include him as a possible candidate to be the Riddler, to give the investigation new direction and pressure Marlowe."

Mitchell agreed that Josh did a bold act and that Mullins believed him in his support of Josh. What would Marlowe say when confronted by Josh?

Titus Banks was standing outside the dock house when Josh, Mitchell and Mullins pulled in. Another car parked next to them.

Seeing Mullins aroused his curiosity. What were Mitchell and Josh doing with Mullins? He recognized the other two as agents from the north dock yesterday. He watched as they boarded *Legal Tender* and go inside.

Edward Marlowe was notified that visitors were

on their way to see him. The matter was urgent. He had seen the visitors approaching and waited for them in the salon when they entered.

"Gentlemen, come in, sit where you can. Make yourselves at home. Hello, Josh, Mitchell, Charlie, Lieutenant." He didn't recognize Kelvin and introduced himself.

"Sir," said Charlie. "Lieutenant Mullins needs to speak to you."

His attention moved to Mullins. "Go ahead. I'm glad you caught me in time. I was headed back to Washington. Less chaotic there," he grinned. "Did you find the so called Riddler? I hope so. I'd like to know why he targeted me. And if he's connected to a foreign group."

"No, Director. We're here for another reason, but I assure you we're doing everything possible to get him, as I'm sure Agent Messina has told you. Mr. Trimble has made a signed statement to me this morning that he saw someone leave Renata Tredanari's yacht at two in the morning on the night she was killed and that person was you."

Marlowe lost his cordial face. Off-guard, and needing to absorb the impact, he went to the galley and leaned against it. He had arrived at the crossroads. Which way to go? Perpetuate the lie, or the truth that could be explained as an innocent visit?

He made the decision.

"I've known Josh Trimble for some time and have always respected him. I filed an affidavit affirming I was on this yacht all night and was substantiated by three other credible and upstanding citizens, including a commandant of the Coast Guard. And all have been murdered. Why did Josh take so long to come forward? Is it because the others are dead? I am now living with additional protection because some serial killer has threatened my life. I will re-state that I did not have anything to do with Renata's murder. Josh Trimble is confused, or a liar."

Mitchell saw rage rise in Josh's eyes. He grabbed Josh's arm and quickly motioned for him to be quiet.

Mullins responded. "He may be, Director, but I will ask direct questions of you again. For the record, did you visit Renata's yacht, for any reason, that night? We know that two men visited her during the hours in question. Were you one of those men?"

Marlowe looked at Josh, then Mullins.

"The answer's easy, Lieutenant. No."

TWENTY-NINE

IN THE PARKING LOT, Mullins was reassuring to Josh. "Mr. Trimble, I know you're disappointed as I am, and know you're concerned about your safety. After Marlowe leaves for Washington, I won't be charged with his safety. To make sure you're protected, I will keep the two squad cars here, one to concentrate on you and your boat. Check with them when you go. If locally, let them drive you.

"I want to meet with the district attorney's office and see what else can be done. I'll call a press conference and publicize your statement. Once that's done, you'll be a media object. You'll be fine if you remain on the grounds. Do you want to be at the press conference?"

"Would it help?" he said, lacking enthusiasm.

"To a good degree. It may indicate you're firm in your resolve and the truth."

Josh looked at Mitchell for guidance. "What do you think, Mitchell?"

"Do what the man says. Become a weapon. Remain visible and stay on the offense and you may put a crack in his defense."

"I'll do it. I can't stay passive."

"Thank you, Mr. Trimble. The squad car will bring

you to the Second Precinct and bring you back." He looked at Mitchell. "You're invited."

"I'll be there."

"Mr. Trimble, would you excuse me one moment."

Mullins held Mitchell by the elbow and guided him towards the squad car. "How long you staying with him."

"Until tomorrow night."

"Taking on the director of the CIA is not a downhill run, as you know. You did a good job. Thank you. How are you doing with the interviews?"

"Had a few, nothing relevant. My only success was convincing Josh to confess."

Mullins looked around the club.

"He was a reluctant witness and came out late. Maybe there's someone else. One more credible witness would convince the DA to take the next step. If Marlowe is accused of murder and didn't kill her, he'd turn honest. He'll be forced to resign and that will be his punishment—a personal disaster and stigma. So far, I've been right about you. I know your efforts will find me the killer."

Mullins talked to the officers of the Second Precinct and gave them instructions. They returned to Josh, who remained where they left him and the Feds who were waiting patiently in their car.

"Again, Mr. Trimble, my gratitude." He got in the car with the Feds and they drove off.

On the way back to Josh, Mitchell requested Mullins to call Adam Farmer to tell him in advance about Josh's statement and have Adam maintain the pressure by keeping the story alive and up front. Mullins agreed.

* * *

Saturday. July 6.
Lake Montauk.

THE DAY IN MONTAUK had come to a close for
Valerie. She was euphoric with the day. After dinner
at a seafood waterfront restaurant, where they
feasted on fresh caught bluefish, they escorted
Valerie to her car. Mario held her hand, Gina and
Matt walked alongside. They reached the car. She
kissed Mario, hugged Gina, kissed Matt on the cheek
and said goodnight. She left.

"Of all the years I've known you," said Matt, watching her red Lexus disappear on Star Island Road.
"There's never been anyone like Valerie for you. If
you don't marry that lady, you're a fool."

"Deficient," added Gina. "I'll no longer think
you're brilliant."

"She is special," reflected Mario, with a broad
smile.

"I'll volunteer to be your best man," said Matt.

"I'll write that down. Let's turn in."

He boarded *Mario-nette,* locked up and went to
his stateroom. The day with Valerie lingered. He had
now given all his love to her; no longer distracted by
his yearning for Renata. His emotions belonged to
Valerie.

Valerie remained on his mind until a final
thought that he loved her deeply and then slept
early. His emotional lovemaking with Valerie had ex-
hausted him.

They had no time to watch television today. They
missed the news conference with Josh and the broad-

cast news. Mario didn't know that Josh had accused Marlowe.

He awakened before seven, showered and shaved and drove to town to buy Sunday Newsday and a copy for Gina and Matt. The headlines and story demanded immediate reading, forcing him to read the articles in his car. *Marlowe at Murder Scene. Witness Comes Forward.* The front page had a full face of Marlowe in black and white and the words in bold red letters—SPIED ON. A photo of Josh was on the third page.

He wondered why Josh decided to come forward at this time. *Why wasn't he any longer frightened of Marlowe?*

What else did he see?

* * *

Saturday.
July 6.

AFTER JOSH AND MITCHELL left for the Second Precinct, Helene sat on the aft deck with a book, with the television turned on mute. A few minutes before the conference, she set the volume.

With the conference over, Helene was less optimistic than Mitchell was regarding Josh's safety. Marlowe was a liar, a fraud, led a cover-up and was an alleged murderer. Unfortunately, only a few knew that. Consoling was that Josh now was visible. That could deter Marlowe from any retaliation.

They decided to have dinner in to avoid Josh having to talk to anyone. Helene volunteered to get six-dozen steamers—perfect with mustard and beer, she added—and salad ingredients.

Josh and Mitchell determined that tonight they'd talk to Titus. At ten o'clock, they left *Coyote* for the south dock and the dock house. They didn't see Titus. One of the assistants informed them that he left at 8:00PM. Slow night.

* * *

Sunday. July 7.
Lake Montauk.

RENATA REPLACED VALERIE in his thoughts as Mario Colarossi boarded *Mario-nette* after dropping the second copy of Newsday on *Bull n' Bare's* cockpit. Gina and Matt were sleeping.

In the wide and beautifully appointed salon with a nautical motif, he sat transfixed to the night Renata was killed. Josh Trimble saw Marlowe. If he saw me, would he have told me about Marlowe? The world now knew there was a second man. How long before it found out it was me? Was there a witness? Was it Josh?

He would deal with Josh when he got back.

He was up that night and couldn't sleep and thought that by opening a bottle of wine, a glass or two would make him drowsy. He tried to convince Valerie to visit him that night for a short while, but her daughters were on *Courtship* and Arthur was nearby on *Legal Tender*. She wouldn't risk it.

The bottle finished, he began to stagger a bit. He walked around clumsily to find balance until he found himself in the enclosed pilothouse. Here is where he captained and steered in inclement weather. His eyes had difficulty focusing on the man leaving *Legal Tender*, and soon realized it was

Marlowe. He was about to go outside and call to him when Marlowe turned right and boarded *Champagne Lady*.

He became infuriated that Marlowe had access to Renata's passion and body and he didn't. He never learned how to cope with her rejection of his continuous romantic overtures. Now, he was here alone and Marlowe was with Renata, and Valerie was with her daughters; both within reach.

Why wasn't Marlowe coming out right away? He waited, and waited. Finally, Marlowe came out looking around like a thief in the night and returned to his yacht.

With thoughts erupting on what might have happened between Ranata and Marlowe, he went back to the galley, opened another bottle of wine, returned to the pilothouse and poured another glass. At this point, the wine could have been spoiled—he wouldn't have known the difference.

He finished half the glass slowly, but in anger when he decided to visit Renata. The time was now to have a talk about her rejections—an alcoholic decision. If Marlowe was good enough for her, he was better. He loved her. Marlowe didn't.

He had defensive thinking remaining to walk close to the yachts on the south side of the dock that provided cover from anyone in the parking lot. He nearly lost his footing. Grabbing the white electric source module kept him on the dock. He boarded *Champagne Lady* and went inside.

The salon was dark and she wasn't there. He was familiar with the layout and after holding the table to release some dizziness, managed to reach the stateroom area. The light was on in her stateroom and the door partially open. He could see cabinets, but not the bed. He approached, blinking to clear his eyes.

Whatever common sense remained in his thoughts forced him to call her name, to announce his arrival. She might have had a gun and shot him as a prowler. No answer, maybe she's in the head.

He called a bit louder . . . no reply. He pushed the door open and saw her sprawled out on the bed naked, passed out with legs apart. An empty champagne glass lay spilled beside her.

He admired his beautiful Renata, his soul mate. She lay before him as a feast to help himself. He nudged her again. She was alive, in a deep sleep, like a coma.

He began to touch her face, yearning. The hands traveled to her breasts, abdomen, lingered on her inner thighs and felt her legs and feet; touching, caressing a delicate object. He kissed her feet and put his mouth over her big toe. She didn't stir. He then kissed her face, not lingering long in one place. He inhaled her exhaled breath and began to tenderly massage her breasts and tongue and mouth her nipples. She stirred, and then settled. Rapture had cleared his mind a bit and was pleased with his reward for loving her.

He stood and backed away from the bed, teetering as he edged towards the door, reluctant to leave. His eyes continued to absorb his naked love.

His heart raced and a new thought stopped his exiting. He mulled the thought and now wanted what he had coming after all the years of yearning. She was there naked, his for the taking.

He removed his pants, managed to get into bed on all fours with her underneath, to avoid putting

weight on her. She was his now and didn't want her
waking to fight him off.

He lowered his lower body and penetrated her,
losing control of tenderness. His rhythm released his
frustration and love for her. She had stirred with dis-
comfort, but he ignored her. He was on the runway
lifting to take off, too late to stop the flight. After
lingering within her for as long as physically capable,
he clumsily managed to leave the bed, kissed her
lips tenderly and put on his pants.

He imitated Marlowe's departing movements on
the dock and re-boarded *Mario-nette,* certain no one
saw him. The drunken stupor couldn't consider re-
morse. He did, the next day.

Mario Colarossi lived with a burning question all
this time; since Renata was alive when he visited her,
Marlowe didn't kill her.

And he didn't kill her.

Who did?

THIRTY

Sunday.
July 7.

IN THE MORNING, *Coyote* left her slip and picked up the club mooring in Lloyd Harbor. For lunch, Josh cruised to Greenwich, Connecticut, to a yacht club. They returned to the Eastern Shore Yacht Club at 6:00PM. The media lurking by the gate in the morning had gone. Helene, Josh and Mitchell had dinner in Huntington Village.

* * *

Lake Montauk.

MARIO COLAROSSI spent the day on the beach in East Hampton with his family, leaving at 4:00PM to return to *Mario-nette* and, with *Bull n' Bare*, to leave for home at 8:00PM. His daughter drove him to Montauk.

Matt wanted to follow *Mario-nette* as a safety factor since Colarossi was traveling alone, and at night. Gina and Matt insisted they travel in tandem.

Colarossi appreciated their concern for him. They would be there to help if something happened.

At 7:45, Matt boarded *Mario-nette* to say his engine was acting up again and won't start. Gina was willing to stay over, to find a mechanic in the morning. He'd go home with Colarossi, return in the morning after his important meeting and cruise back with Gina. Colarossi agreed, happy to have Matt as company.

The weekend transients had begun to leave since morning, vacating their rented slips. By the time *Mario-nette* was ready to leave, only their two boats remained on the isolated dock.

Night was approaching and the western orange sky was fading. Gina untied the docking lines, waved goodbye and watched *Mario-nette* enter the channel to reach Block Island Sound. Colarossi blew his horn for her in farewell.

"Don't concern yourself over Gina, Mario. She's off tomorrow and isn't thrilled about boating at night. Not many people, besides you. Believe me, she was glad the engine failed."

"I'm concerned about her being alone on that dock."

"Not to worry. She can take care of herself and knows how to use the shotgun."

In the inlet, they passed the Coast Guard station, the commercial fishing fleet and restaurants on the left, then the jetty towards the black and white bell buoy. There, they'd turn west towards The Race whose lighthouse beckoned. The waypoints to Huntington and The Race had been plotted.

They were on the top deck on this warm and pleasant night. Colarossi sat in the captain's chair by the controls, Matt, in the chair next to him. Night visibility was clear and the lights along the shore were obvious landmarks to a familiar sailor. The area was familiar to Matt and Mario, having been out here numerous times before. Ahead, across Block Island Sound, were the clustered lights of Watch Hill, Rhode Island and the sparse and scattered lights of Fishers Island.

Mario-nette passed the bell buoy and proceeded north to make a wide sweep of the fishing nets that were somewhere to the west. The lights of Montauk slipped further away. Colarossi began his turn and revved up to fifteen knots, his comfortable cruising speed. He was about to connect the autopilot when Matt said, "Turn right, Mario. Go out towards Block Island."

Colarossi turned to question the strange request to go the opposite direction. "Let's take a ride, Mario." Matt was now standing behind his chair holding a gun with a silencer.

Colarossi was more surprised than panicked.

"Do as I say, Mario. Please." Colarossi slowed down and turned northeasterly.

"What the hell is this, Matt?" He maintained control of himself. Guns pointed at him were not a new experience and knew that Matt wouldn't hurt him, much less kill him.

"I was asked to give you a warning. They knew I'd be spending some time with you this weekend and decided it would be better if we talked rather than them visiting you."

"You don't need a gun to give me a warning. What's the problem?"

Matt continued to point the weapon. "It's for emphasis. I'm to tell you there are too many bodies around your territory and they believe you're responsible. They aren't happy about that. Your picture is in the papers, plus the re-surfacing of the radioactive waste matter. That's negative publicity. They also aren't happy about that."

Colarossi was now becoming concerned, but saw Matt's action as a warning gesture—knew him long to feel threatened by him.

"I wasn't involved with those riddles and killings. No one has accused me of that. Now, put that damn thing down. I'll go see them personally and explain. You made your point. And I got the message."

Matt maintained his position. "They won't believe you weren't involved. I know you weren't involved. Actually, Mario, I verified that *you* were killing those people."

"What?"

"They had already come to that conclusion. It was a perfect opportunity to blame you. And they believed me. Everything worked out perfect. Just perfect." Before Colarossi could ask for an explanation, he added, "I haven't given you the message, yet. As soon as I do, I'll put the gun away. I promise."

Colarossi breathed easier, but remained confused by his lies. He was in no position to control the direction of the conversation. Before he could get his explanation, Matt fired two shots.

"That's the message, Mario . . .and I almost forgot to say that the first one was for them. More importantly, the second was for my brother. Time finally ran out."

Colarossi fell dead against the console, bullets in his head and neck.

Matt eased the throttles and slowed. Other boats and land were far off. He rushed below for a docking line. He returned and propped up Colarossi and tied him to the captain's chair.

"The good news, Mario. I won an argument on your behalf with them and they agreed not to throw you overboard the way the others were killed—to leave you here, to set an example. They liked that. This way you'll have a funeral when you're found and they'll all come and lament for you, with flowers galore. Gina and I will be there and we'll console Valerie. I will grieve for you, Mario, because I've come to like you, in spite of my hate. But honor is honor and I've waited and plotted a long time."

Matt traveled for another mile at increased speed then swung wide to go south towards the Montauk lighthouse, connected the autopilot and went below to turn on the salon and stateroom lights to show there was life aboard.

He returned and made an adjustment to the autopilot to steer wide of the lighthouse and Montauk Point.

"Sylvio!" he yelled to the night, "I have honored you, my brother! Rest in peace!"

He was satisfied, accomplished. Looking behind in the dark, he saw a boat coming towards him. He increased speed to twenty-two knots and went into the dark Atlantic towards the obscured horizon that blended with the dark sky, into the fishing waters of Montauk's fleet.

Three boats were in the distance to port, showing red lights, and heading for shore. They were far away for Matt to be concerned. The boat behind continued to follow, showing its red and green lights.

Seven miles into the Atlantic, the only boat around was the one following. He slowed to twelve knots. The other boat was now to his starboard beam, fifty or so yards away, traveling a parallel course.

Matt rechecked that the autopilot was connected. He had no destination, or specific compass heading in mind, just south into the vast Atlantic Ocean.

He put on a life preserver with a night light attached and waved to the other boat whose lights went off and on once to return the signal. Matt climbed on the rail and dove off, stretching out to avoid the propellers. He surfaced and began swimming towards the approaching trailing boat.

The *Bull n' Bare* had veered towards the blinking light. Gina pulled alongside and helped him climb aboard. He removed the life vest and the wet clothes, toweled off and put on the clothes Gina had ready. When she came out of the inlet, the *Marionette's* salon and stateroom lights were signals to Gina that it was over and for her to easily identify *Marionette* in the darkness.

They stood a while, watching the *Mario-nette* head for the lost horizon, its lights shrinking with distance.

"He never suspected," said Matt. "I did love him, regardless."

Gina cupped his face, kissed him and said, "He was getting out of control. And you had a family obligation to satisfy. This was the perfect reason."

"I'm glad we had the weekend together. I've always enjoyed being with him."

"Did you tell him that you told them he was doing all the killings?"

"Yes, just before he got the messages."

"We finally did the right thing," Gina said. "You let him live too long. There's no need to be at the yacht club anymore, is there?"

"We'll finish the season, then sell the boat. Now that they are dead, the club served its purpose."

* * *

–Helene and Mitchell left after dinner without talking further with Titus.

–Josh paced sleepless and troubled until the sun began to peek beyond the hills and he slept.

–Edward Marlowe again sought the refuge of his office to avoid responding to Josh Trimble's testimony.

–Titus didn't go to work on Monday. When the club office called his home, no one answered.

–The *Mario-nette* motored south, soon to enter the blue waters of the Gulf Stream.

THIRTY-ONE

BEFORE IMMERSING INTO his project and concept for his next book, Mitchell entered all he could remember into the yacht club diary; bits of conversation, Josh's confession, Mullins, Marlowe's reaction, everything that occurred for the four days.

He had been consistent maintaining this record. When the case ends and the killer is caught, he'd give Josh the notes and newspaper articles and encourage him to do the book. A good portion of the book—organization—will have been achieved.

Josh received his fifteen minutes of fame at the conference. The book will ensure him a best seller; the insides look at the famous murders. The creative endeavor would be his leap into fame and more dollars. That should motivate him to write without having to use fiction. Josh deserved this success and Mitchell would do all he could to help a close friend.

* * *

GINA FERRARA AND Matt DiBiasi arrived at the yacht club at noon. After their excursion into the Atlantic, they returned to their slip, chatted with neighbors at another dock and had dinner at the club restaurant to establish their alibis that Mario left Sunday night, that they spent the night in Montauk and left Monday morning.

During the day, they emoted their concern that Mario hadn't arrived ahead of them. Titus confirmed that *Mario-nette* did not return and leave again. Others assumed he probably stopped overnight elsewhere.

* * *

VALERIE DRYDEN called Mario at home and at the boat after his office said he wasn't in. Marie Bailey, at the club, told her the *Marion-ette* hadn't arrived as yet. Nervous and concerned, Valerie kept calling the boat, his home and restaurants. Why wasn't Mario communicating? He had the latest communication technology.

* * *

TITUS LOCKED himself in his house all day Monday refusing to answer the phone, needing to be alone. He had seen Josh's press conference. What good did it do? Marlowe remained free and in Washington. If a reputable university professor was incredible when he said he saw Marlowe, no one would believe him if he came forward to tell about Marlowe and Colarossi.

The newscaster on News 12, the Cablevision all news channel that covered Long Island news like a comb, confirmed that Josh had little impact. More witnesses verified Marlowe told the truth and allegedly was when he called Josh a liar. Some media wanted to know—Why was he doing this to Marlowe?

Talk shows started their speculative tainting, showing profiles of Josh, his marriage and career. A media sickness complained Titus.

What chance did he have? What social standing
did an old sailor have against the media's need to
ravage? They would expose his history and distort
the Perth rape incident. He would be crucified, he
concluded. That's why he decided to stay home, to
fortify his thinking and erase the memory portion of
his mind that he saw Renata's visitors.

And hope no one blames Renata's death on him.

* * *

MULLINS, CIA AGENT CHARLIE MESSINA and
FBI Agent Kelvin Jackson met with the District Attorney, played the tape again, replayed the press
conference, reviewed all club data related to Marlowe
and the unanimous result was they needed more
substance to arrest. The DA, a long time friend of
Marlowe's, wanted to know if Trimble had a personal
vendetta against Marlowe.

"No," defended Mullins. "Mitchell Pappas, whom
I've talked to you about and who encouraged Trimble
to come in, substantiates his creditability. I believe
him. If Pappas weren't persuasive, Trimble would not
have come in. He was afraid. Marlowe's guilty. We
have to pressure him."

"Then get me more evidence."

Mullins snapped his fingers. "Just like that?"

"Faster."

* * *

TUESDAY PROVED to be a more dramatic and emotional day for Josh Trimble than coming forward to testify and attending the press conference. Renata's sister and brother-in-law, Sophia and George Slater, with a captain, were coming to take *Champagne Lady* to Florida.

Sophia had called Josh yesterday. Josh said he'd arrange for a mechanic to be here at 8:00AM to begin his inspection.

Sophia, Renata's younger sister, bore a strong family resemblance. Looking at her, Josh kept superimposing Renata's image. George Slater owned an accounting firm in Boca Raton whose clients primarily were computer companies in Florida's 'Silicon Beach.'

The door to *Champagne Lady* was open when Sophia and George and their captain, Nate Wheeler, arrived. The mechanic was below. Josh greeted them and they boarded. Josh waited on the aft deck while they went below. Sophia and George returned. Sophia's eyes were red and teary. She leaned against the railing.

"That was difficult," she said.

"Come to my boat," said Josh. "The diver's expected soon to clean the bottom. The mechanic is working. We'll have to allow them a few hours. Then a sea trial and you're off."

"I need to do some food shopping, plus," Sophia said. "I've brought a little of everything, including bed sheets. We passed a supermarket down the road, Josh. Is that where I should go?"

"That's where I go. They also have a pharmacy."

Sophia left. George and Josh went to *Coyote*.

George was of slight build, about forty-five, with a receding hairline.

"How's Sophia doing?" asked Josh.

"She hasn't recovered. They were close. It was difficult when she went below and saw Renata's personal items. If you recall after the funeral, she couldn't face getting on the boat so soon. The passing of time made it a bit easier. She's reaching acceptance. The same when we went to Renata's apartment. We'll have to make a decision on that soon. We may hold on to it."

In an hour, Sophia was waving from the parking lot. They went to carry the packages. Within another hour, *Champagne Lady* was ready for her sea trial. The captain and mechanic were satisfied with her performance.

After the sea trial, it was time for the *Champagne Lady* to leave her berth to move to a new neighborhood, new neighbors. Josh bade them farewell and gave Sophia a tender hug, as if she was Renata.

"Thank you for everything, Josh," said Sophia, "and for being a good friend to my sister."

"I'm glad I could help. Renata will be missed. Have a safe voyage."

"It should be. We told the captain we prefer the Intercoastal Waterway."

"That should be comfortable."

With a heavy heart, Josh untied the docking lines that held Renata's memory close. He released the last line with sadness as *Champagne Lady* pulled out of her slip. Josh waved farewell to the *Champagne Lady* and the champagne lady who owned her.

As she turned into the channel after blowing her horn, Josh boarded *Coyote* and went to the bow for a final look.

With dampened eyes, he watched her go away from him until she disappeared past the green buoy.

* * *

VALERIE DRYDEN'S distress reached alarming proportions by Tuesday night. Mario couldn't be located. She called the marinas at major cruising ports from Nantucket to Newport, from Block Island to Essex to Port Jefferson. No one had seen *Mario-nette.*

She began to think the worst—that he had an accident at sea. He could be anchored somewhere on The Long Island Sound. Wouldn't he call someone? Was he sick? Maybe he had a heart attack or a stroke and couldn't move to call for help. She called the Coast Guard and the police to report him overdue at his destination . . . that he was missing.

* * *

ON TUESDAY NIGHT, Director Edward Marlowe appeared on CNN's Larry King Show and was interviewed for a half-hour about the club murders, Josh Trimble and the radioactive waste incident.

He was an excellent speaker before the cameras, and impressive. His version was easily accepted that he told the truth.

THIRTY-TWO

Wednesday.

THE GULF STREAM had drifted *Mario-nette* eastward as she continued her south-southeast journey as the sun rose fully on the horizon, spraying the golden glow of early morning on the water. *Marionette* gracefully parted the moderately calm and clear sea on the way to her destiny.

Her voyage to nowhere was about to end at the Kitchen Shoals, north of St. George's Island, Bermuda.

Her misguided course towards the shoals didn't go unnoticed. A local fishing boat near the Mills Breaker Channel tried to warn her by radio that she was about to go aground and to take the buoy to starboard.

Getting no response, they increased speed towards her to help for she'll surely sink or get hung up on the shoals.

* * *

Same day.

TITUS RETURNED to work. He had called the Commodore to say he had a stomach virus.

At noon, Josh called the dock house and invited Titus for a beer and lunch. Titus readily accepted.

"I've plenty of beer and food," offered Josh. "Just bring yourself."

Titus felt good about the invitation. He felt he had gotten closer to Josh ever since the flooding incident. The tie between them had strengthened. When Titus entered the salon, the guest surprised him. Mitchell Pappas was on the couch.

Why didn't Josh tell him? He wouldn't have come to face his damn questions. He wasn't the answer man!

"Hi, Mitchell. Good to see you." Titus became leery.

"Same here, Titus."

"Are we going to have a confrontation?"

"Not this time. I'm keeping Josh company. He's had a tough time since exposing Marlowe."

"He did what he had to do," said Titus.

"Grab a seat, Titus," said Josh. "Here's a beer. Turkey sandwich?"

"Perfect. And mayo."

Josh remained in the galley preparing lunch, making a double order of everything.

"Josh is taking a beating, Titus. Marlowe was on Larry King last night attacking Josh's credibility. Marlowe has witnesses to support him. Josh has no one."

Josh brought extra beers and the extra sand-

wiches and placed the tray on the coffee table. He
sat.

"Now, we have Josh regretting that he told the
truth," continued Mitchell. "If Marlowe also turns
out to be the Riddler, he's got bigger problems. We
need your help, Titus. We have to find evidence to
help Josh. What will help Josh is another witness. And
there aren't any."

Titus' suspicion rose. "How do you think I can
help?" His suspicion increased.

"By keeping your ears open. Listen for anything
some members may say. You know, innuendoes."

"That's simple, but sounds like fantasy. So, that's
not what you want from me." *Damn! I've been had!*

"You're right, Titus, it's not. You were convinced
Colarossi was going to kill Josh the other day. Why
would you think that? Josh saw Marlowe. Did you see
Colarossi? Did you see Marlowe and Colarossi? Are
you a supporting witness for Josh?"

Titus became irate and upset. "I'm not anything,
dammit!" He got up and left.

"Well," said Josh. "That was weak, not your normal finesse and subtlety."

"Consider that the opening bell. We have to start
rubbing his sticks for the fire to ignite. Tonight, before dinner, I'll hound him again, and the same after work. I'll be a mosquito under his net."

"Creative paragraph, Mitchell." Josh lifted his
beer to toast. "Here's to Mitchell. Josh Trimble's junk
yard dog."

"I need to call Mullins, to check in."

He waited to be transferred.

"Lieutenant Mullins."

"Mitchell Pappas, Lieutenant. I'm at the yacht
club with Josh Trimble. I'm checking in with noth-

ing new, but pursuing a strong lead that may support Josh's testimony."

"Another witness?"

"Possibly."

"I'm glad you called. Saves me another call to
you. We've been notified by the Bermuda police and
our State Department that they discovered Mario
Colarossi dead on his yacht."

"What's that?" said a shocked Mitchell.

"His yacht grounded on a shoal. He was found by
fishermen, shot twice and tied to his captain's chair.
He was executed. Rubbed out."

"And obviously, no one knows who did it."
Mitchell covered the phone and mouthed to Josh
that Colarossi was dead. He made a gun with his
thumb and forefinger and pretended to pull the
imaginary trigger. Josh became attentive.

"I can guess," said Mullins. "He was hit by his own."

"That's another mystery for you to solve."

"We've talked to Gina Ferrara and Matthew
DiBiasi who spent the weekend with him in Montauk.
They have alibis. Good riddance to Colarossi. You may
want to tell Josh Trimble since you're with him. You'll
be hearing about Colarossi soon. We're releasing the
information to the media. I've called Adam and you
at home and left a message. What does that do to
your theories?"

"I'll re-evaluate and let you know."

"I have a few more calls to make. We'll talk later."

Mitchell hung up as an impatient Josh urged,
"What happened?"

"Mario Colarossi was found dead in Bermuda,
executed. His yacht ran aground on a shoal."

Josh sat back, dumbstruck. "Marlowe. It had to

be Marlowe. Now he's the only survivor of the radio-active waste scandal."

"I don't think so, Professor. Colarossi got hit for other reasons." Josh remained upset. "Are we getting weaker, or are we stronger by his death."

"His death may be our ace in the hole with Titus. Maybe he was afraid to speak against Colarossi. Afraid as you were against Marlowe."

"I think that's a long shot."

"Yes, but let's take it. Let's tell him for the reaction."

They went to the south dock. Titus was at the end of the fuel dock, about to ferry two members out to a mooring. They went down the aluminum ramp, called out to Titus to wait, and he did, annoyed at seeing them. He couldn't avoid them and Mitchell's badgering. Why make a scene with others present. They boarded the launch. Josh knew the couple and said hello. Titus was quiet.

He untied the lines and backed out, turned, steered towards the channel, crossed the channel and came alongside a 37' sailboat, *Kalliope*. Titus held the sailboat's stanchion to keep the launch close to the hull to accommodate his passengers' departure.

When Titus pulled away, Mitchell said, "Titus, Lieutenant Mullins just informed me that Mario Colarossi is dead. Shot twice. Executed. *Marionette* was found on a shoal in Bermuda and his body was on board."

Titus didn't respond, concentrating on steering around the mooring field boats to reach the channel.

"He's dead, Titus," Mitchell reiterated. "It should be on the radio and television news before the day is over. What does that mean to you, Titus? Your friend,

Josh, whom you tried to save from Colarossi needs your help. Friends have to be there when needed. Josh needs you. Colarossi can't harm you now."

Titus remained intent as he crossed the channel and steered to the launch's berth. He deftly eased in docking position and tied one line. After tying the second line, he switched off the ignition. Mitchell and Josh exited and waited on the dock to see what Titus would do. Titus followed, deep in thought. Mitchell took his mood as a hopeful sign. Titus wasn't hurrying away to avoid them. Then Titus approached.

"Josh."

"Yes?"

"I saw Marlowe."

Josh broke into a broad grin. "Thanks, Titus. You are a friend. That means a lot to me. More than your gesture to save me from Colarossi."

"And Colarossi? Did you see him?" asked Mitchell, pleased that his hounding was productive.

Titus didn't hesitate. "Him, too."

"Are you willing to make a statement to Mullins?"

"Yes. I will support Josh as soon as my assistants finish with their lunch break."

THIRTY-THREE

SINCE VALERIE DRYDEN reported Mario Colarossi missing, Lieutenant Ken Mullins called to tell her what happened and how he died. He also said something about her signing some form, or other, but she wasn't listening completely.

Valerie—traumatized and trying to act unemotional to Mullins—covered her mouth to hide the pain and then became hysterical with grief after she hung up. The depth of her grief surprised her daughters. Valerie showed less for their father.

Her daughter, Tina, called Valerie's doctor for a prescription to calm her.

* * *

LIEUTENANT MULLINS was meeting with two detectives and the Feds. The phone rang, but he wouldn't answer. His meeting on Colarossi was important. The phone stopped and started again, and stopped. Shortly, an officer was knocking on the door. Mullins stopped talking.

"What already?" he called out. The door opened.

"I regret the interruption, sir. Mr. Pappas needs to talk to you. It's urgent."

"All right, put him through on line one and hold all other calls. Thank you." The officer left.

He looked at his guests. "Hold on, gentlemen. One of our best weapons says it's urgent." The phone rang. He answered.

"Are we winning the war out there?"

"Are you free now to see me, Lieutenant?"

"For you, I'll stop my meeting. Where are you?"

"About a mile away. We'll be right there."

"Someone with you?"

"Yes, Josh Trimble and Titus Banks."

"I'll be waiting." He hung up. "Guys, this meeting is temporarily suspended." He addressed his detectives. "Harry, Ward. Take all this stuff on Colarossi and his litter and start the process." They gathered the material and left. "Charlie, Kelvin. If he offers another clue, I'll erect a statue to him in front of this building."

"No," said Kelvin, smiling. "What you should do is give him your job."

"Ha, ha. Where's the tape recorder? I don't know if we'll need it, but have it ready. He was trying to get another witness."

"Another witness to what?" asked Kelvin.

Mullins shrugged. "Let him surprise us."

"It's back here on the table," said Kelvin.

Kelvin examined the recorder. "Needs tape." Mullins opened a desk draw, took out a tape and flipped it to him.

Minutes later, an officer, followed by Titus and Josh escorted in Mitchell. Without a word, Mullins directed them to sit at the three empty chairs opposite the Feds.

"Go ahead, Mr. Pappas," said Mullins impatiently his curiosity peaked. It's your floor. We'll listen."

"This is Titus Banks, gentlemen. Dock Master of the Eastern Shore Yacht Club. You may want to turn the tape recorder on. Titus has something important to say."

Mullins was stimulated by the request that may mean additional evidence. He turned the recorder on and spoke into the microphone, following the same routine he did with Josh. Mitchell requested the microphone. He got it.

"I am Mitchell Pappas," he said, leaning in. "Mr. Banks has come to me with information at his own free will that has a bearing on the yacht club murders. As I have with Josh Trimble, I can verify that he's responsible and believe what he says. He hasn't spoken out prior to this because he feared for his life and his philosophy in life is to avoid getting involved directly in anything, other than his job. Those are his reasons. Have I stated that correctly Titus?"

"Yes, you have." Titus looked nervous to Mitchell.

"This is Josh Trimble," he said, leaning in. "I also vouch for him. I have known him many years."

Mullins and the Feds were in suspense. Titus was fidgety, collecting his thoughts.

"Titus," said Mitchell. "Why don't you begin by telling your name and the basics to get you started? Don't be nervous. Just say what you have to say as if we're having a conversation."

"Okay." He cleared his throat. Kelvin pushed the microphone closer to Titus. "Before I start. Is it true that Mario Colarossi is dead? That he was murdered? Shot? That his yacht is in Bermuda?"

"Yes, it's true. Mario Colarossi is dead," replied Mullins. Titus looked at Mitchell apologetically. "I wanted to make sure he was cause it wasn't on the car radio."

"No problem, Titus," said Mitchell. "I'm glad you asked. Go when ready."

"I'm ready. My name is Titus Banks and I've been the dock master for the Eastern Shore Yacht Club for the past eight years. I am familiar with all the members of the club and their boats as I come in contact with them on club business, or socially.

"On the night Renata Tredanari was killed . . . I'm sorry, but I don't remember the date . . . at around two in the morning, I saw some activity around the *Champagne Lady*. That's Renata Tredanari's yacht. I was in the dock house, unable to sleep, alone with the lights off to look out at the quiet marina scene. I do that a lot because I find it relaxing, especially when I can't sleep, when I'm staying overnight at the club. I do that usually on the weekends. Without the lights on, the view is better." He talked slowly, but Mullins and the Feds hung on every word.

"I should clarify that the dock house is directly opposite *Champagne Lady* across the marina. What I saw was Edward Marlowe leaving his yacht, *Legal Tender* and boarding the *Champagne Lady*. After a while, I saw him leave and go back to his yacht. That's who I saw." Titus leaned back in the chair.

There wasn't a sound in the room.

CIA Agent Charlie Messina's heart sank. Mullins spoke up when it appeared that Titus had finished speaking.

"Mr. Banks, you are positive the person you saw was Edward Marlowe."

Titus cleared his throat and leaned in. Positive. Edward Marlowe, Director of the Central Intelligence Agency, so there's no mistake who I'm talking about."

"Is there anything else, Mr. Banks? Anything you'd like to add?" queried Mullins, assuming Titus was finished with his stunning testimony. Titus nodded.

"I didn't think much about it at the time because I knew Marlowe and Renata were intimate. Nothing was different or suspicious about his going to her boat. I figured he was going for a piece. You know what I mean?" He made a faint grin that was rejected. "I considered Marlowe's coming and going an activity that came and passed—nothing out of the ordinary.

"In another five minutes, or so, I saw another person come off his yacht, who may have had too much to drink cause he staggered a little and almost fell off the dock, and he also went to the *Champagne Lady* and boarded." Mullins and the Feds perked up. "That second person that the press referred to as the second man . . . after you announced that you had two different specimens of semen, came back out of *Champagne Lady* and went back to his yacht. That person was Mario Colarossi."

The silence was thicker and the jaws lower. The recorder kept recording. Nobody moved. Then Mullins looked to Mitchell for credibility and confirmation, hoping Titus was real. *What a find!* Mitchell conveyed by nodding that he was genuine.

Mullins found his voice because Titus didn't continue.

"Again, is there anything else Mr. Banks?" He got a hell of an answer to that question before. Maybe there was more.

Titus contemplated the question. "For now, no." He had told Mitchell and Josh the same thing. There was no need to go further. He fulfilled his obligation to Titus.

"This is the truth?" Mullins asked. "You saw what you say you saw? If so, please repeat."

"I saw Edward Marlowe, Director of the Central Intelligence Agency and Mario Colarossi board *Champagne Lady* and saw them leave . . . on the night Renata Tredanari was killed . . . at about two in the morning. That's when I saw them."

"Would you be willing to sign a sworn statement to that effect?" said Mullins.

"Yes. I'll sign to verify what I said. I swear that is the truth."

"Are you familiar, Mr. Banks, with what's going on at the club regarding the murders, not just of Renata Tredanari, but the others?"

"Yes, I am aware and have attended all the emergency meetings at the club. But I don't know who killed Commandant Deever, or Alvin Horatio, or Arthur Dryden. I haven't a clue. I only know about Renata Tredanari. And I've read all the papers and seen most of the newscasts. I'm pretty current as far as what's public."

"Coming back to Director Marlowe and Mario Colarossi," continued Mullins. "Since you are an eyewitness to their being at the scene of the crime, who do you believe killed Renata Tredanari? Let me expand on that speculation a moment before you answer. If Marlowe killed her, then she was dead when Colarossi came in. You said he staggered. Then he must have had sex with a dead person. Too drunk to know better, but the knife in her heart would be obvious.

"Therefore, it may be logical that Marlowe had sex with her and left, then Colarossi had sex and then killed her. And if he did, it doesn't matter as much because he's dead. Based on your visual sight-ing therefore, on how they acted when they came out, which one do you think killed her?"

Titus stalled.

"Take a guess," urged Mullins.

Titus' eyes were darting, evaluating what he should do to help end his nightmares. The opportunity was timely. His mind would be rid of the tormenting pollution.

His audience waited.

Titus continued to massage the thoughts that would stun everyone in the room. He leaned towards the microphone again.

"I have another confession to make. There was a third person."

THIRTY-FOUR

VALERIE DRYDEN'S OLDEST daughter, Tina, drove to the pharmacy by the mall to pick up a prescription for her. Valerie was beginning to recover. She switched on the news channel for any announcements, or new information. She also listened to a radio news station hoping to hear further about her Mario.

How did it happen? Gina and Matt said they would follow him home when she expressed concern about his traveling alone. Why didn't they? Where are they? How did the killer get on his yacht? Didn't they help him cast off?

She picked up the phone and called Gina's office. Gina was in court today, she was told. She called Matt. He was on his way to an investment meeting and may be back in a few days if all goes on schedule. Frustrated, she wanted to call Mario's daughters, but decided they wouldn't know anything.

Why did they kill him? Why now when she was free to have him forever? She began to cry at her lost future with Mario.

Her daughters understood grieving for a long time friend, particularly the way he was murdered. The extent of the grieving continued to baffle them.

What if the *Mario-nette* didn't go aground in Bermuda? How far into the Sargasso Sea and the South Atlantic could she go with her fuel capacity? Mario may not have been found for months until he drifted to some shore. Could he have drifted into the Antarctic? She wasn't interested in those thoughts and swept them away. She had to think of anything else to alleviate the disaster that befell her.

She was lying across the sofa covering her reddened eyes when her daughter, Elizabeth, came into the room to say that Lieutenant Mullins was at the door and needed to speak with her.

"He probably has additional information to tell me about Mario. And he also wanted me to sign something because I reported him missing, making me the primary person. Whatever . . . let him in." She changed her mind. "Better yet, I'll go to the door. Tell him I'll be right there."

Elizabeth left. Valerie looked in the mirror and adjusted her hair. She looked terrible, tired from sleeplessness. A little make-up might help, but her depression rejected the idea. She accepted her face. Under the circumstances, she was in mourning.

She tried to look spirited when she went to the foyer. Elizabeth stepped aside when she arrived. Mullins was in the doorway and another man, in a business suit was behind him.

"Hello, Lieutenant. Thanks for calling before about Mario. Do you have any new information? Do you have the form for me to sign?"

"Mrs. Valerie Dryden. You are under arrest for the murder of Renata Tredanari."

THIRTY=FIVE

VALERIE'S DAUGHTER, Elizabeth, screamed and covered her mouth with both hands and her eyes widened while horror forced her to lean against the wall for support.

Indignant at the accusation, Valerie retorted, "Is this some kind of joke?"

"We have a witness who saw you leaving Ms. Tredanari's boat the night she was killed. You were the last to leave." The other detective took out handcuffs and moved closer to Valerie. Valerie backed up. "Mrs. Dryden, you have the right to remain silent . . ." Mullins continued the Miranda disclaimer while nodding to his detective to handcuff her.

"This is insane!" objected Valerie. "Who said that? I was never on her boat! Never!"

"The dockmaster, Titus Banks identified you."

"He's lying! He probably did it and is blaming me! This is a mistake!" she exclaimed, as the detective forced her arms behind her. "Maybe he's the one who killed my husband. You should be arresting him!" She turned to her daughter. "Elizabeth, call Roger at the firm and tell him what's going on!" Elizabeth continued hysterical. "Hurry!" her mother urged. "Move!"

Her mother's orders moved her and she rushed to the kitchen phone.

Mullins and his detective escorted the protesting Valerie to the waiting squad car. The squad car was pulling out of the driveway as Elizabeth reached the front door.

As she sat handcuffed next to Ken Mullins, Valerie Dryden watched her daughter's hysterics in front of the house as she sat handcuffed next to Ken Mullins. She looked away, unable to bear her child's agony.

* * *

ON THE NIGHT Renata died, Valerie was on her yacht with her daughters when awakened to use the head facilities. Unable to return to sleep, and rather than lay awake in bed, she went to the salon to watch television. The cool evening beckoned and she opened the aft door before turning on the set. The fresh night air was soothing.

To her surprise, she saw Mario Colarossi staggering on the dock towards her and almost fall in the water. At first, she thought he was coming to see her and was concerned because her daughters were on board.

Then she saw him turn right and board *Champagne Lady* and enter. She waited and watched until he left. She loved Mario, but he wanted Renata. She had known that for a long time. She became crazed with anger that Mario would visit her. There could be no happy future for her as long as he wanted Renata. And Valerie wanted all of him.

She took a steak knife from the galley wanting *to only threaten her.* She looked for the police and agents in the parking area. They were out of sight. Staying low and close to the dock's edge, she stealthily went to *Champagne Lady,* went below to the stateroom and saw Renata sprawled on the bed, passed out. Traces of semen by her vagina were proof of Mario's infidelity.

Madness took over.

Without hesitating, she took a small throw pillow with her left hand and covered Renata's face and plunged the knife into her heart with the right hand. The body bolted from the shock and she pressed the pillow firmly not to see Renata's facial reaction, to suffocate her at the same time.

When Renata stopped moving, she wiped the pillow against her clothes to remove any fingerprints, let it fall to the floor and kicked it away. She took off her top and wiped the prints off the knife. Then she wiped most of Renata's body and bed in case Mario left prints, careful not to touch blood. After killing for him, she didn't want him arrested. She dressed and left, careful to be unseen as she returned to *Courtship.*

She drank a glass of vodka and put the murder out of her mind, as if it never happened. She remembered to throw the rest of the steak knives overboard.

* * *

POLICE DIVERS, probing the murky bottom, found four of the matching steak knives.

Confronted with the evidence and a witness, Valerie adamantly stated she had nothing to do with Arthur's death.

Only Renata's.

* * *

AS SOON AS Mullins returned to the Second Precinct, he arranged for a press conference, deeming it most urgent. Mitchell and Josh attended and stood up front, off to the side.

This time, the Police Commissioner, the District Attorney and the County Executive stood before a room full of the media to announce the following, to which they later provided details:

–The killer of Renata Tredanari has been apprehended and has confessed, and that murder case has been solved.

–Mr. Titus Banks has also confessed to being a witness in seeing Director Edward Marlowe leave Ms. Tredanari's boat that evening, corroborating the Josh Trimble testimony.

–Mario Colarossi visited Ms. Tredanari that night and was seen by Titus Banks. That explains the two semen samples.

The District Attorney, when asked if he would arrest Marlowe, replied, "We have the killer of Renata Tredanari. Director Marlowe did not aid, or abet. He visited. If anything, Director Marlowe has trouble with the truth. We will review his involvement further, particularly in the area of obstruction of justice."

Lieutenant Mullins now stood before the battery of microphones with a barrage of camera flashes going off.

"I will answer all your questions at the end. I'm not going anywhere. You'll get whatever you need. We have a lot of news today. Please hold your questions.

"If you haven't heard already from our earlier

release, Mario Colarossi was a gangland victim, shot twice, tied to a chair on his boat and put to sea where the boat ran aground in Bermuda.

"Mario Colarossi was involved with events in the past where he had ties and dealings with the Riddler's victims, Alvin Horatio, Commandant Deever and Arthur Dryden, the husband of Valerie Dryden, who confessed to murdering Renata Tredanari.

"After reviewing all the material collected, it is our conclusion that Mario Colarossi killed, or had killed, Alvin Horatio, Arthur Dryden and Commandant Deever using the Tredanari murder as an excuse to exterminate his ex-associates, the players involved in the radioactive waste scandal.

"I can confidently state that Mario Colarossi wrote those riddles. *He* was the Riddler. The Riddler case is closed."

That created a rumbling. Impatient hands went up and voices raised, calling for attention. Mullins ignored them and spoke louder.

"Now, why was Colarossi killed? Colarossi belonged to organized crime that usually gets rid of enemies in a manner Colarossi killed his. Make the corpse disappear.

"Being familiar with how this organization works, I can tell you that Mario Colarossi was killed for killing those people, for getting too much publicity, for giving the organization a bad . . . let's say, reputation." There was some laughter. "To wrap it up, the Tredanari case is closed and resolved. The yacht club case is closed and resolved. The Riddler is dead. All logic and evidence leads to that conclusion.

"At this time, I wish to thank Mr. Josh Trimble, who is here, for courageously coming forward with his testimony. And to Titus Banks, as well—who's not here." He pointed Josh out. "And particularly, the famous author, Mr. Mitchell Pappas, whose counsel and investigative assistance helped to resolve these cases." He pointed Mitchell out. Mitchell smiled and waved. The question and answer period began.

* * *

–THE EVENING NEWS was filled with the substance and revelations of the conference.

–Mullins received accolades from his superiors, as did the Feds. Agent Charlie Messina and Kelvin Jackson would return to Washington . . . and away from Mullins' pastries.

–The Commodore and club members were delighted the murders were over that they weren't murdered in the process and life would go back to normal. The club's cruise to Newport remained scheduled for the end of July.

* * *

DIRECTOR EDWARD MARLOWE cancelled all meetings and appointments when he heard that the Suffolk Police were planning a press conference on further developments on the yacht club murders, and be carried live by CNN. He told his executive assistant, Betsy Hobart, to go home. He adjusted his phones to ring busy if anyone called. No need to tape the press conference. Maybe they finally caught the Riddler who threatened him.

He was uncomfortable on his ice floe. Hell lay ahead, as did the unexpected.

He impatiently waited until the announcer said: "We take you now live to Long Island and the press conference regarding the yacht club murders. Entering the room are . . ." Marlowe's mind went off course from his thoughts. *Everyone's there!* " . . .and Lieutenant Mullins of the Suffolk Homicide Squad. The conference began and ended.

He was doomed.

Two witnesses!

He sat numb, mummified. He was now at the edge of hell.

Very little ice remained.

He locked his door to keep the outside world away. He reviewed what he had done repeatedly and wished he had another chance, to correct his lies. To tell the truth, that it was a harmless visit with a lover. He could have withstood the political assault. The President would have defended him. They were friends.

He had lit his own fuse when he lied. Two witnesses! *How could there be two witnesses at that hour of the night?*

He wasn't interested in his ex-associates and Colarossi—only his survival. They're dead. Who cares?

He refused to answer the knocks on his door, knocks from senior aides to determine if he had seen the broadcast. He remained in his office until ten o'clock, and then went home.

The President's chief of staff was waiting for him in front of his house when he pulled into the driveway.

The ice floe had melted.

The next day, Edward Marlowe, Director of the Central Intelligence Agency submitted a letter of resignation to the President of the United States.

THIRTY-SIX

WHEN MITCHELL ARRIVED home that evening, he logged recent events into his yacht club notes and diary with enthusiasm. The story was told— a beginning and an end. The police had Renata's killer and the Riddler was dead. The murder cases were solved at last and the killing was over.

As he entered and reviewed both cases, he realized the yacht club battlefield was littered with the many who had fallen—the dead and the wounded.

The dead: Renata Tredanari.

Arthur Dreyden.

Alvin Horatio.

Commandant Deever.

Mario Colarossi.

The wounded: Edward Marlowe . . .wounded forever publicly.

Valerie Dryden—facing the death penalty.

The tarnished: The Eastern Shore Yacht Club.

The President and his Administration.

The Central Intelligence Agency.

And the many wounded family and business members of the dead and wounded.

His notes were becoming voluminous. Tomorrow and the next day, he'd devote time to putting everything in logical sequence with dates and time of occurrence, including recalling conversation as accurately as possible. At evening's end, he was satisfied with his recollections and participation.

He was asked to help. And he did.

He had helped a friend in need.

What came from it were a national murder case and a sense of personal and professional satisfaction in helping Mullins to close the cases.

A book had to be done by Josh. Now that he helped solve the mysteries, Mitchell's saliva for a book was flowing, to be written soon while interest was high. That was added motivation to complete and update his research immediately for Josh.

* * *

–TITUS REHIRED the two assistants.

–Charlie Messina and Kelvin Jackson received organizational commendations in Washington for their participation in the cases.

–*Mario-nette* was to be salvaged and towed to a marina for repairs. A crew will return her to the yacht club.

–Lieutenant Mullins was becoming a media darling, as were the celebrity members of the club.

–Josh was happy that the police boat and squad cars would be leaving, returning the club to normal so he could enjoy the rest of the summer without turmoil. All he wanted was to go back to his private world, away from media attention. He needed that. He'd meet with Mitchell and Helene and discuss a book deal, having the rest of the summer to write. He'd try to convince Mitchell to accept a co-authorship. After all, he had already done most of the work.

–Adam Farmer received a bonus and added stature by his ability to get an exclusive and by leading a national news story. His headline articles also attracted the attention of the television talk shows. NBC's *Dateline,* wanted to do a story on him.

* * *

THE IMPACT OF the press conference, of Mullins stating that Mitchell was involved in the solutions, also attracted the variety of media.

The next day, the calls came to Helene's office. Some shows wanted Helene and Mitchell since both were involved. She'd get back to them, Helene replied. Mitchell's publisher called to say that they were planning a marketing campaign around Mitchell to re-issue his books, individually and as sets.

They asked Helene if he was going to write the book on the yacht club murders. She said, no, but Josh Trimble would, with Mitchell helping. She'd come in on Monday and talk about an advance for Josh Trimble. The advance would be much higher if Mitchell's name was on the cover as a co-author, said the publisher. Much more? Much. That might be arranged, Helene added . . . not at all optimistic about Mitchell agreeing.

Mitchell spent the next two days involved with his notes. Mitchell wasn't interested in over-shadowing Josh by his being a co-author. Instead, he'd write a foreword for the book and help to promote it wherever he could, including on television. The publisher can advertise—With a foreword by Mitchell Pappas— if he needed to use his name. He would help a friend any way he could. The yacht club was Josh's life and world and the events were his story to write.

On Sunday night, with all the notes in the computer and catalogued, Mitchell printed a copy of the numerous pages for his own use and review. He settled back in his reading chair in the living room and began the review—to determine strengths and weaknesses.

Something in the notes wasn't reading well.

Loopholes, the kind that run through his analytical evaluation that should be checked to avoid inconsistencies in dialogue, or actions that arouse suspicions—the kind that haunt you until you get an answer, no matter how meaningless the answer—the kind that asks Josh if he was the second man who supposedly raped and killed Renata. He had to ask Josh those tough questions.

He stopped what he was doing, disturbed that the notes were leading him into a certain direction. But the loopholes were there. He picked up a note pad, started again from the first page and began to note the troublesome theories. He definitely needed more information in certain areas to round out the notes.

The original notes, from start to finish, were obviously what had occurred. That's not the perspective he was forced to follow. He went through the reviewing process and the further he traveled, the more chaotic his theories.

The notes weren't serving as a history, as was their purpose.

They were functioning as new theory and leads.

He paced the room, then the apartment—his method of stimulating the process. He convinced himself that the direction he was going had to be fiction, yet explored. He needed reality and facts only. His thinking wasn't right. Was it mental fatigue from excessive information and note taking? That had to be the reason. He stopped and started again. After an hour, the conclusion was the same.

The key was Commandant Deever.

And the Coast Guard.

He had to get to the Coast Guard station at Eaton's Neck.

He couldn't be right!

The Riddler was still alive!

THIRTY=SEVEN

THE PLAY WAS OVER. The man had already placed the lamp with the single light bulb in the middle of the stage. The curtains were drawn and the audience was filing out. Hold it! Where is everyone going?—The show's not over. The fat lady hasn't sung yet!

There was no sleep, only hyper conflict and tension. He had crossed the threshold of his body needing sleep; alive and vibrant and under mind control to continue its energy source ready for a new day. The second wind was upon him.

Getting his second wind wasn't a new experience. On numerous occasions, he'd work through the night, charged with enthusiasm, or anticipation of a coming event, or tension and try as he might, sleep was evasive. Then, by the end of the new day, his mind and body would weaken and shut down.

He needed to reach Mullins. That's the first procedure.

And needed more information and background on Titus Banks and Matthew DiBiasi.

The weekend had tempered the yacht club murders. The focus of the nation and media would soon switch to other matters, other forms of tragedy entertainment, to be consumed by other people's crisis and tragedies, to be riveted to their damn tubes awaiting the outcome of a trial, or political scandal and disgrace.

Mullins had termed it before, his tension concluded. We had become a nation of coliseum Romans, cheering the gore and inhumanity. Let the lions eat—as long as it isn't me, or mine. Tell me how others are suffering!

In his own way, he was one of the modern days Romans. He was glued to the television set through all the tragedies and in the conflict with Iraq, impatient to see the modern weapons unleash destruction and death. The best damn television ever! *I'm losing my mind.* The second wind was blowing stronger. *I've got to sleep! Why am I condemning the world?*

He took a hot shower to allow the heat to bring him down, to ease the tension, to think normal, nonviolent and rational.

He was up. Sleep would not come. But he knew what to do today. The evaluation had already been done. All he had to do was follow previous decisions. He didn't have to be mentally alert, or creative. What was the first thing? *I have to call Mullins.*

Breakfast cereal, or the traditional breakfast wouldn't suffice to get through the day. He needed food shock treatment.

He made a huge steak and eggs for breakfast and had a strong cup of coffee with honey. When finished, he felt he could leap tall buildings.

At nine o'clock, he called the Second Precinct and asked for Mullins. He was informed Mullins no longer operated from there, that the case ended and he returned to the Suffolk Homicide Squad's offices in Yaphank.

"You are the first person to know that for the first time in years, I slept through the night," said Mullins.

"Then we have a trade-off. I caught your disease. For the first time in years, I didn't. When was the last time you had steak and eggs for breakfast?"

"Never. What are you going to do? Have cereal for dinner?" A relaxed Mullins laughed heartily. "How have you been? I'll bet you're more popular than ever."

"Not with my wife, I'm not."

"What can I do for you? Just ask. You made me look good."

"I'm going through my notes and files on the case and lack certain data and was hoping you'd help."

"Notes? Does that mean you'll do a book? Who do you think will play me in the movie?"

Mitchell started to laugh. Mullins was relaxed. No longer tense and every decision wasn't life, or death.

"Jack Nicholson will do you justice. And when the time is right, we'll do an interview."

"No kidding? He's a good choice. Sorry for the distraction. How can I help?"

"I need background information on Titus Banks and Matthew DiBiasi, the guy who spent the weekend with Colarossi. I only know Titus served in the navy. DiBiasi, only that he's an investor. And include Gina Ferrara, his fiancée."

"I'll ask the Naval Department for Banks' data. That should take a few days. I'll put urgent on it. I know the other two. First, they had alibis in Montauk, so I can't charge them for Colarossi. We now know that he and Colarossi socialized frequently at the club and elsewhere. We believe he's connected to one of Colarossi's New York City organizations. Gina Ferrara is a criminal attorney, affiliated with a firm that has represented some goons we've indicted, and didn't."

"Can you determine what DiBiasi invests in?"

"That may be difficult. I'll inquire. Anything else?"

"I need permission to visit Deever's office and have the cooperation of the Coast Guard by providing me with certain unclassified information."

"Should I ask what that's for? Deever's dead and gone and his killer's dead."

"Background for my notes. If I find something your files should include, I will definitely call you."

"To an author, the aftereffect details are important. For me, the case is closed. My record for the year remains perfect. It's time for other problems. Hold on, I'll call on the other phone."

Mullins placed Mitchell on hold. To tell Mullins the new theories was premature without any evidence. Mullins would not appreciate a false alarm in his case-solving environment. Mullins returned.

"When do you want to go? It's okay. Give me a date and time."

"Today. Around one o'clock. And directions from the expressway."

"Hold again."

In a few seconds, Mullins said, "You're on. Ask for Captain Kowalski. I told him you were continuing the investigation for me. Take down these directions."

He left New York City at eleven o'clock to allow adequate time to be on time, or early. The directions took him north through the town of Northport.

Going through the town, he remembered seeing Colarossi's and Titus' names on Mullins' list as those living in Northport.

He followed the zigzag local roads that headed north to Asharoken Avenue and the Coast Guard Station located on the edge of the bluffs.

After parking in the visitor's area, he diverted his mission to appreciate the expansive views of The Sound and Connecticut. He had looked forward to being here when he, Josh and Titus were on Coast Guard Auxiliary duty and hoped to meet with Commandant Deever.

He was expected, received cordially, asked to see certain records in Commandant Deever's office and received full assistance and cooperation.

He found what he was looking for.

THIRTY-EIGHT

HE LEFT EATON'S NECK and the Coast Guard station and headed south, reversing his directions. Having his information, he wasn't ready to act. He needed more time. After passing the town of Northport and reaching Route 25A, Fort Salonga Road, he made a right to his new destination, the Eastern Shore Yacht Club.

He didn't park by the north dock as usual when visiting Josh. Instead, he parked by the clubhouse, wanting to talk with Titus Banks first.

The club had three docks now, the third one being completed last week. Many of the new slips were occupied. The police were gone. The club was back to its quiet, private environment on the waterfront. The hillside homes were no longer a threat.

He could see *Coyote's* stern and the closed doors. Josh was either out, or had the air conditioning on. He looked for his absent car. At the dock house, he was informed by a dock assistant that Titus was in the machine shop, on the other side of the pool building. He found Titus welding two mooring chains. When finished, Titus cut the flame, raised the welding mask and saw Mitchell at the open garage type entrance.

"Well, hello Mitchell. If you're looking for Josh, he went out to Riverhead to do some discount shopping."

"I didn't see his car. Actually, I need to speak with you."

"More questions? I thought all that ended." He came out of the shop and removed the mask, placing it against the wall.

"Only some details to fill in my notes."

"Doing a book?" he inquired.

"Josh may be. I'm keeping a diary for him."

"Will I be in it?"

"Of course. You were major in solving the Renata case."

Titus liked that. "Then I'll look forward to reading it. How can I help? Ask questions." He seemed at ease with Mitchell now that the threats to his life had vanished.

"When did you start Coast Guard Auxiliary duty?"

"About three years, or so ago."

"Did you go out of your way to join?"

"No. They came after me."

"Who recruited you?"

"Commandant Deever."

"Why?"

"He found out I had a naval background and kept after me."

"Did Matt DiBiasi ever do Auxiliary duty?"

"I don't think so. Matt never volunteered for anything. Had no time."

"On the night you saw Marlowe, Colarossi and Valerie, did you see Matt DiBiasi? At any time?"

"No. I know he slept on his boat."

"Did you see Josh?"

"No. When he saw Marlowe, he had to be in the

shadows and the light doesn't penetrate far from the dock."

"The reason I ask is because it took you a while to tell Mullins about Valerie. Information has to be drawn out of you. While in the navy, did you ever have occasion to be temporarily assigned for duty to the Coast Guard?"

"Never."

"You never met Commandant Deever until he took over at Eaton's Neck?"

"That's correct. Strange question, Mitchell."

"Only background, Titus. You can be full of surprises. Just took a wild stab. If I don't make sense, it's from lack of sleep. You mentioned someone once falsely accused you. Is that something you'd want mentioned?"

"No. That's dead and buried. Let it lie."

"How are things around here?"

"Back to normal. The weekend was lively again. I even enjoyed listening to those damn tennis racquets. *Champagne Lady* left for Florida, so the last of Renata is gone. Josh and I plan to visit her grave tomorrow to pay our respects. Other than that, life goes on. Better for some. Worse for others."

"The two of you visiting Renata will be a wonderful gesture, Titus. It's good to remember former friends, especially when their families are far away. That's what friends should do. Tell Josh, I stopped by and I'll call him tomorrow. But before I go, one thing."

"Shoot."

"What can you tell me about Matthew DiBiasi as a club member?"

"Not here often. As I said, he was usually with

Mario and didn't volunteer. He was also friendly with
Renata. I know he visited her grave a while back."

"Matt visited Renata's grave?" he asked, rather
surprised.

"Yes. He told me he did. I don't remember when
though. Right after she died, I think because he
missed her funeral. He was on the West Coast somewhere. Left the day after she was found."

"Thanks, Titus. I'll be talking to you soon. I'm
glad I talked to you. You were a well of information
today."

Titus returned to his welding. Mitchell left. The
second wind wasn't blowing strong. He was beginning to feel numb, glad that Josh wasn't there. He
was satisfied with Titus. The talk helped with what
he had to do.

On the way to the expressway, he decided to stop
at the Book Revue bookstore in Huntington Village
and purchase a book on the works of Alfred, Lord
Tennyson to add to his library.

On the road again, he called Adam Farmer. Adam
was happy to hear from him. They chatted about the
case and how grateful Adam was for the exclusive
articles. Mitchell told him he needed information,
background to round out his notes.

"I have little on the man who spent the weekend
with Colarossi. His name is Matt DiBiasi. Do me a
favor and go to your library computer and cross reference anything on him and his last name." Mitchell
gave him his car phone number. "I'll be home in
about an hour, or so."

Adam called in a half-hour as Mitchell was passing Cross Island Parkway.

"You are not going to believe this. You must be
psychic. During the radioactive waste thing, two of

Colarossi's employees died mysteriously. One of them, a barge captain, was Sylvio DiBiasi. I cross-checked the obituaries and it turns out that he had a brother named Matthew."

Mitchell grinned from the uncanny luck. He recalled Colarossi saying, when he and Josh had dinner with him, that revenge is best when you least expect it and when its aged. He also recalled a conversation with Helene when he first got involved and him saying he'd take the covers off some garbage cans and see what's inside. DiBiasi's can added to last minute discovery.

"Mr. Pappas. You think DiBiasi killed Colarossi for revenge to avenge his brother? How about Deever? He wrote the Coast Guard report. You think DiBiasi killed him? Maybe DiBiasi is the Riddler instead of Colarossi. That makes sense."

"You have a fertile mind, Adam. My opinion on those won't arrest him. Mullins confirmed he has an alibi for Colarossi's rub out. The information you gave me, confirming that Sylvio was his brother, widens other avenues that I'm looking into now. I found a reference to a Sylvio DiBiasi in Deever's files. I assumed he and Matt were related. I'm no longer surprised by anything that happens, or by anyone. The next time you write an article on the subject, include this new information on DiBiasi. Let your readers believe that DiBiasi is a possible hit man. You won't be far from wrong. You may be doing more future articles on him. In the meantime, when I finish accumulating his data, DiBiasi may surprise you. I'll provide that to you. Thanks for the information, Adam. I'll be rooting for you to win the Pulitzer." He ended the connection.

By the time he reached the Triboro Bridge, his

energy level had decreased and a yawn came. He increased the air conditioning and sang to stay awake.

He learned a lot today, an awful lot.

He learned what he needed from the Coast Guard.

He learned what he needed about Matthew DiBiasi.

And he learned what he needed to know from Titus.

The walk home from the garage provided momentum to stay awake. At home, he again began to evaluate and verify his notes; pending what information Mullins can add about DiBiasi and Titus. He had to be sure, positive before he took the final step. On second thoughts, he was certain. He had sufficient information to proceed with confidence. Tomorrow would be the better time. Fatigue was encroaching, but he kept fighting sleep.

Then he read Alfred, Lord Tennyson until the second wind stopped blowing and his head fell on the pages.

CHAPTER THIRTY=NINE

AWAKENING IN HIS bed at 5:00AM, he didn't remember getting there and being alone. Last night, Helene had nudged him to half consciousness, helped him fall into bed and he fell awkwardly across the bed. Heavy to move in that position, she slept on the sofa.

After a few half-hearted exercises, he felt revived and returned to Tennyson, needing to find the appropriate passage before leaving home, ready to add the final chapter to his notes.

Mullins didn't call last night. Driving to Long Island under a gray sky, he called Mullins while passing the expressway exit to Glen Cove Road and entering 'Death Valley', the four mile stretch between Exits 39 and 40.

"I don't have the information on Titus Banks and Matthew DiBiasi. Probably today."

"I'll wait. I have what I need for now. I didn't call for that. What's your schedule for today?"

"I should be here all day. No new homicides reported yet. Cleaning the paper work and more paper work. Why? What are you up to?"

"You'll know when I call you back. If you must go out, leave word where I can reach you. It's important that we meet later."

"What's the subject? Is it about your book?"

"I'll tell you when I call again."

He ended the conversation with the curious detective and continued his trip as he passed an orange Astro Moving and Storage van. Upon reaching his destination, he parked and read Newsday and The New York Times. At the appropriate time, he called and spoke to Mullins. Then he attempted the crossword puzzles as he sat in his vehicle.

* * *

THE DAY CONTINUED morbid and gray. The clouds tumbled and the warm southern wind rustled dried leaves. Rain should have been falling; the symptoms were there. Sometime today, the rain will fall in scattered areas.

* * *

HE CAME AGAIN to the cemetery to be alone with Renata, and was now far from the wilted flower posture of an earlier visit.

Now, he was closer to her, valiant for her, her knight. He stood tall before her. There remained one more deed to accomplish for her. Then the promises will have been fulfilled.

This time, he brought a folding chair to sit and talk to her, her favorite champagne and two glasses and, most important, two dozen red roses. He placed the bottle behind the metal plaque. He spread the roses around the unopened bottle and placed the champagne glasses on the plaque—to share a toast together. He planned to visit awhile; convinced the rain would bypass this region. If wrong, he'd sit in the car and wait for the rain to pass. Today, he wasn't concerned with wearing sunglasses, the boating cap or being recognized. The yacht club murders were solved. He had succeeded and was free to visit his Renata without restraint.

Then he sat, facing the plaque, his back to the road, the world and all living things. He was alone in his world with Renata, reminiscing and stirring memories to bring her to life, to share precious moments again. He closed his eyes, sat back in the chair for several minutes and let the visions perform to his contentment.

His reverie and images ended when his eyes suddenly opened, jarred by an intruder, and then his body eased.

The familiar voice from behind ended his privacy.

The interruption was accepted with disappointment and passive resignation and he sat without moving, without turning because the voice said the perfect words to end his journey of revenge for Renata.

The words were the inevitable ending, for they told the truth and were spoken with poetic feeling as when written by England's poet laureate over one hundred years ago.

"Let no man dream but that I love thee still," and repeated with added emphasis, "Let no man dream but that I love thee still. Alfred, Lord Tennyson."

Renata's knight swayed slightly back and forth with approval and responded, "To love one maiden only, and worship her by years of golden deeds. Tennyson, also."

He continued to face the plaque.

No need to see the face of the voice.

The owner of the voice approached him and walked past and around the chair, positioning himself behind the roses ringed champagne to face him. He dropped to one knee to be eye level with him and said, "Well, Professor. Here we are. The Riddler and I."

Josh's attitude remained resigned discovery, with acceptance of Mitchell's presence and his conclusion. "I avenged her with golden deeds, for I loved the maiden. This ending was ordained, wasn't it? I hoped it wouldn't be. How did you know?"

"A few loopholes here and there."

"Ah, the eternal loopholes."

"I was reviewing the notes and some aspects required a further look—to close questions needing substance—and certain actions of yours seemed to establish a pattern. Once I began to list them, separate them, I needed to know more."

"I didn't think I made that many provable inconsistencies. I thought I was pretty precise about that."

"You weren't objective in your thinking. I was."

"And what did you need to know that made this unscheduled confrontation a reality? You already had the ending. Everyone else accepted Colarossi."

"I did, also, at first. After we learned about the Horatio riddle, we discussed alerting Deever. I believe your words were—There's no need to rush to warn him. The killer will probably precede any attack with a cryptic message. You convinced me. That was in keeping with previous riddles.

"Then on Sunday, June twenty-third, on Auxiliary duty with Titus, you called Deever's office for us to visit. You did make the call. I found out yesterday that Deever never worked on Sundays. I now know you knew that."

Josh remained passive, both hands gripping the ends of the armrests, chin on chest. Then he said, "Point of order. That's classified as hearsay. Not good substance."

Mitchell continued, undeterred. "And there was one that told the truth. The truth I didn't want to find, kept hoping I wouldn't find. On Friday, June twenty-eight, Lieutenant Mullins called to tell me the Rudyard Kipling riddle was for Deever. Then I called you. You told me you were going to call Deever and alert him. You placed me on hold. When you returned, you said Deever wasn't there, that you left word for him to call me at home or you on your yacht. And that his wife was out of town."

"I did say all that."

"I went to the Coast Guard station yesterday and checked Deever's phone records. There is *no* record that you ever called him on that day. Which means you didn't call because you had already killed him. Hung him off the buoy. You picked him up in Northport. He was off-duty and in civilian clothes. You were certain of security that night."

"Very few people on the dock. And it was dark," offered Josh. "Otherwise, I would have taken him to dinner and waited for another opportunity. I didn't want it to happen so quickly. I wanted him to live with the thought that he was prey."

"And he probably told you his wife was away visiting her mother in Columbus, Ohio, or you heard his wife was gone. You called him at home and you invited him out. These were major loopholes, Professor, where Deever was concerned. You got careless, or over confident with him."

Josh shook his head. "Not exactly that way. He told me that his wife was out of town at Horatio's funeral and I invited him out since he was alone. I never warned him about Marlowe. The timing was opportune and he looked forward to the trip across the Sound."

"How did you subdue him and the others?"

"I have that rifle. You want the details for your notes, their final moments how they begged and pleaded? Who whined the most? What I said to them?"

"No, not at this time. I can't imagine them refusing to follow orders against that high-powered rifle. One way, or another, you tied their hands and got them overboard."

"I also taped their mouths so they couldn't scream for help before I pushed them over."

"In retrospect, your continuing refusal to come forward strained credibility until you realized you couldn't complete your revenge against Marlowe. He was closely guarded and mostly in Washington.

"You sent Mullins the Marlowe riddle to call attention to Marlowe and then you came forward to accuse him. You planned that well. You also wanted to sacrifice Titus, telling me he lied about Renata. Fortunately, Titus confirmed your story after Colarossi died. As for your revenge, that was nearly accomplished when Marlowe toppled in disgrace."

"That was temporary," added Josh. "To get him to resign and then he wouldn't have government protection. He was next in order to complete my . . . deeds for Renata."

"No, Professor," Mitchell corrected, "for your *obsession*. You told Colarossi about Marlowe, to use him as a cover so it would appear he was the avenger, the Riddler. You knew he was affiliated and you used underworld methods to execute them even though you didn't want the bodies found. Once Dryden and Horatio were found, it didn't matter if they found Deever's body."

"Partly correct. The problem was, I couldn't find literature more appropriate and easy as Kipling's, 'they were going to hang Danny Deever'. I had to hang Douglas Deever to stay true to the riddle. Dryden and Horatio were easily convinced to take a trip across to Norwalk for dinner. We had done that before on their yachts. In both instances, I insisted we go on mine. I couldn't risk Deever at the club because of increased security. Meeting him in Northport was safer."

"About Northport," said Mitchell. "The Northport postmarks were to add blame to Colarossi? Or was it Titus?"

"Mario. To be consistent."

"The Marlowe riddle and solution were sent by overnight mail from Hicksville and Long Island City. You wanted the focus on Marlowe while he was visiting the club for the July Fourth weekend. That's why you agreed to bear witness after the weekend was over, why you delayed. You planned to confess on Saturday and blame the increased protection. Scheduling Sag Harbor was a ploy.

"You needed timely and prompt deliveries, unlike the Deever riddle that was four days in arriving. When you first told me about the murders, you were believable. You used me, Professor, as you did the others. You used me to convince Mullins that Marlowe and Colarossi were the killers. I was your front to hide your revenge. Your abusing me was secondary to your obsession with Renata. I resented that at first but I accept that now."

"Please accept my apologies also, Mitchell. I love you and Helene too much to hurt you. I thought I had succeeded blaming Colarossi. Damn near did, didn't I? If you didn't probe, we would have lived happily ever after. Mullins closed the case. The world believed Colarossi was guilty. There wouldn't have been future riddles for Marlowe because the Riddler was dead. I would have gotten Marlowe eventually. Are your notes complete now?"

"Not entirely. I'm seeking background on Titus and DiBiasi. I think DiBiasi killed Colarossi. His brother was the captain of one of Colarossi's barges and he died mysteriously. A bit of revenge there, also—so much revenge in the tiny world of one yacht club. So much obsessive hate and love."

Mitchell's legs were cramping and he stood, ligaments crackling, rubbing his knees and brushing off his pants; some stubborn ground evidence remained.

"I didn't want Dryden's and Horatio's bodies found," Josh said, late on the subject, and remaining in the same position. "They lied for Marlowe. They didn't deserve decent funerals. I hated them for protecting him and don't regret what I did. They were liars and frauds."

Mitchell immediately added, "And because they were making love to Renata and had something of Renata you never had. That had to be added motive."

"That, too. Ate my insides. I resented and envied

her visitors. I would have loved her with my heart and soul. Have you told Helene? Does she know?"

"No one knows the whole story. Only you and I." Mitchell began to walk back and forth to ease the cramps.

"You'll have to write that book now since you re-solved the ending," said Josh. "No need to add fic-tion. Love does make one do strange things, doesn't it?" he reflected. "As I said about Colarossi, his love would kill for Renata. Not her. And my love avenged her. No love could greater be than the love I had for Renata. The police weren't pursuing Marlowe when I believed he killed Renata. It was up to me and needed you to catch Marlowe, or blame Colarossi. Which is what happened. Valerie was a shocker, wasn't she?"

"As you are. More so."

Josh nodded in silent agreement. "Well, if Marlowe told the truth from the beginning, there would be no need for revenge to drown Deever, Horatio and Dryden. Valerie tarnished my cause, didn't she? What now?" Josh added, taking a deep breath. "Do I chase you around the cemetery and fight and roll on the ground until I do you in, and no one else will know?" He attempted a difficult smile.

"Is that what you want?" replied Mitchell, con-tinuing his pacing.

"You know better."

"I thought I did, Professor. What happened to Titus? He said yesterday you both were coming here today."

"He mentioned your conversation when I re-turned from Riverhead. I talked him out of coming. I wanted to be alone with Renata. I couldn't stand

looking at the empty slip. Do me a favor and stop
pacing. Don't be so tense."

Mitchell stopped pacing and stood before him.

"I made a tragedy list yesterday of the dead and
wounded, starting with Renata to put the tragedies
in perspective. Helene and I will now add our names
to that list, and yours and Melanie's, and your future
son-in-law—five more victims. Your deadly initiative
and revenge voyage left a wide wake."

"You're talking nautical again. Liars were protecting Marlowe. The police weren't doing anything. I
had to." He looked resigned. "I had to," he repeated
in his defense as he looked at Renata's plaque. He
looked up again. "You must ask Melanie to forgive
me before I see her. I ask again. What now? Do we
forget this conversation now that you found the missing piece to the puzzle?"

"We can't do that, Professor."

"I didn't think so, unfortunately."

"It's not a good movie ending, no chase scene or
anything exciting, but Lieutenant Mullins is waiting
in his car down the road for us to finish our talk."
Mitchell pointed to his left.

Josh turned to see Mullins, about eighty yards away
on a crossroad, standing by the car's fender and a
squad car with two officers behind him. They waited
patiently.

"A boat chase should be the movie ending," said
Josh. "In a stormy sea, where I eventually escape,
never to be seen again, lolling somewhere in the Vir-
gin Islands or the South Seas. You'd better call Mullins
and hand him the last piece on a silver platter. I need
a favor. Go to *Coyote* and bring my pictures of Renata
next time we meet. The key is in the car. In the glove
compartment."

"I'll do that. We'll talk again, soon." Mitchell's voice was less than conversational level.

The notes were finishing.

The final pages were beginning to turn.

Josh leaned forward, rose slowly and collapsed the chair. They stood facing each other in silence as Mitchell delayed in signaling Mullins.

Mitchell, restraining his heart wrenching emotions, went to Josh and extended his right hand to offer continuing friendship. Josh grasped it tightly in surrender and with love.

Mitchell pulled him closer and gave him a hug, and held Josh for a few seconds as his eyes became blurred. The words choked in his throat.

"You killed me, Professor. You killed me. You killed the both of us."

＊ ＊ ＊

MITCHELL WATCHED THE squad car heading for the cemetery exit as he stood with Mullins near his car.

Mitchell had notified Mullins while waiting in the Pinelawn parking area. Mitchell didn't explain the specifics; said he'd do that when he arrived. Mullins came and parked by the Pinelawn railroad station. Mitchell explained by car phone and Mullins agreed to the arrangement. Had Josh failed to arrive at the cemetery, they would have gone to the yacht club and had the confrontation on *Coyote*, also in private. Considering the weather, Mitchell preferred the cemetery today.

When Josh's car entered the cemetery, he called Mullins and Mullins gave Mitchell a lift to the road leading to the gravesite.

"All's well that ends terribly," said Mullins. "I'm sorry. I know he was a good friend and how difficult this was. I'll see that his car is returned to the club."

"I appreciate you understanding that I needed to meet with him alone. Something I had to do. Mainly, it's ended."

"That's the important thing," said Mullins, heaving a sigh. "I don't know when I'll see you again, and it may not be the appropriate time to say this, but there is a reward. You and Titus Banks."

Mitchell shrugged. "If so, I'll send my share to Josh's daughter, Melanie, and tell her I'm repaying a loan, or something. I guess this makes me somewhat of a bad guy to her for turning in her father, and a close friend."

Mullins patted his back. "You've stopped the killing. It's no consolation, but it makes you a continuing hero." Mullins sensed the personal anguish Mitchell was experiencing and wanted to alleviate his burden temporarily by adding lighter fare. "As I said, I knew you'd find the killer for me. And you know what that makes me?"

Mitchell looked at him as if to ask—What?

"A genius. An absolute genius!"

Mitchell tried, but it was hard to smile.

He looked back towards Renata's grave at the unopened bottle of champagne, the glasses and roses that a romantic lover had brought for her; one who felt a love from his soul, who worshipped and adored her at arms length.

With mind still current with Tennyson readings, he couldn't help but recall the famous Tennyson lines the Professor could have spoken to define the ending and his final separation from Renata. To fur-

EOD

ther justify his love and deeds—'Tis better to have loved and lost . . . Then never to have loved at all'.

The rain came at last to wash Tennyson away and end its daylong threat, and to coax them into the car for Mullins to drive Mitchell back to the parking area for his car.

And then for Mitchell's long ride home to tell Helene.

The rain fell a bit harder on the windshield. It was a good day for sadness and to be in a cemetery.

* * *